SMITH BROS.

ROB MACDONALD

PARK
BENCH
PRESS

SMITH BROS.
© 2026 Rob Macdonald

ISBN: 978-1-7644472-0-1

Published by Park Bench Press
www.parkbenchpress.com.au

Printed on demand in the country where this edition was purchased.

First Edition

For Dad
The funniest man I've known
&
Fraser
I sent this to you to read. Then you died.

ONE

Jim Smith stood in a small room at the back of the brightly lit Peaceful Gardens chapel and pressed the big red button on the sparse console in front of him. It controlled the curtains either side of the shiny casket that sat, set slightly back, in a small, central alcove at the front of the room. The casket itself was adorned by a grotesquely gaudy arrangement of flowers - an eye-watering dispute of rhododendrons and chrysanthemums. As the red felt drapes started to draw together, Jim also pushed play on the screen of the tablet under the console and the chapel speakers roared to life, drowning out the sniffles of the bereaved with the blaring mariachi horns that mark the unmistakable beginning of Johnny Cash's *Ring of Fire*.

Jim grew annoyed as he watched the curtains jerking in a stop-start manner, catching on their rails as they edged closer together. They should have been gliding like sharp scissors through paper given the chapel build had only been completed three months or so previously, not to mention the fact that Jim had deposited the best part of a can of WD40 on them just that morning in an effort to improve their operation. They had been a bane in Jim's life in recent weeks due primarily to the reluctance of the responsible tradesman, Barry McWirder from Barry McWirder Curtains and Blinds, to take responsibility and fix the problem. It subsequently meant, despite several calls to the relevant Ombudsmen, that a trip to the small claims court wasn't off the table. At least the new speakers, part of a twenty thousand dollar audio-visual package that Jim had insisted upon installing, sounded good. He surreptitiously nudged the volume up two more notches as 'The Man In Black' sang about going down, down, down…

Although the music drew a few disapproving looks from the more conservative element of the congregation, broad smiles crossed the faces of the majority of those in the chapel. Jim had tried his best in his meetings with the family to steer the song choice towards something more traditional – *Wind Beneath My Wings* or anything by Josh Groban (*You Raise Me Up*, perhaps?) – but this had been just one of an extensive list of typically roguish final wishes from local larrikin Frank Collinton. The long time local butcher, former patron saint of the mighty Nuggets Rugby League Club and man in who's honour half the town had gathered today, certainly was a character.

Jim was pretty sure that Frank's wake would soon be filled with side-splitting stories from Frank's life, such as the time he put a live pig in a particularly disliked police constable's car, or that hilarious occasion when he mixed in some laxatives with the mince he used in a batch of sausages for the rival Bandicoots' end of season awards night and BBQ. And who could forget when he set off some fireworks leftover from the Annual Show inside the hall at Mac Tennant's fortieth?

Yep, he sure was a bit of a wag that Frank.

As the song slowly faded out and solemn silence once again filled the room, the mourners started to stand and make their way from the chapel, led by Frank's newly minted widow Maureen. Jim quickly adjusted his tie, smoothed down the sides of his jacket and contorted his face into his well-practiced smile. It was an expression that conveyed sympathy, empathy, compassion and kindness and was one hundred percent contrived. It's not that Jim didn't genuinely like Frank when he was alive, it's just that after twelve years in the funeral game, Jim just didn't have much genuine emotion left to give now that he was dead.

"I'm so sorry again for your loss, Maureen," Jim said, as he gently took her hands in his.

"Thank you, Jim. They broke the mould with my Frank, they did," Maureen replied.

"That they did Maureen," Jim said through his smile. "Don't worry, we'll be sure to take great care of him".

Having finally cleared the chapel of Frank Collinton's mourners with a reminder to the stragglers that, prior to his passing, Frank had arranged for a five hundred dollar tab to be placed on the bar at the bowlo, Jim closed and locked the main doors before making his way through the drawn curtains to a drab, utilitarian room at the rear of the building.

"About bloody time, Jim."

Standing in the middle of the room was Mick Smith, Jim's older brother. Mick was a good foot taller than Jim and almost a foot broader. He was casually resting his elbows on Frank's Collinton's coffin. The casket was even fancier up close. The rich mahogany was polished to within an inch of its life. Gone from it was the flower arrangement, which now sat half-sticking out of a large green waste bin in the corner. The lid of the casket was now also wide open, revealing Frank Collinton lying peacefully on the plush, silk lining. He was dressed in his best suit – which, it must be said, didn't say much for his other suits.

Mick knew Frank well from his time as the star of the Nuggets' famed back-to-back grand final wins of a decade or so before but had always tired of Frank's constant praise. Frank was known to regale anyone who would stand still long enough with stories of Mick's footballing heroics. 'A tantalising mix of Eric Grothe, Arti Beetson, Wally Lewis with a dash of Mal Meninga thrown in for good measure!' was his preferred way of introducing Mick as a player before invariably launching into embellished tales of his exploits on the field. Mick took a second and looked down at Frank's body in a brief moment of reflection.

"I thought I was going to have to shift the annoying bastard myself," Mick said, with a slight grin.

"Yeah, sorry mate. They wouldn't leave."

Jim walked over and slid his arms under Frank Collinton's legs as Mick took a firm hold of his shoulders. On the count of three, they heaved his lifeless carcass out of the coffin and into a plain box of similar dimensions, constructed out of stiff cardboard, that was sitting next to it on an ambulance gurney. It never failed to surprise Jim how heavy and difficult it was to lift a dead weight and even though Frank was sixty kilograms soaking wet, Jim lost his grip and Frank's legs thumped to the floor. The sudden drop twisted Frank's shoulders free of Mick's hands and the deceased butcher's lifeless body crashed to the ground where it lay in a contorted heap.

"Jesus Jim! You're useless as tits on a bull sometimes."

"I'm sorry Mick. He just slipped."

The brothers bent down and grabbed whatever

they could get the best purchase on. Jim opted for two hands in Frank's belt while Mick gripped him with one hand in the lapel of his suit and one hand firmly on the back of his collar. With a brief, ungainly effort, they managed to heave him off the ground and into the box.

"I'll get him over to the crematorium. I do love it when they go for the cremo. It makes the whole thing much easier," Mick said. He slid a lid, also made of cardboard, onto the box and secured it with a couple of carefully placed strips of packing tape.

"You're right to get this one cleaned up?" Mick asked, nodding in the direction of the shiny mahogany casket.

"Yeah, of course, Mick," Jim said.

"Beauty. See you at the bowlo later? Seems rude not to raise a glass to old Frank here, funny prick that he was," Mick said, tapping the top of the box.

And with that, Mick wheeled Frank Collinton's body out into a plain white van parked at the rear of the chapel but not before cautiously sticking his head around the corner to make sure there weren't any stragglers from the funeral still milling about. Five minutes later, Mick was pulling up at the crematorium. It was housed in a non-descript building on the edge of what constituted a small industrial area down one of the back roads out of town. Three and a half hours after that, Frank Collinton's body was cooling in a steel tray, a mix of ash, cardboard and the polyester from his best suit.

Jim, meanwhile, had loaded the now empty mahogany casket into the back of a similarly non-descript van and was making the five minute drive in the opposite direction, back towards Prosperity's main street.

The locals all had their opinions on the name of their town but most figured it was some sort of queer irony. Settled in the 1850's during the area's gold rush, the town of Prosperity had long ago shed any traits associated with its name. First came the closure of the local tannery, and then the Bingham's Boot factory shut its doors. However, it was the ongoing drought - the longest any of the old blokes in town could remember - that had been the real kick in the teeth. In fact, there was a certain amount of envy amongst the townsfolk cast in the direction of Jim and Mick - for no matter how bad everything else got, people still kicked the bucket on the regular.

The only thing that had been keeping the doors of Prosperity open in the past couple of years had been the construction of The Oasis. But even that hadn't been without considerable controversy. Built about ten kilometres out of town, down by the now almost dry river, The Oasis was conceived and marketed as a one hundred room adult theme park, which was a polite way of saying: medieval-themed brothel. It was kind of like the movie *Westworld*. Only without the killer robots.

The development had caused a fissure in the town between those who saw it as a jobs panacea on one side and those who feared an influx of unsavoury characters on the other. Not to mention the moral outrage from the small but vocal church community, where it had become somewhat of a cause celebre that had resulted in agreement and cooperation between the Catholic and Anglican congregations of a manner rarely seen since King Henry the eighth split from Rome.

Jim passed a large billboard advertising The Oasis as he swung around the war memorial round-a-bout and into Prosperity's main street. He noticed that someone had defaced the hoarding with one of the many "NOasis" posters that had begun cropping up around town in protest. Personally, Jim was on the fence about the whole thing. He'd never really been the type to pick sides. At high school he picked up the nickname "Splinters" for always sitting on the fence. Indeed, in large part it had been his circumspect and peaceable nature that had served him well as an undertaker. However, he did think to himself that all the recent protests seemed too little too late to have any real hope of forcing a change. The horse had well and truly bolted – after all, The Oasis was due to open in only a few weeks.

The main drag of Prosperity began at the war memorial and ran for the best part of eighteen hundred meters before petering out just past the Royal Hotel. Jim drove the van down the largely quiet main street before he took a right at the second of five intersections about a third of the way along the main road. He almost immediately swung a left into what was essentially a rear lane that ran along the back of the shops and slowed the van to a stop. He fished around in the centre console amongst old receipts, empty mint tins and the odd coin, for a remote control. He pointed the remote at a large roller door at the rear of one of the buildings that faced the main street and clicked the button a few times. Finally, the door began screeching open and Jim drove the van inside.

Jim wheeled the shiny casket from the back of the van into the funeral home's mortuary. The room was clinical and cold, with lots of stainless steel and a floor that could be easily hosed out. Along one wall were about a dozen refrigerated drawers for storing bodies. The number of drawers was probably overkill given they usually had one, maybe two bodies at any one time but Jim liked to be prepared for the "just in case", particularly given some of the people in the area made it difficult to rule out a sudden spate of unexplained deaths occurring at any moment. He flicked on the fluorescent lights, which sprung to life with a low hum, and got to work.

Jim and Mick had been around the funeral business all their lives, it was in their blood. Their dad, Sid, had been an undertaker as had his dad before him. During school holidays growing up - in the summer at least when Mick wasn't playing footy – the brothers would help dig and prepare the graves. Mick didn't mind the physical stuff, in fact he quite enjoyed it but Jim's personality was always better suited to the business, something their dad had recognised early on. Jim's partiality for funerals really solidified around the time he ran the service for their beloved cattle dog Mollie, after she came off second best in an argument with a particularly distempered brown snake. Jim organised the flowers, wrote and printed the service booklets, arranged for a condolence book and chose the music - John Denver's *Take Me Home Country Roads*. All at the age of seven.

Indeed, it was a nineteen-year-old Jim who took over the business after Sid's sudden passing. In accordance with Sid's will, Mick was to get the family farm and Jim was handed the keys to Smith Family Funerals. At the time it seemed a fair and equitable division of Sid's assets. The farm was about ten minutes out of town and was made up of about four hundred acres of fair to middling land that was capable of sustaining about a hundred head of cattle if there was water about. The funeral business came with the keys to the building on the main street and a pretty much guaranteed future revenue stream. There were no other assets of any significance to disperse which was a good thing as there were also no other beneficiaries. Sid's wife and the boys' mother, Glenda, had disappeared years before in the company of a rather debonair travelling knife salesman and no one in the family had heard from her since. Many in town put Sid's passing down to a broken heart. His doctors attributed it more accurately to an acute cardiac event most likely brought about by Sid's predilection for cigarettes, cheap scotch and neenish tarts.

Jim had a successful first few years as the solo captain at the helm, which was not that surprising given Smith Family Funerals where the only funeral business in town. However, it wasn't long before Mick wanted in. Mick had always banked on making it big in the National Rugby League but when a 3am altercation in a Sydney pub had left him with a broken orbital, a torn anterior cruciate ligament and, worse, a reputation as a troublemaker, he'd been forced to give up that dream and return home with his tail between his legs. Given that he had spent most of his life focussed on playing footy, Mick had realised pretty quickly that he really knew "fuck-all about farming", as he put it. When the drought really started to bite, he was left with few other options than to turn to the family business for a helping hand.

Jim was happy to have his older brother on board, well at least happy enough (Jim always thought it might have been nice of Mick to cut him into the farm as a bit of a quid-pro-quo but that was a conversation Mick had managed to successfully put off for the best part of a decade). The only issue for Jim was one of pure economics - there were now two mouths to feed at the top of the food chain and the good people of Prosperity were still dying at the same rate as ever.

While the notion of somehow increasing the local

death rate did fleetingly cross Jim's mind - a highly virulent gastro bug somehow circulated amongst the local branch of the Country Women's Association, perhaps - he ultimately stumbled upon a scheme so obvious he wasn't entirely sure why it hadn't come to him years earlier. The real money in his business had always been in the caskets. However, once they were buried in the dirt or burned to ashes, that was the end of them - all that money, gone forever. It had always seemed a such a waste to Jim but he also understood that, human nature being what it was, people always liked the idea of giving their loved ones a nice final resting place. His idea? To simply swap the bodies out of the expensive caskets and into cheap boxes prior to burial or cremation. A quick scrub and a spray of disinfectant later and the luxury model was ready for re-sale, awaiting the next grieving loved ones who walked through the doors, ready to pay top dollar.

While it had taken a little while to work out the mechanics for how to do it for clients who opted to be buried – in the end a rather simple bait and switch was devised – for those who opted to be cremated, Jim and Mick were able to test the concept almost immediately. The brothers worked out that the casket could be substituted extremely easily after the service, as they had just done for Frank Collinton, for a cheap, flammable cardboard box. Even better, like all perfect crimes, there was absolutely no evidence that remained after it had been through the furnace.

By now, Jim was well practiced at cleaning the caskets and had this one spick and span, with all evidence of its previous occupant Frank completely removed, within fifteen minutes. He threw in a sachet of lavender-heavy potpourri just to be on the safe side and made his way through the doors that lead into the main part of the building, switching off the morgue lights as he went. He conducted a quick inspection around the office to make sure nothing was out of place and there were no prying eyes. It was a habit he had picked up over the years as a consequence of the low level guilt he had acquired over the scam. He made his way to the front door, punched in the code to set the alarm and stepped outside and onto the footpath.

The front façade of the building was far and away the grandest on the street. Built from large blocks of sandstone, it had belonged to one of the six banks that had been built during Prosperity's heady gold rush days but was the only one that had survived the intervening hundred and fifty years. Jim locked the doors behind him and briefly looked up and admired the ornate gold lettering on the glass above the door before setting out on the short walk to the bowlo to raise a glass to the departed Frank Collinton.

The late afternoon sun caught the gold lettering behind him as he left. It glistened as it spelt out simply: "Smith Bros."

TWO

Down the far end of a wood-panelled corridor inside the 1970's eyesore of a structure formally known as the Prosperity Ranges Municipal Council Building, Mayor Terry McInerny reclined in his plush faux-leather office chair and rubbed his hand over his engorged belly. His white business shirt stretched taught across his mid-section as he perused the latest copy of the local newspaper, the Prosperity Ranges Argus. He was particularly interested in the front-page article 'Mayor McInerny Makes Moves'. Apart from appreciating the alliteration in the headline, Terry was particularly enamoured of the article itself, even though by any objective measure it was a nauseatingly saccharine puff piece detailing the achievements of his fourth term as mayor. He had always enjoyed positive coverage in the local rag, in large part due to McInerny Motors and Machinery, the mayor's local farm machinery business, being a major advertiser. However, today's article was particularly sycophantic, praising him as the town's saviour for having overseen the jobs mini-boom associated with The Oasis development. It could well have been headlined 'Mayor McInerny: Modern Messiah'.

Terry finished the article and loafed quietly in his chair, marinating in self-satisfaction before tossing the newspaper on his desk, having little interest in any of the other stories. He drummed his fingers on his inflated balloon of a belly, producing a dull percussive sound. As if part of a bodily call and response, his stomach answered with a loud gurgle from deep within. It belched and spluttered. The mayor considered making a dash to the bathroom to relive himself for the third time that morning, his roiling stomach just the tip of the iceberg of his creeping hangover. The crapulence had been hard earned the previous evening, courtesy of the two bottles of red wine the mayor had indulged in. Although a non-traditional pairing, the bold Barossa Shiraz had diligently washed down the succulent five-course Chinese meal Mayor McInerny had enthusiastically devoured while watching the season finale of his favourite English small town police procedural on the television.

As his stomach aggressively burped once more, he took a quick glance at his watch to check the time. It was 11.24am. His next appointment wasn't until 11.30. Terry did a quick calculation in his head and was just about to make a dash to the bathroom when his phone buzzed.

"Yes?" he said, gruffly.

"You're 11.30 is here, Terry," his secretary replied.

Terry hung up the phone and fixed his tie. He made a cursory attempt at tidying up some of the documents strewn across his desk, adding them hastily to the towering stacks of papers already teetering on the edges of the table. He went to put the copy of the Argus away before reconsidering. Instead, he placed it prominently in the middle of the desk with his front-page article conspicuously displayed.

McInerny then sat back and quickly pulled out his mobile phone and held it to his ear. He had just settled into his position as the door to the mayor's office abruptly swung open and in walked his 11.30.

Christian Palfreeman sashayed into the room, his six-foot-two frame dressed in an immaculate navy suit that was most probably custom Italian and most definitely uncomfortably out of place in Prosperity. Palfreeman's heavily tanned face appeared as tailored as his suit. His high cheekbones were almost obscenely dewy, a consequence of a rigidly adhered-to skin care regimen (and a rumoured fondness for Botox). A pair of square-framed glasses sat comfortably on his face and his salt and pepper hair was kept at a manicured shoulder length, in the manner of a wealthy Italian man-about-town. The upshot of the sum of all these parts was that it made it almost impossible to accurately guess Palfreeman's age. Mayor McInerny had him pegged as being somewhere between forty and fifty-five. Age aside, one thing everyone could agree on was that he was an uncommonly attractive man.

Following a few steps behind Palfreeman was Aleks Keshishian. Unlike Palfreeman, Aleks was uncommonly un-attractive. He struggled to get over five foot, even with the considerable Cuban heels on his ubiquitous black cowboy boots and preferred tight black jeans to go with his tight black, slightly shiny, collared shirts, that stretched over his barrel-chest. Aleks also suffered from male pattern baldness, and dyed the remaining hair on the sides and back of his head jet black, which had the unintended consequence of accentuating the shininess of the rest of his dome. His face was dominated by a boxer's nose which spread across it, while his ears were grotesquely cauliflowered from years of Greco-Roman wrestling in his native Armenia. In other words, as far as gangsters went, he was straight out of Central Casting.

"…yes…yes. I appreciate the compliment minister. Yes…" McInerny said into his phone. He looked up at Palfreeman and rolled his eyes, making a silent talking gesture with his free hand before smiling and enthusiastically waving his guest into the room.

"I'm really sorry, minister but I'm going to have to leave you there. Someone very important has just arrived. Of course. See you then."

McInerny placed his phone on his desk.

"Sorry about that. Bloody politicians. Give 'em the tiniest bit of power and they think they're the most important people in the world! Am I right?" McInerny said, bursting into a loud, guttural laugh.

"Indeed," Palfreeman replied.

Aleks Keshishian closed the door to the office and perched himself on a sideboard that ran along the length of the rear wall. Due to his vertical challenges, he had to do a little jump to get up on to it and managed to knock over a photo of a beaming McInerny holding up a large barramundi. The picture smashed to the ground, sending glass shattering across the threadbare maroon carpet. Aleks was unmoved, the loud crash barley eliciting a reaction beyond an almost imperceptible raise of an eyebrow.

"Shit!" Terry shrieked, genuinely shocked by the sound of the unexpected destruction.

"You'll give me a heart attack!"

Palfreeman considered the remark briefly and surveyed the vision of splendid health in the form of the mayor in front of him. He certainly couldn't rule it out as a distinct possibility.

"Mayor McInerny, thank you for making the time to see me again," Palfreeman said, as he made his way, hand outstretched, towards the mayor.

"Apologies for Aleks. He does have a penchant for breaking things."

The way he said 'penchant', with a slightly affected emphasis, amused the mayor. He was definitely the only person in Prosperity he'd ever heard use the word.

"It's all good. I'll have someone clean it up later," McInerny said, as he reached across the desk and shook Palfreeman's hand. It was an effort for the big man that required him to rest his stomach on the desk and brace himself with the other arm to prevent toppling headfirst towards his guest.

"Please, take a seat."

Palfreeman did as requested, then crossed his legs and unbuttoned his suit jacket in a fluid and well-practiced manner. He smiled his thousand-watt smile at the mayor, locking his eyes on to McInerny's like a tractor beam in *Star Wars*.

"I don't intend taking up too much of your time, Terry. I know you're a very busy man."

His eyes lowered slowly and deliberately towards the front page of the paper on the desk, forcing McInerny's eyes to follow. A sudden warm shock of embarrassment flooded the mayor's body. He shifted uncomfortably in his seat as his face started to blush.

"Bloody local rag. Wouldn't know the right end of a pen most of them," The Mayor said. He sheepishly removed the paper from the desk and placed it, rather theatrically, into a wire waste paper basket next to the desk.

"The old, circular filing cabinet is the best place for it!" He tried to laugh but his normally rowdy roar got caught in his throat, held back by a bout of unexpected self-consciousness.

"Good for us though in some ways. Very positive coverage of The Oasis again. They've got my back. And I…um… scratch their back. And then as I scratch your back …well you get what I'm saying. "

"Of course," Palfreeman said.

"And while I think of it, don't worry about all those 'NOasis' posters going up around the town. I've had a chat with the local cops about it and I've also been on to the council clean-up crews who've assured me that they'll remove them all. Bloody barefoot greenie vandals!"

"I appreciate your efforts, Terry. As always," Palfreeman said. "Now, to the purpose of my coming here today. As we are getting very close to the grand opening of our little venture, I just want to make sure that nothing gets in the way at the last minute. That there are no loose ends."

"Loose ends?"

"Yes. Hitches. Glitches. Problems. Stumbling blocks. Impediments. Complications. Obstacles. Hold-ups. Snags. Setbacks…loose ends."

McInerny took a moment's pause to think.

"As far as council is concerned, we're all good to go, Christian," he said.

"That's reassuring to hear. And how about you and me, though? And the small matter of the paper trail I spoke with you about last time?"

An air of quiet tension filled the room.

Terry McInerny had first been introduced to Christian Palfreeman five years earlier at the much-touted debut art exhibition of the well-liked local veterinarian Dr George Hibbert. At the time, Dr Hibbert was considered somewhat of a 'catch' by the local womenfolk, a result of his classical good looks, easy charm and, perhaps more pertinently, the fact that he was still single on the verge of turning thirty. As such, there had been quite a buzz around town when it had become known that not only was Dr Hibbert a mighty fine vet but also a budding creative who had long held desires to forge a reputation as a contemporary artist.

Dr Hibbert's debut exhibition *The Dreams Of What Might Have Been*, was met with what could most politely be referred to as a 'mixed' response, that went some way towards diminishing his eligible bachelor status. Borrowing heavily from celebrated UK artist Damien Hirst, Dr Hibbert had assembled a collection of animals suspended in formaldehyde. Unlike Hirst, however, whose works featured whole or segmented beasts, Dr Hibbert had taken his vision a step further by first dissecting and then re-assembling a veritable menagerie of animals into new creations. There was the domestic cat with what appeared to be the wings of a macaw; the half-sheep / half-sheepdog that, if anyone had been forced to vote, would no doubt have won a people's choice award (if not for the art itself then for the cleverness of the animal pairing). The centrepiece for the show featured a fully-grown kangaroo sporting a complete set of cow udders that was titled, rather spectacularly: *KangaMoo*. The

Argus perhaps summed the exhibition up best in their review the following day which simply carried the headline "Art?".

Palfreeman had impressed everyone on the day with his generous offer to purchase the bulk of the artworks on the proviso that Dr Hibbert donated fifty percent to save the Prosperity Bowling Club in which the exhibition was being held. Due to declining memberships and lack of rain, the two greens had been left to fall into disrepair and had become by that point more weed than grass, rendering it a bowling club in name only. Faced with a distinct lack of alternative buyers, Dr Hibbert happily accepted the offer. What made the generosity of the purchase even more remarkable was the fact that hardly anyone in attendance at the time, including the mayor, had any idea who Christian Palfreeman was.

However, Terry McInerny knew he wanted to find out.

The very next day, McInerny found himself sitting across from Palfreeman in his mayoral office, listening to his bold plans to redevelop an old gold mining site out near the river and with it bring a much-needed cash injection into the struggling town. Conspicuously, no mention of the whole 'medieval themed-brothel' was forthcoming that day. So, when Christian Palfreeman sought Terry McInerny's support for The Oasis project at the conclusion of the meeting, it was granted enthusiastically and without hesitation.

Over the ensuing five years, the two had met countless times, both in official and not so official capacities. Hundreds of emails had been exchanged, text messages had been sent and dozens of documents had been signed. Now, taken in isolation none of these by themselves were an issue. However, when viewed as a whole, things started to take on a murkier picture. The expensive bottles of wine in thanks for supporting the initial development documents at council. The all-expenses paid holiday in Noosa following Terry's support for the first amendments to expand the development. The dinners at the best restaurants in Sydney. The multi hour, multi lady evenings at Aleks Keshishian's popular inner-city den of sin The Red Room. And so the list went on.

Now, neither McInerny nor Palfreeman were fools and they were very careful to make sure that there was never anything explicit in any of the correspondence. However, it wouldn't have taken much for a forensic investigator worth half his salt to put two and two together and come up with "corruption".

Given all that, Palfreeman had been dumbfounded to learn in their previous meeting that not only had McInerny kept all the emails between the two of them but that they were sitting on a publicly accessible server right there in the council building.

McInerny smiled a self-satisfied smile.

"All good big cheese. I got in touch with my nephew, Graham - hell of a tech whizz that boy. I'm not sure what he's doing most of the time but he spends all day on his computer. Anyway, it took a fair bit for this old luddite here to get my head around stuff but he helped talk me through it and I managed to get everything off the server and onto a USB stick."

Palfreemen tensed slightly in his seat. Enlisting a nephew wasn't exactly what he had envisioned. McInerny spotted his unease and held his hand out to placate him.

"Now before you jump to any conclusions, the nephew had no idea what I was asking him about. In terms of specifics, at least. We just talked hypotheticals. As far as he thinks I was just trying to get all the porn off my computer. So he's all good."

"And the USB device?" Palfreeman asked.

"It's in a very safe place. Don't you worry about that," Terry replied, beaming.

The tension in the room appreciably dissipated as Palfreeman allowed his face to relax into a smile.

"That's very good to hear, Terry."

Palfreeman braced himself on the arms of his chair and stood up.

"Once again Mayor McInerny, I can only thank you for your support of The Oasis. I look forward to properly showing you my appreciation on opening night."

He reached out his hand to the mayor.

"Not at all Christian. It's my pleasure."

The mayor shook his hand and gave him a big wink in the acknowledgement that, as previously agreed,

Palfreeman's opening night appreciation was to take the form of a full evening running amok at The Oasis in the best medieval fashion McInerny could muster.

Christian Palfreeman buttoned his suit jacket, bid a final farewell and made his way out of the mayor's office. Aleks Keshishian hopped down off the sideboard and followed, not bothering to avoid the broken picture on the floor, crunching the glass shards under the heels of his cowboy boots as he left.

Once outside the council building, as they made their way to the matte black Mercedes sedan with the dark tinted windows parked and waiting in the handicapped space at the foot of the entry stairs, Christian Palfreeman turned to Aleks Keshishian.

"No loose ends, Aleks."

THREE

Twenty years before, the main street of Prosperity had been, rather unbelievably given its current circumstances, home to no less than three Chinese restaurants: The Lotus Garden, The Imperial Peking and The Golden Palace. All three restaurants had boasted loyal and passionate clientele, devoted to their restaurant of choice and fervently opposed to the remaining two dining establishments. This was despite each venue sharing almost identical twenty page menus.

When the local tannery had been forced to shut its doors due in large part, somewhat ironically, to cheap Chinese imports, the three restaurants found themselves in a sudden battle for survival. With the town no longer able to support all three as going concerns, it was prawn toast at twenty paces as each proprietor tried to outdo the others in attracting customers. Lunch specials, dinner specials, three mains with rice, four mains with rice - nothing was off limits. In what the Prosperity Ranges Argus dubbed 'The Great Wonton Wars' there could be only one winner in the battle for the town's lovers of Mongolian lamb, honey chicken and special fried rice. After a surprisingly brief but bitter conflict, that winner was Mrs Lee Chang, proud owner and head chef of The Lotus Garden.

Having proved victorious, Mrs Chang was very careful not to gloat publicly about her success as she was acutely aware of the lingering tensions in the town and the damage that had been done in the pursuit of victory (particularly the nasty rumour that somehow circulated about The Imperial Peking's use of roadkill in their Sweet and Sour Pork). Ever the astute businesswoman, Lee Chang recognised the need for change. In an effort to heal the wounds that had riven the community and encourage all of Prosperity's devotees of authentic(*ish*) Chinese fare to feel comfortable eating in her restaurant regardless of their prior affiliations, Mrs Chang decided that the only right thing to do would be to rename The Lotus Garden in the spirit of peace. And so it was, after a brief renovation that included the addition of two imposing - some might even say triumphant - gold painted guardian lions by the entrance, Lee's New Golden Imperial Lotus Garden opened its doors.

So it was that Sam Chang, eldest and only son of Mrs Lee Chang, found himself twenty years later, standing in the kitchen of Lee's New Golden

Imperial Lotus Garden putting the finishing touches on an experimental version of sizzling beef, when his phone rang.

"Detective Chang," Sam said, answering the phone as he wiped his beading forehead with a red and white chequered tea towel.

"It's Riley, Sam. Glad I caught you. Are you at the restaurant?"

On the phone was Constable Grace Riley, a fresh-faced, diligent cop who had been stationed by herself at the small, part time police outpost in Prosperity for the past three months. It had been some years since the town had had a properly staffed police station, with most of the heavy lifting now being done out of the local area command in Bathurst, about fifty kilometres away. Many in the force saw the posting as a career ender for a young cop. Riley was determined to prove those naysayers wrong.

Detective Sam Chang was one of those based full-time out of Bathurst. However, he still lived in Prosperity, where the Chang family name had roots stretching back several generations, all the way back to the time of the goldfields. When his mother, Mrs Lee Chang had died a few years back, she made him promise to keep the restaurant doors open. Being the loyal son that he was, the deathbed burden hadn't left him much choice even if he'd wanted to leave town. Thankfully for Sam, he held no desire to. He had spent every spare minute since his mother's passing, toiling in the kitchen to keep the woks burning hot.

If he was honest with himself, Sam secretly enjoyed it. It was his method of cleansing himself, in a way, of the often grimy and unsavoury business of his day job. Plus, to the surprise of many, it just so happened that Detective Chang turned out an exceptionally good Beef and Black Bean.

"Cooking up a storm as per usual. What's going on?" Sam said.

"You better get down to Misty's."

On the second week of each month, Misty Gerrard booked out the three end rooms upstairs at the Royal Hotel for the purposes of her travelling brothel. This had been the case for as long as Sam had been a cop and he had never had much trouble from the place aside from the occasional drunk punter getting out of line and causing a ruckus. But for the most part, Misty's served a need and went under the radar. Unusually for Sam, this was the second time this week he'd found himself making the three minute walk down the main street from the restaurant to the Royal Hotel to pay a visit to Misty's. He'd been forced to have a chat with Misty a few days prior about the 'NOasis' posters that had been springing up around Prosperity. She denied all involvement, of course, though she expressed sympathy for the cause - the imminent opening of The Oasis threatened to sound a death knell for her business.

But this time was different.

Waiting for Sam outside the entrance to the Royal Hotel was Constable Riley. She made some brief pleasantries before leading him through the sparsely patronaged main bar of the Royal towards the stairs that found their way up to the accommodation on the first floor.

"So where did they find him?" Sam asked, as they rounded the landing and made their way down the hall, past the small rooms that hung off each side.

"In the shared bathroom at the end of the hall. He had just finished a session with one of Misty's workers…" Constable Riley paused to refer to her notebook.

"…a 26-year-old who goes by Candy. Obviously not her real name. He had stepped out to the bathroom to clean himself up but when he still hadn't come out twenty minutes later, Misty went in to check and found him on the floor, deceased."

"And the ambos?"

"They're still at least half an hour away. There was a pretty big MVA on the other side of Bathurst, apparently. When they got word that he was dead… well, no longer much of a rush, I guess. You know how things are."

"You wouldn't want to actually need them, hey?" Sam said, shaking his head.

"But I spoke with the forensics boys and they are coming out at some point. Given who it is and all," Riley said.

Detective Chang approached the door to the shared

bathroom. It was open, having been chocked ajar with a small rubber wedge.

"Make sure no one else comes in here until the ambos or forensics turn up," Chang said. He stepped through the door leaving Riley to stand sentry outside.

Sam initially struggled to get himself into the room. Although it served as the shared bathroom for half of the ten rooms at the Royal Hotel, it was by no means a generous space. It was made even smaller by the hulking body lying face down in the middle of the floor. Dressed in a suit minus the jacket, the lifeless mass took up a large part of the area between the washbasin and the two stalls that housed the toilet and shower respectively. It required some considered foot placement for Sam to make his way past the body and into the comparatively open space in the corner beyond. From there, he turned and surveyed the room. Nothing appeared out of place. No broken glass, no cracked tiles, no splatters of blood on the walls. In fact, it could have passed for perfectly ordinary - if not for the massive dead body lying in the middle of the floor.

He knelt down beside the motionless mass and looked for any signs of wounds or injuries. There weren't any clearly apparent. As habit and training would have him do, he placed his fingers on the side of the neck and checked for a pulse. He turned the wrist of his other hand to count the time on his watch. After a good thirty seconds, confronted by many questions and very few answers, at least one thing was clear to Detective Chang - Mayor Terry McInerny was definitely dead.

Sam rose to his feet and examined the room again. On the far wall there was a large frosted window that let a beam of natural light into the bathroom. He took the two steps it took to bridge the distance to the window and peered out. It overlooked the main street but the view outside was barely discernible through the opaqueness of the frosting, which rendered everything outside as little more than soft shapes and coloured blobs. The window was completely sealed into the frame, meaning the only way to open it would be by putting something through one of the panes. Which left the door he had come through as the only way in or out of the room.

He returned to the mayor's body and searched the pockets of his pants, trying his best not to disturb things too much. The pockets were empty. Sam figured that his wallet, keys, phone and other sundries would probably be found still in his jacket, wherever that was. He knew the forensics team would be there soon to document the scene properly but Sam pulled his phone from his pocket and snapped a few photos for his own files. A couple of the body. A few of the room. One of the obscured view out the window.

Constable Riley stuck her head through the door and called out to Detective Chang.

"Everything good, boss?"

Sam looked up and made his way back to the

doorway to the shared bathroom where Riley was eagerly waiting.

"So, heart attack you reckon?"

It was the obvious conclusion and one that had already come to the front of Sam's mind. The mayor was hardly a picture of health. Sam reckoned he'd have to have weighed at least a hundred and forty kilograms and he knew from his frequent meals at Lee's New Golden Imperial Lotus Garden that he had an extraordinary capacity for food and alcohol. Couple that with an hour's exertion with Candy - not her real name - and it made sense that his overburdened heart would have waved the white flag.

"It's possible," Sam said, "but we'll wait for the official word."

He scanned the hall past Riley and saw Misty standing a few doors down consoling a pretty young woman who Sam presumed was Candy. He waited until Misty felt his stare and looked towards him. He gestured for her to approach.

Misty Gerrard appeared as if she'd stepped straight out of a 1950's rockabilly poster. Her platinum-blonde curls fell just below her shoulders, tied back with a bright red headscarf - the same bold shade as her lipstick. Her skin was so pale it was almost translucent, as if she had never set foot under the Australian sun (in truth, she only ventured outside beneath a parasol - part precaution, part pretension). She wore a calf-length navy dress patterned with crisp white polka dots, its halter-top cut perfectly framing the colourful sleeve of tattoos that ran down her right arm.

"Two times in the same week, detective. I must've killed a Chinaman," she said with a wink and a cheeky smile.

Sam cocked his head slightly and raised an eyebrow but largely let the comment slide.

"Tell me what you know, Misty."

Misty proceeded to tell him the basic outline of events and they matched pretty well with the story he had already heard from Constable Riley. Mayor McInerny had just finished a vigorous hour with Candy – not her real name – when he had gone into the bathroom to freshen up. When he hadn't come back out after twenty minutes, Misty went in to make sure if everything was okay and found him on the floor. She'd checked his pulse and when she couldn't find one she called triple zero.

"It was bound to happen someday. The bloke was a whale," Misty said. "And Candy's one of my best girls - a true professional. She would've given him a proper session, even if she couldn't stand the sight of him. She's really cut up about it, the poor thing."

"Was anyone else here? What about your other girls?" Sam asked.

"Things were actually a little slow so I'd sent the other two girls off for an early dinner," Misty replied.

"Any chance we'll find drugs in his system?"

Misty's hands went to her hips.

"I don't know what the fuck you'll find in his system, detective, probably a whole roast pork!" Misty said, defensively.

"You know I run a clean operation, Sam. And my girls know I won't put up with that shit. So if you find gear in Jabba The Hut in there, it's on him. But my guess? His heart just exploded on him."

"I'm going to have to take a look in the room the mayor and Candy used."

"Be my guest. Take your time - this whole carry-on has stuffed my business for the day anyway."

"Which one was it?" Sam asked.

"Number 6. Second there on the left."

Room number six was not much bigger than the shared bathroom. A queen-sized bed dominated the space, its sheets still messy and unmade from the mayor's dalliance with Candy. There was a pair of matching bedside tables. A bowl of condoms and a pump pack of lubricant sat on the top of one. On the other was a portable Bluetooth speaker that Sam assumed was used to set the mood. Wedged behind the door was a heavy wooden cupboard that ran the length of the wall and made it impossible to open the door all the way.

Sam pulled the cupboard doors wide. There wasn't much inside apart from some dusty spare blankets, two thin and yellowed spare pillows and, on a quilted, pink coat hanger, one oversized suit jacket.

Sam pulled out his phone again and snapped a few more photos to document what he had found in the cupboard. He then removed the jacket from the hanger and laid it on the bed before searching all the pockets and laying out the contents on the ruffled bedspread next to it.

"Riley, can you come here please?" Sam shouted.

"You called?" Riley said, arriving at the door, moments later.

"Have you got any evidence bags in your car?"

"Sure do. I'll pop down and grab some," Riley said, already half-way down the hall.

Sam took another couple of photos of the jacket and its contents. There was the mayor's wallet, his phone, an absurdly large set of keys, a half-finished tin of mints, a local pharmacy receipt for Viagra and an assortment of loose business cards. The detective checked the images on his phone and was struck by how similar they looked to some of the flat-lays he had seen people post on social media.

He left the items where they were and headed back into the hallway to find Candy. He wasn't expecting her story to be much different to the one he had already heard but as she was the last one to see the mayor alive he needed to tick the boxes. As expected, Candy's story aligned with the version Sam already knew. The mayor had arrived around three o'clock and had asked for Candy by name. Apparently, he always visited Misty's when he heard she was in town. Nothing had struck her as being out of the ordinary, he was sweaty and out of breath as he always was and had insisted that she called him Big Mac as was his wont - he enjoyed either that or Titanic Terry. Afterward, when he went to freshen up, she had scrolled on her phone for a while, browsing resort deals in Fiji for a long-dreamed-of vacation and ordering some face cream from her favourite online shop. But when he didn't return, she went to find Misty in the room a few down, which served as her office, and asked her to go and check on him.

"He was a bit of a pig, but he was harmless enough. Except when he wanted to be on top…" Candy said, finishing up her story.

"Thank you. Did my colleague, Constable Riley, get your details earlier?"

"Sure did, Boss!"

It was Riley, who had returned carrying a few large brown paper evidence bags.

Sam politely released Candy and let her on her way. He took the evidence bags from Riley and, back in room 6, started carefully placing the mayor's jacket and contents inside them, being sure to label the bags as he went.

Riley watched him as he worked.

"Do you think there's more to this, Sam?" Riley asked.

"Probably not," Sam replied, sealing up the last bag.

"I'll take all this and bring it in to the station with me tomorrow. Are you right to wait here until the forensic guys turn up and… do what they have to do?"

"Definitely."

"I'll just be at the restaurant if you need me," Sam said, as he grabbed hold of the evidence bags and made his way from the room.

"Oh…" he remembered, half turning back to Riley. "When they're all done, give Smith Bros. a call and get them to come and collect his body."

FOUR

The Carrington was the top-of-the-range casket in the Smith Bros. funeral catalogue and, while perhaps prone to the usual marketing hyperbole, carried the following description below its glossy picture:

Hewn from majestic Oak, the Carrington offers resplendence like no other casket. Hand-carved detailing, a rich high-gloss finish, and brass handles with platinum accents and golden inlays combine to create an aesthetic that evokes memories of the pharaohs. The plush interior features quilted, pure-white satin fabric to ensure your loved one has the most peaceful forever slumber one could ever hope for.

It was the only fitting choice for Mayor Terry McInerny.

Jim Smith was clearly thrilled with the choice of the

Carrington. At a recommended retail price of $7899 it was a nice little earner - especially since the replica box the mayor was to be actually buried in came in at a couple of hundred bucks, all the trimmings included. The high-resolution image decals stuck to the MDF shell created a surprisingly realistic proxy for the real casket and once the moulded plastic handles were attached, it took a very close inspection to spot the ruse. It worked so well in fact, that in all the years of running the scam, Jim had yet to have anyone raise any suspicions. Tears and grief, it turned out, were willing and reliable accomplices.

The Smith Bros. had received the call to collect the mayor's body from the Royal Hotel at about 7.30pm on the Monday evening. Dr Enrico 'Ricky' Cociarelli - who, although only in his mid-thirties, was a pallid, unusually skinny man save for a disproportionate paunch that gave him a silhouette not too dissimilar to E.T. - arrived to examine the body at approximately 8.45pm.

Dr Cociarelli had first hung out his shingle in Prosperity only a few years earlier and from the outset it was clear that he fancied himself as somewhat of a Don Juan. The stark reality was that he was almost universally viewed by the women in town as more of a 'Don't Wanna'. Indeed, his reputation had been rapidly trending toward that of a lecherous reprobate until fate provide an opportunity for him to redeem himself.

When local five-year-old Jayden Hicks fell into

an abandoned mineshaft, it had been Dr Enrico Cociarelli who had climbed down after him, set his badly broken leg and carried him back up to safety. Although the scuttlebutt at the time was that he had been quite forcefully resistant to rendering assistance initially - something to do with claustrophobia and bone spurs - The Prosperity Ranges Argus chose to ignore those whispers and instead lead with a front page headline the following day trumpeting: 'Cociarelli's Conspicuous Courage'.

While his redemption arc took the form of tolerance more than celebration, it did result in a short-lived but intense dalliance with Brenda Dalwhinney, a thrice-divorced pharmacy assistant at the Prosperity Discount Chemist. Their tumultuous time together was marked by frequent public arguments largely due to Brenda's fiery, borderline violent, and possessive personality. While inevitably detrimental to the longevity of the relationship, there was a silver lining for the wider community - Brenda's parting promise to cut Ricky Cocciarelli's "balls off with a rusty knife" and shove them so far up his arse he'd "be wearing them as earrings" if she ever saw him with another woman, effectively put an end to his harassment of the good women of Prosperity.

Dr Cociarelli's usual demeanour when attending the Smith Bros morgue always made Jim and Mick fell as though the good doctor had been summoned away from something far more enjoyable. He approached this part of his job with about the same enthusiasm as an anaphylactic bee-keeper approaching a hive without a protective suit. This evening was no different. But when he departed after less than fifteen minutes - a period that had involved the quick drawing of a blood sample and what could best be described as a cursory examination of the mayor's body - even the brothers were slightly surprised. Despite his long list of less agreeable traits, one thing that everyone in the community had consensus upon was the doctor's reputation for thoroughness, no matter how reluctantly he may generally have gone about it.

The official cause of death later recorded by Dr Cociarelli was myocardial infarction brought on by vigorous exercise and precipitated by underlying hypertension, chronic morbid obesity, extremely high cholesterol and diabetes. He noted the mayor's blood revealed a high-range blood alcohol reading, the presence of sildenafil citrate (the active ingredient in Viagra) and diazepam, more commonly known as Valium.

Ten days later, the mayor's funeral was an extravagant affair, at least by the more traditional standards more commonly experienced in Prosperity. To the surprise of many, Terry McInerny had left detailed and clearly long-considered plans for his send off. Everything from the Morris dancers celebrating the arrival of his casket to the full pipe band to lead the procession from the church had been thoroughly researched, with preferred suppliers identified and deposits paid, well in advance of his demise.

Detective Chang arrived at the Smith Bros. Peaceful Gardens chapel just before the scheduled 11am start time and stood at the back of the room. It would have been his preferred spot even if there had been room for him to take a seat, which there wasn't. It was standing room only. Despite his many foibles, the mayor clearly remained a popular figure in the community.

Chang liked the back of the room for one main reason - it provided a vantage point from which he could survey the congregation easily and casually. He obviously didn't want to advertise that he was monitoring the residents of Prosperity but he'd learnt over the years that he could learn a lot by observation. It was always telling who was sitting with whom and sometimes, more importantly, who was making a point of setting some distance between themselves and others. And McInerny's send-off had certainly drawn an interesting crowd worth his once over.

The local state and federal members of parliament sat with the rest of the Prosperity Ranges council in the front rows, where they could be clearly seen by their constituents. Off to one side, Misty Gerrard, dressed rather demurely by her standards in a dark green three-quarter sleeve A-line dress, sat next to a stony-faced young woman who Sam took a moment to recognise as Candy, the last person to see the mayor alive. Without her work make up, Candy looked considerably younger, with softer features that gave her the appearance of a homely kindergarten teacher. Filling much of the rest of the front half of the chapel were the various committee members representing the slew of community organisations in town; The Country Women's Association, The Progress Association, The School of Arts Committee, The Park Committee, The Prosperity Public School P&C, the Prosperity Ranges Secondary College P&C, The Lions Club, the Rotary Branch, The War Memorial Preservation committee… plus various representatives of the local sporting clubs and affiliated groups from across the region. Detective Chang had often considered Prosperity to be the most over committeed town in the country. Seeing them all together like this, Sam quietly mused about the devastating power vacuum that would be left in the town should a stray asteroid strike the chapel at that very moment.

Outside of the various dignitaries, the remainder of the seats in the chapel were taken up by general members of the public who had come to pay their respects. The quiet hubbub among the congregation was suddenly overtaken by a blast of music that took Sam a little by surprise. He couldn't help but think it was a little on the loud side for the occasion, not helped by the fact that he was standing directly beneath a huge speaker mounted on the wall. Sam immediately recognised the track. It was *Spirit in the Sky* by Norman Greenbaum.

Sam tried his hardest to fight an almost irresistible compulsion to start dancing. A shimmy at the very least. Perhaps even throw in a little hip twist. He loved music and always struggled to keep his dancing on the inside. He reminded himself where he was and managed to restrain himself, just. Thankfully, Constable Riley provided a welcome distraction as she hurried through the front doors in full police uniform and scanned the room looking for him. Sam raised his hand as discreetly as he could to gain her attention. She eventually spotted him and urgently made her way over to him.

"I'm so sorry I'm late, boss," she said, slightly out of breath.

"I had to park miles away. The bloody carpark was chockers."

Sam's attention was suddenly drawn to a slight commotion in one of the rows towards the front.

"Looks like you're not the only tardy one."

Aleks Keshishian, dressed in his usual black shiny shirt and black jeans - for once situation appropriate - was rather forcefully ushering the ladies from the CWA to their feet. John Harnsuckle, long-time president of the primary school P&C, who was seated in the row behind, made a brief attempt to intervene, only to retreat after a withering glare from Keshishian forced a rapid change of heart. As the shocked and harried ladies gave up their seats,

Christian Palfreeman nonchalantly made his way to take one up. Dressed immaculately in a tailored Gieves and Hawke Suit from London's Saville Row, Palfreeman acted oblivious to the disturbance his late arrival had caused. Aleks slid into a seat next to his boss while two other men who had followed behind them into the chapel - almost identical in look and dress as Keshishian - occupied the remaining seats.

Sam had had little to do with Palfreeman and Keshishian since their arrival in Prosperity, apart from the NOasis poster complaints and dealing with the occasional theft of building equipment from The Oasis site during construction. However, he knew of them and Keshishian's band of Armenian 'associates', known collectively about town as the Kardashians. Riley made a move as if she was about to make her presence felt but Sam caught her arm just in time.

"There's no point, Riley. By the time you get all the way down there you'd just be causing more of a scene."

Sam reached inside his jacket pocket and pulled out a small black notepad and ballpoint pen. He clicked the top of the pen and quickly busied himself writing something. To Riley looking on, she could have sworn he was keeping time with the music as he wrote. And with a flourish that all but confirmed Riley's suspicion, Sam tore a piece of paper from the pad and handed it to his junior colleague.

"I need you to take this outside and place it on the

Kardashians' car," Sam said, leaning in to Riley to avoid having to shout over the music.

"Which one is it?"

"I'm guessing it will be a late model European sedan, probably black and most definitely parked illegally somewhere near the front door. They don't strike me as the types of people to park and walk"

Riley unfolded the piece of paper and quickly read it. She smiled broadly.

"Consider it done, boss."

Riley exited through the front doors of the chapel, leaving the music behind, and stepped into the bright sunshine outside. She pulled down her sunglasses from the top of her head and searched left and right, trying to identify the Kardashians' vehicle. It didn't take her long. Parked almost next to the front door in a fifteen-minute loading zone was a black Mercedes S560.

Riley walked the few steps to the car and placed the paper under the wiper on the front windscreen of the sleek German sedan before flashing a satisfied smile and making her way back inside with a spring in her step. The fine for $191 spelled out the transgression clearly: 'Park contrary to signage' with an additional note added to the bottom - 'More than Tea and Scones' (the motto of the Prosperity Ranges branch of the Country Women's Association).

Coming in at over two and three-quarter hours,

Terry McInerny's send-off set a record for the longest funeral of Jim Smith's career. The service booklet alone was eighteen pages. Each of the three eulogies, although supposedly capped at seven minutes per speech, collectively ran for almost an hour. The slide show took up another twelve minutes and once the hymns, readings and musical interludes were thrown in, many of the mourners were beginning to question the merits of attending.

As the congregation patiently endured the complete nine-minute version of Guns 'n' Roses' *November Rain*, a favourite of the late mayor's and the last item on the order of service, Jim's mind started to drift to his next job at hand - the far more difficult task of switching the mayor out of the Carrington and into the cheap burial likeness that was already waiting in the back of the van. All while en route to the cemetery. While Jim and Mick were generally well practised at the swap by this time, they had never had to deal with a man of the mayor's size before. In order to help facilitate the exchange, Mick had cobbled together what amounted to a small electronic hoist in the back of the van. As Slash's guitar solo soared, so did Jim's anxiety. His palms grew clammy despite Mick's breezy assurances that the contraption would hold. The truth was, they hadn't had time to test the new rig before the funeral. One thing Jim hated more than anything was being less than completely prepared. And if the logistics weren't troubling him enough, Jim couldn't help but fixate on the fact that they had never tried to pull it off in front of such a large and diverse crowd before.

And especially not in front of a crowd that included Detective Sam Chang.

FIVE

The inside of the Peaceful Gardens was suddenly less then peaceful, as it filled with the rousing pipes and staccato drums of the Prosperity Ranges Pipe Band. They performed with gusto as the congregation stood to begin the procession of the mayor's casket from the chapel. In a move welcomed by his many friends and acquaintances, a collective decision had been reached prior to the mayor's funeral for his pallbearers to be comprised of players from the Nuggets Rugby League first grade side.

However, even the chosen six - the burliest of the burley - struggled to carry the mayor's body down the aisle and out to the waiting van. The task was made more difficult still by the pressing issue of getting all forty pipers and drummers out through the double doors and into the open air, a task not helped by the mournfully slow tempo of the chosen hymn *Amazing Grace*. Although they only had to carry the hefty casket a distance of no more than fifty metres, the young men were already visibly wilting by the thirty metre mark, as the casket began wabbling and shaking under the strain.

Jim stood waiting at the open rear doors of the van when a sudden panic gripped him. The pallbearers were lurching toward him, the mayor's bulk threatening disaster with every step. It wasn't so much the potential indignity of dropping the mayor in front of such a crowd that worried him but rather, if the casket did fall, with so much weight inside it, the Carrington wouldn't stand a chance. Jim could already see their plans unravelling - once the box was damaged, there'd be no chance of reselling it and all their preparations would be for nothing.

In an effort to avert disaster, Jim broke with protocol and rushed to provide an extra set of hands. He grabbed the handle at the front of the casket and managed to steady the ship, enabling them to reach the van in one piece.

"Well, that was close to an unmitigated fucking disaster!" Jim said as he scrambled into the back of the van with the casket and pulled the doors closed behind him.

Mick, who was sitting in relative comfort behind the wheel, seemed rather unmoved.

"Never in doubt, brother," Mick said, looking through the rear vision mirror, smiling.

"Thanks for your help by the way," Jim muttered as he made his way towards the front of the van.

"You're meant to be the big, strong, footy player one remember?" Jim said, as he huffed and wiped his brow. "Now, get back here. I'll drive."

"Relax, you're back there now, so you may as well stay put," Mick said. "Besides, everyone's watching the van. It'll look sus".

Jim looked out through the front windscreen. Mick was right, all eyes did seem to be on them

"Bloody hell," he said, hanging his head.

The van shuddered to life as Mick turned the ignition.

"It's fine. I'll talk you through it."

It wasn't so much that Jim hadn't handled the casket swap before, even though Mick was better suited to it given his size, Jim had certainly done his fair share over the years. It was just in this instance, Jim had simply assumed that as Mick had built the special contraption they were using for the mayor, that he would be the one best placed to operate it.

"It's seven minutes to the cemetery," Mick said, as he pulled the van out of the chapel's circular driveway and eased it out on to the road. "But if I drive slow enough, I reckon I can probably stretch that to about eight and a half."

Resigned, Jim reluctantly made his way back towards the mayor's casket. He took his phone from his pocket. As he removed his jacket and hung it over a small hook on the inside wall of the van, he spoke to his phone and asked it to set a timer for eight minutes.

He then took a deep breath and got to work.

He pulled back a maroon velvet blanket that had been used to obscure the dummy casket at the end of the van furthest from the rear doors and began to wrestle it into place next to the real thing. In the tight, airless quarters of the back of the van, this manoeuvre was no mean feat. By the time Jim had it lined up parallel alongside the original, he was already breaking into a decent sweat. Large dark patches were forming under his arms and his shirt was beginning to stick to his back.

"You'd want to get a wriggle on, mate. If I drive any slower I'll be going backwards!" Mick said, piping up from the front seat.

A quick eyeroll was all the time Jim could spend on his brother's helpful interjection. He removed the large flower arrangement sitting on top of the casket and carefully put it to one side, conscious of keeping it as undisturbed as possible in order for it to be able to reclaim its position in as pristine condition as possible. He then cautiously began unclasping the lid of the Carrington and gently opened it up.

Terry McInerny was dressed in a sharp three-piece pin stripe suit with red satin tie, topped off with a pair of pristine white patent leather brogues. The careful refrigeration of the mayor had held the natural processes of decay at bay and Jim couldn't help but think that he actually looked fairly decent, all things considered. The blue-grey hue of his skin wasn't too dissimilar to his complexion when he was alive and the discreetly placed pouches of potpourri were doing an admirable job of keeping the unmistakable smell of death obscured. What hadn't changed was his size. If at all possible, he looked even bigger, his body wedged in hard against the sides of the casket to fit.

"Okay, now you've got it open, find the tabs up by his shoulders and down by his thighs and pull on them," Mick said, flicking his eyes between the road and the rear vision mirror to keep an equally attentive eye on both.

It didn't take long to find the yellow tabs that Mick was referring to. Jim did as instructed and pulled on them. They were attached to large green heavy-duty tow straps that stretched taut underneath the mayor's body.

"Now, hook the wall straps to the loose ends using the carabiners."

Jim reached towards one side of the van and took hold of one of two similar tow straps that had been bolted to the side panel of the vehicle. He held open the latch of the carabiner and slid it through the end of its corresponding strap in the casket. He then repeated the process once more on the same side and then performed the same task twice more on the other side until all four straps were secured.

Jim quickly stole a look at his phone. The timer only had two minutes and fourteen seconds left. He was acutely aware that it was taking too long.

"Time to fire up the winches, Jim. You're gunna

have to be careful to get them both going at the same time to keep the straps level. You don't want the big fella sliding off as you lift him!"

Mounted on the floor on the nearside of the casket were two portable winches that Mick had picked up from the local auto superstore. The ends of the tow ropes had already been fed around the spools. Sitting next to each winch were hand-held remote controls to operate them. Jim picked one up in each hand and cautiously moved his thumbs into position over the respective control buttons.

"You'd want to hurry up, mate. We're about to pull into the cemetery," Mick said, for the first time betraying a hint of urgency in his voice.

Jim did his best to shut his brother out as he cautiously pushed the buttons. The winches sprang into action and began winding in the tow straps, slowly taking up the slack until they pulled tight underneath the mayor. The winches resisted for a moment under the strain before Jim noticed Terry McInerny's body ever so gently start to levitate.

At first, Jim cursed the sluggish pace of the winches as the mayor slowly levitated out of the casket. But he quickly thanked his lucky stars. Although Jim had been meticulous in trying to keep the winches winding in tandem, he hadn't allowed for enough difference in girth between the mayor's upper torso and his legs. This had resulted in his body emerging from the Carrington on an increasingly steep angle and it was in imminent danger of sliding off the straps.

"You've got about sixty seconds, Jim!"

Trying his best not to panic, Jim quickly stopped the torso winch while keeping the lower winch going to allow the legs to catch up. From there it didn't take him long to adjust his method and get a handle on feathering the winches to keep them in unison. Soon, the hulking frame was clear of the casket and suspended precariously in the air like some kind of magician's illusion.

"Slide him across the straps mate and get him in that box as quick as you can. I'm running out of runway here!"

This was the part Jim had always been nervous about. Getting the mayor in the air was one thing, moving him safely across the straps was another thing entirely. He grabbed hold of the mayor as tightly as he could and tried to slip him across the straps. After a couple of firm tugs that required almost all the effort Jim could rouse, he knew he was in trouble. In theory, it should have been easy enough to slide him along the taut straps but despite the best efforts of the winches, there was still enough natural give in them to make it all but impossible.

"Thirty seconds, mate. Get him in that fucking box!"

"Would you just shut up for once!" Jim shouted back.

Jim made a split-second decision and abandoned the idea of sliding the body. Instead, he reached over and grabbed the far side of the mayor and leant back to gain some leverage. He used all his strength and body weight to try to roll the body over towards him and bring it up on to its side. He struggled but finally managed to get the mayor up on one shoulder. But the cadaver passed its tipping point much faster than Jim had allowed for and it came tumbling over, hurtling in Jim's direction with terrifying momentum. In the scramble to get out of the way, Jim found himself lying on his back inside the cheap box. He was now looking straight up at the massive corpse, suspended, face down, above him. The supporting straps had shifted in all the action and the mayor was now delicately held by one strap across his neck at one end and one across his ankles at the other. With the body now bowed in the middle, Jim could feel the mayor's belly pressing against his own. The mayor's arms flopped down either side of Jim, all but trapping him completely.

Suddenly, Jim's phone sprang to life in a series of chiming bells. The eight-minute timer was up.

"Shit!" Jim said, panic vibrating through him.

He frantically looked around to try to find a way out. He spied a small gap between the mayor's body and the top of the casket and managed to squeeze his hand through, wincing as he scraped his arm along the sharp edge, before forcing his elbow then his shoulder into the gap. He desperately stretched his arm as far as he could manage, his fingers reaching just long enough to touch the side of the van. He walked his fingers from side to side until he found one of the strap fasteners. He wrapped his hand around it tightly and, pressing his own body against the mayor's, he tugged and wriggled and slowly pulled himself free.

But it had cost him precious seconds. Time he didn't have.

"Shit, shit, shit!"

Jim looked at the precariously hanging mayor. There was no way he was going to be able to roll him onto his back and lower him into the box in the next few seconds. This was rapidly turning into a cluster fuck.

"What do I do?" Jim screamed, turning to his brother.

He suddenly felt the van aggressively accelerate under him then lurch violently as it launched over a speed bump. Jim turned to see the mayor's body momentarily become airborne, reminding him of people flying around weightless in a Zero Gravity Plane he'd seen once on YouTube, before unceremoniously crashing facedown through the straps and into the box beneath it.

"Just put the lid on and dress it up," Mick said, pleased with himself.

Jim looked at the awkwardly positioned mayor, lying face-down in a tangle in the box. He couldn't help but feel guilty. Despite everything, he had always tried to be respectful to the dead and treat them with compassion.

"We can't bury him like this, Mick. Can't you go around the block or something?" Jim said, pleading.

"I mean, at least give me a minute or two to figure something out."

"No chance, Jim. There are no more minutes left."

Jim could feel the van slowing. He knew his brother was right but hated what he was about to do.

He straightened the mayor up as best he could and slid on the box's lid. He hastily fastened it in place with the simple hooks that secured it, as the van came to a gradual stop before the engine switched off.

Jim heard the front door open and close and then the crunch of his brother's footsteps on the gravel outside, as he made his way down the side of the van. He hastily reached for the flower arrangement - that remained remarkably intact - and slid it back into position on the mayor's new casket so as to complete the look of the previous Carrington.

Next, he grabbed the still suspended straps swaying above him and fumbled with shaking fingers to open the carabiners. He could hear the muffled sound of his brother talking with mourners at the rear of the van as he finally managed to unhook them, sending the straps swinging like pendulums in opposite directions and coming to rest against the sides of the van. He scrambled on the floor for the maroon velvet blanket and hurriedly spread it over the actual Carrington to conceal it.

Finally, as the rear doors swung open, flooding

the back of the van with the brightness of the day outside, Jim slid back on his jacket and pickled up his still chiming phone. He turned off the timer before sliding the phone back into his inside breast pocket as Mick grabbed the handle on the rear of the mayor's new casket and started to drag it out the back doors.

As he climbed out of the back of the van, still trying to catch his breath, Jim felt a firm slap on his shoulder. It was Mick's way of telling him he'd done a good job. But Jim couldn't shake the feeling of tightness in his chest from his surging anxiety. The same thought kept circulating in his head. Around and around. The thought that they'd never tried to pull off the switch in front of such a large crowd, for such a high-profile client. And never when they knew the police were going to be watching on.

Thankfully for the brothers, the majority of the mourners were still gathering themselves in the parking lot by the time they got the casket graveside. It gave them time to transfer the box from the gurney to the mechanical lowering system that held the casket above the grave (it was this bit of machinery that had been Mick's inspiration for the winch set-up that Jim had just wrangled with). The design of the contraption being what it was, once in place, the casket sat partially in the grave below the ground level. Combined with the oversized flower arrangement on top, once it was in situ, there was remarkably little of the actual casket left visible to betray the deception.

Half an hour later, following a touching committal from the local Anglican minister, despite the mayor's often professed atheism, and a rather earnestly melodramatic reading of W.H Auden's *Funeral Blues* by twelve year old local girl Maddi Bourke – recipient of the mayor's young citizen of the year award* - all evidence of the scam was buried under six feet of earth.

Jim had tried to play it cool but kept a keen eye on Detective Chang throughout proceedings. To his relief, Chang, positioned toward the rear of the gathering, spent most of the time watching the crowd, giving the casket only a cursory glance.

Despite this, and even though none of the other eighty odd people in attendance had seemed to notice anything amiss, Jim couldn't shake his anxiety completely.

Something was gnawing at him.

Something was making him unsettled.

Something told him that the whole thing wasn't finished with just yet.

*Maddi Bourke had won her young citizen of the year award for her local fundraising efforts in support of threatened Sumatran Orangutans. However, her victory hadn't come without controversy. A minor scandal had erupted when it was discovered that the cheap fundraising chocolates that formed the backbone of young Maddi's campaign were, unfortunately, made with palm oil derived from the very plantations threatening the Orangutans. With the Argus ready to run a front-page story "Fundraising or Fund-RAZING?" it was only a last-minute intervention by the mayor that saw the story killed. As it so happened, Terry had become quite partial to the chocolates in question and had in fact ordered at least two dozen boxes from Maddi, making up the lion's share of the $117 eventually raised. This, naturally, led to some quiet murmurs about a seeming conflict of interest - or of potential currying favour at the very least - following the mayor's announcement of Maddi's prize.

SIX

Christian Palfreeman sat in the rear of his Mercedes S560 and stared out the heavily tinted window as the last buildings on the main street of Prosperity gave way to the scrubby farmland on the edge of town. He massaged his brow to try to ease the pain of the tension headache that had been building all day. Funerals had never been his favourite kind of social gathering but the Greta Thunberg impersonator butchering W.H Auden's poetry graveside had had him considering jumping in the casket with the mayor. Palfreeman had always counted 'Four Weddings and a Funeral' in his top five favourite films of all time, in large part due to the touching scene during which *Funeral Blues* is recited in the movie's eponymous send off. Indeed, he had briefly considered using it for his own service one day.

"It's meant to be 'Scribbling on the sky the message 'He is Dead'. Not 'Scribbling on the sky the message

'He. Is. *Deeaaaaaad,*'" Palfreeman said, doing his best to capture Maddi's dramatic rendition that was more suited perhaps for a highly commended at the local eisteddfod rather than the formal occasion of a mayor's burial. He rubbed his head more intensely before lashing out and pounding the window in frustration.

"For fuck's sake, how hard is it?"

Aleks Keshishian, who was sharing the back seat with Palfreeman, briefly looked up from his phone before resuming his interest in the screen. Yet another rhetorical outburst from his boss that required no input from him. Besides, his attention was firmly with the self-help guru Gary Vaynerchuk and his keynote address about ignoring negative feedback in business called: *Fuck you, no one cares about your feelings.*

A thick vein was starting to rise on Palfreeman's forehead and he began scrambling to loosen his tie. He was soon shifting wildly in his seat as he struggled with the knot and smeared sweat across his trousers in a vain attempt to dry his palms.

"I need some water." Palfreeman said, with rising desperation.

"I need some fucking water!"

Aleks again looked up from his screen, paused the video, and casually tapped the driver on the shoulder and motioned for him to pull over.

The Mercedes slid to a stop on the gravel shoulder and was briefly swallowed up in a cloud of dust.

When the dust settled, Palfreeman was already out of the car and pacing back and forth like a startled giraffe.

"Aleks! Water!" Palfreeman shouted, without breaking from his manic dance.

Aleks was in no hurry to rush to the rescue. Like a paramedic at a crash scene, he calmly made his way around the front of the car and offered a bottle of Italian sparkling water to his panicked superior.

Palfreeman snatched the water from his grasp and fought with the lid while trying to remove it. The whole scene had an air of pantomime about it. After a furious few seconds of effort, he handed the still closed bottle back to Aleks, who simply twisted the cap and opened the bottle with a loud *fizz* and passed it back to Palfreeman. As he hungrily inhaled its carbonated contents, Aleks placed a reassuring hand on his back.

"Remember to breathe, Christian," Aleks said, in a calm voice, rich with his gravelly Armenian accent. "In through the nose - two…three…four. Out through the mouth - two…three…four."

But Palfreeman suddenly erupted with an expulsion of water. It sprayed from his mouth and nose in a violent, fizzy torrent.

"Jesus Christ, it's fucking sparkling you dickhead!" Christian said with a splutter. "You could have warned me. I almost bloody choked to death!"

Unmoved, Aleks continued counting in the same slow, measured way.

"In - two…three…four. Out - two…three…four"

Palfreeman tried the water again, more cautiously this time. He gradually began timing his breath to the count.

"In - two…three…four. Out - two…three…four"

Slowly a measure of calm started to return to the situation.

"This is good, Christian. This will be over soon. Remember your mantra."

Palfreeman looked up for the first time and turned to Aleks with doe like eyes.

"Yes, my mantra."

Christian took a moment to compose himself and let out one long cathartic breath then began, his voice quiet to begin with.

"These feelings are real but they will not hurt me."

He repeated even louder.

"These feelings are real but they will not hurt me"

Aleks checked his watch, his nose wrinkling in disinterest.

"THESE FEELINGS ARE REAL BUT THEY WILL NOT HURT ME!"

Palfreeman was now standing tall and shouting to the open sky. He broke into a wide smile and laughter tumbled out of him uncontrollably.

"We're late," Aleks said, as he started to make his way back around to his side of the car only to stop short. It was only now that he noticed the fine Constable Riley had placed under the windscreen wiper. He removed it, quickly read it, then scrunched it into a ball and tossed it over his shoulder, emotionless.

As Aleks slid back into his seat, Palfreeman remained outside. His laughter quickly trailed off and he took a second to compose himself. He straightened his tie, combed his hair into place with his fingers and climbed back into the Mercedes.

Once the doors were closed, the driver put the car into gear and put his foot on the accelerator. The tires spun for a second in the gravel before bighting hard and launching the vehicle back onto the main road. Palfreeman continued to straighten himself up as his composure finally fully returned. He reached into his pocket and produced a tin of breath mints. He popped three into his palm and threw them into his mouth.

"Mint?" he said to Aleks, offering the tin in his direction.

Aleks gave a small, almost imperceptible shake of his head.

"My apologies for that little… episode just now. I've been under a hell of a lot of stress recently," Palfreeman said, finally feeling in control once again. "With The Oasis opening. With the whole thing with the mayor. And then that bloody insufferable funeral."

"I really need to get back into my daily yoga practice," Palfreeman continued, "and commit to meditation again. You know, really provide an outlet for controlling my anxieties. Master my inner self again."

"Kick-boxing," Aleks replied, "I find kicking the shit out of something very good for release. Kickboxing and sex. The best for these…anxieties."

"I'll take that on board," Palfreeman said, as he looked out the window just in time to see a large, brand new advertising hoarding for The Oasis on the side of the highway. It featured an artist's rendition of a scantily clad, buxom medieval maiden standing by a pool of inviting azure water in an otherwise barren desert. Emblazoned across the top was the slogan '*Quench All Your Desires*'.

Christian winced. He'd argued back and forth with the marketing team about the word *quench*. His gut feeling had been that too many people wouldn't know what it meant. Especially around these parts. But the team had prosecuted a convincing argument that it was language in keeping with the entire theme of the place and he'd ended up relenting. However, now seeing it on the billboard for the first time had him convinced that he'd been right all along.

"Aleks, remind me when we get to the office to change that fucking sign as soon as we can. I want a new one up before the opening next week. Also, remind me to fire the fucking marketing team!"

And with that, Christian Palfreeman felt his power fully returned.

"Now, I'm only going to ask this once and then I don't want to discuss it again Aleks. The mayor's USB is taken care of yes? No loose ends?"

"100 percent. No loose ends, Christian."

"Good, Aleks. Very good," Palfreeman said.

Aleks Keshishian had good reason for his confidence. The night before he had personally overseen the break-in at the Smith Bros. funeral home. He had then made sure that it was he who had carefully placed the USB inside the casket under the mayor's body. As far as Aleks was concerned, the device was now buried beneath a couple of tonnes of soil, inside a sealed box, under a two-hundred-kilogram deceased mayor. Sure, it would have been easier to just crush the small device under one of the Cuban heels of his boots, but he thoroughly enjoyed the romance of burying the sins with the sinner. And he quietly savoured the added thrill of the wholly unnecessary risk of it all.

Aleks sat in quiet contentment as the black Mercedes continued heading away from Prosperity for the next fifteen minutes. It rapidly approached the bridge that crossed the dry riverbed before it took a sudden hard right turn onto a well-maintained dirt road and lost itself in the cloud of dust kicked up by the tyres.

A sign slowly emerged from the settling dirt. It was the same busty maiden, this time with her arm outstretched and index finger extended, pointing down the road the Mercedes had just taken.

Your Private Oasis Awaits. Entrance 1km.

SEVEN

Your Perfect job Awaits. Apply at The Oasis Now.
Tracy Smith had been sitting on her computer at the rustic farm table in her kitchen for the past hour, staring at her laptop. Her long, sandy blonde hair was pulled back into a messy ponytail and she was still wearing her neon accented activewear from her daily workout. Tracy had always been fastidious about maintaining her figure and still kept her favourite outfit from when she was twenty. It served as a kind of yardstick. Even though the fashion - a ripped, wide-leg pair of jeans and a nude crop top - was horribly out of date, whether she could still fit into it remained her body's litmus test. Tracy had, up until recently, travelled daily to her gym, an almost two hour round trip into Bathurst. It was worth it for the full complement of classes on offer, everything from Body Attack to spin classes to a proprietary functional fitness programme set to 70's music

simply called *FUNKtional*, her guilty pleasure. It also didn't hurt that her personal trainer Matt was easy on the eye, even if his regular form correction often strayed into handsy territory.

However, Tracy had lately been forced into following free workout videos on YouTube after Mick had abruptly stopped paying for her gym membership. No matter how much she tried to convince herself to the contrary, online tutorials just didn't hit the same.

She had only meant to sit at the computer for a few minutes to indulge in her usual routine of checking social media while she cooled down post workout. However, today she had soon found herself, almost absent mindedly at first, scouring the local jobs website. One listing had already pulled her back several times - the post advertising opportunities at The Oasis. Tracy knew all about The Oasis - her good friend Cath's husband was the site foreman during construction - so she'd been wary at first about exactly what sort of 'jobs' were on offer. But the wanted ad seemed pretty stock standard and read like any new hospitality venue looking for staff. There were positions for chefs, front of house roles, bar staff, cleaning crews, valets and porters. Not a single one of them had even a hint of anything unseemly. Tracy figured the hiring of the 'specialist' staff would most likely be handled by a different, more niche department.

Tracy looked up from the computer as she heard

the screen door at the side of the house open - the hinges resisting with a loud squeak - then close with a jarring rattle on the door frame.

"Mick," Tracy said, calling out to the next room, "can you come in here a sec?"

Mick hopped into the room on one foot, still trying to pull off one of his work boots. His dark blue drill shirt bore large sweat-marks under each arm and in a quintessential 'v' shape over his chest, testament to his day's toil on the farm.

"The fucking electric fence wasn't working down in the far paddock," Mick began, throwing his boot out of the room, back towards the front door.

"The stupid bloody cows were all mixed in with 'Old Man' Harrigan's. It was a fucking shit show trying to separate that lot. And the old codger Harrigan is about as useful as a one-armed paper hanger."

Mick grabbed a glass off the bench and filled it with water from the kitchen tap and thirstily gulped it down.

"Then it took me the best part of half a day to fix the buggered fence. And then I almost electrocuted myself half a dozen times trying to get the fucking energiser to work properly. I tell you Trace, I'm not built for this farm crap."

"Yeah, no shit," Tracy said, under her breath.

"What was that?"

"Sounds shit," Tracy said, speaking up.

Mick pulled up a chair next to his wife at the table.

"Now, what did you want? I'm desperate for a shower. I stink like a kebab."

"I'm thinking about getting a job," Tracy said. "Get a bit more money coming in."

Mick's head dropped.

"What have we talked about? You don't need to do that. I know things haven't exactly panned out like I promised, Trace. But things will turn around. The drought's got to break sooner or later. Then we can re-stock and get this place back to what it was. Until then, the funeral stuff will keep us afloat."

"But it's not enough, Mick."

Mick slammed his fist on the table in a sudden outburst of anger. Tracy jumped in her chair.

"It never is, is it?!" Mick snapped, his voice cracking hard like a whip.

Tracy slid her chair back and stood up. She grabbed Mick's glass off the bench and marched to the fridge. She opened the door and reached for the nozzle on the cask of Fruity Lexia sitting on the middle shelf, filling her glass almost to the brim. Shutting the fridge door, she leant back against the bench and took a large sip.

"I was meant to be a WAG, Mick," she said, bitterly. "Look at me - day drinking in activewear after doing free YouTube workouts 'cause I can't afford a fucking gym membership."

Mick's eyes fell to the laptop and he slid it over so he could see the screen properly. It took him about two seconds to connect 'jobs' with 'The Oasis'. His blood began to boil.

"So what? You're going to be a bloody hooker are you? Great career choice, Trace!" Mick yelled.

"At least I might get some attention then, Mick," Tracy spat back.

Mick's eyes filled with tears, a mix of anger and his own deep feelings of failure.

"No wife of mine…"

Tracy cut him off.

"As if I would ever be a hooker, Mick. Read it properly, dickhead."

Mick looked at the laptop screen again. He wiped his eyes with the back of his hands to clear the welling tears so he could make out the words without feeling like he was reading through swimming goggles filled half filled with water. Tracy could feel the tension easing. Tracy's voice softened.

"I just figured I could pour beers or something. That place has the only jobs going around here," Tracy said.

"What, work behind the bar?"

"Yeah, I've been getting my own drinks, and yours for that matter, for years so it's not like I don't have experience. Or maybe I could work just cleaning rooms or something."

Tracy finished her drink with a large gulp as Mick eased himself back onto his chair. Tracy set her glass down and joined Mick back at the table.

"I'm sorry, Trace. I don't mean to be like this. I just always thought our lives would be footy and fame, not funerals and this bloody farm," Mick said.

Tracy looked at her husband, hunched over. He was a shadow of the man she'd first fallen for. She knew that he kept up his old bravado around town, always the local hero. Shoulders wide enough to carry the whole town. Even in front of his brother. But Tracy had seen first-hand how much his failure to crack the big time of the National Rugby League had taken out of him. How much it had hollowed him out.

When they had first met, he was the guy everyone talked about. Every bloke wanted to be him. Every girl wanted to be with him. He was head and shoulders above all the other league players in the local competition, and everyone knew it. He had talent scouts from most of the big clubs courting him. They offered him the world. And she'd been there since almost the beginning. Tracy wasn't naïve enough to think that there hadn't been other girls along the way. She knew for a fact that Sharnee Maitland used to give him blow jobs behind the sheds if he had a good game. Which was most weeks (the slapper). But she'd stuck with him. Mostly because she loved him. Although there had always been a part of her that had hoped he'd be her ticket out of town.

And for a brief moment he was.

After Mick had been signed up on a three-year contract, to great celebration in town, she had joined him in Sydney in a one-bed apartment just off Bondi

Road in the city's east. While Mick had put in a solid pre-season with the team over the summer, Tracy had put in a pre-season of her own, lapping up the beach lifestyle. She was a regular on the Bondi to Bronte walk and had her spot picked out on the sand at North Bondi beach. She regularly hosted her friends from home at the North Bondi RSL and almost had Mick convinced of the idea of them getting a puppy - a staffie, of course. She had also started to appear here and there in the social pages, occurrences that suitably stroked her ego. With the season just around the corner and Mick, by all reports, training the house down, Tracy could taste her future. And she couldn't have been more certain that it was exactly who she was meant to be.

The night it all unravelled for them both had actually started out wonderfully. Mick had surprised Tracy with a bunch of lilies - her favourite flowers - despite the fact that they gave him terrible hay fever. This was followed by a romantic dinner at the finger wharf at Woolloomooloo, after which they strolled up the hill to King's Cross to meet up with some of the other guys from Mick's team.

Tracy and Mick were slow dancing to Seal's *Kissed By A Rose* when the scuffle broke out. One of Mick's teammates had unwittingly been hitting on the girlfriend of a bikie with a hair-trigger control of his emotions. Mick had crossed the dance floor to break things up when he'd been king hit from behind. His eye had swollen shut almost immediately. Tracy had her wits about her enough to grab hold of Mick and extract him from the mêlée and out of the nightclub before any more punches were thrown. She was keenly aware of the negative media backlash that usually accompanied incidents involving footballers at 3am in the Cross. Unfortunately for Mick, the reduced vision from his newly broken eye-socket meant that he failed to see the wonky paver sticking up by the famous El Alamein fountain outside. If the searing pain from his anterior cruciate ligament rupturing in his knee hadn't sobered Mick up, the cold water of the fountain surely had, as he tripped and tumbled headlong into the shallow pool. The photos of a soaking wet Mick being helped from the fountain were all over the papers the next morning. Even the Argus had run them under the headline 'Smith Makes Sydney Splash'.

Needless to say, the club hadn't been happy. Even though everyone had backed Mick and Tracy's story that painted Mick as concerned bystander at worst if not the innocent victim of a vicious coward punch, the club had to be seen to make a stand. The incident came at the worst possible time for both Mick, the club and the National Rugby League, occurring as it did during an offseason that seemed to have lurched from crisis to crisis. First had been the leaked video of a star player caught in a compromising sexual act with his teammate's stepmother in the toilets of a popular eastern suburbs pub. Then there had been the team-building golf day that had descended into chaos when a couple of the players thought it would be hilarious to defecate in the fourteenth *and* fifteenth holes. And when an Australia day BBQ resulted in accusations of drug taking, sexual misconduct and animal cruelty, the talking heads in the media were baying for blood.

The circumstances being what they were, the club fined Mick thirty-five thousand dollars, an amount that made up a large part of the first year of his rookie contract. Mick had tried to take it on the chin but the first six months of rehab on his knee had been tough mentally. He couldn't help but feel like he'd been made a scapegoat. The media had been relentless, holding him up as a symbol of everything wrong with the modern game and the entitlement of its young, overpaid players. He put on weight. He started skipping his physio appointments. Tracy had found it hard to watch as they both realised their dreams were slipping away. Ultimately, it had been unsurprising when the club finally cut him loose during the following off season with Mick never having donned the jersey on the field.

Returning to Prosperity had been tough for Mick. The big fish in the little pond again. Sure, he never had to buy a beer at the pub but that wasn't enough to make up for the fact that he was always going to be the guy that should've made it - but didn't.

'The best player never to play in the NRL' was how Frank Collinton used to describe him with such pride. A little piece of Mick died each time he heard it.

Tracy looked across the table at him now and didn't want to pity him but she couldn't help it. She reached out her hand out and placed it over his.

"It's just a job, Mick. And we could really use the extra cash."

They sat in silence for a moment before Mick pulled his hand back.

"I'm going to go take that shower."

EIGHT

Sam Chang stood over the flaming hot wok in the kitchen of Lee's New Golden Imperial Lotus Garden and wiped his sweating brow with a tea towel he kept thrown over his shoulder. It hadn't been an unusually busy night - a few takeaway orders of the typical mixed entrée, honey chicken, Mongolian lamb, special fried rice variety - but he always felt a little bit more heat when Marnie Rochambeau was dining.

To the people of Prosperity, the diminutive Marnie was somewhat of an enigma wrapped in a riddle, wrapped in a mystery, wrapped in another riddle. No one could remember when Marnie had first shown up in town; some swore blind they had memories of growing up with her as a kid more than half a century ago, while others were willing to put their house on the fact that she had only turned up a few years back. However, the backstory that seemed to excite the town's imagination most was the one that portrayed Marnie as the eccentric wealthy widow of a long-deceased textile millionaire who had sought out a quiet rural refuge to see out her dotage as an antidote to her previous gilded existence. People pointed to her fierce grey bob, preference for a popped collar and her ubiquitous string of pearls as undeniable supporting evidence. Many a whisper suggested that she would have looked more at home in the high-end boutiques of Sydney or Melbourne than in Danielle's Discount Designs, the local dress shop (and novelty gift store) on the main street of Prosperity.

Marnie kept largely to herself. She lived in a small cottage on one of the back streets in town and spent much of her time tending to her garden where she had nurtured an array of fabulous flowering plants including her spectacular dahlias that often took first prize at the annual Prosperity show. Sam had made a habit of walking out of his way on a semi-regular basis under the pretence of inspecting her flowers in order to conduct a sort of low-key welfare check. He never went in to her house but would smile and say hello if he happened upon her in the garden as he passed.

Marnie had intrigued Sam since the first time she had eaten in his restaurant. It wasn't so much that she ordered Zha Jiang Mian (Beijing fried sauce noodles) off menu but more so that she had placed her request in flawless mandarin. Sam had been shocked and thrilled all at the same time but Marnie had brushed it off with the same nonchalance to which Sam had now grown accustomed.

'You don't live as long as me without picking up a few things along the way' was the way Marnie had explained herself.

Sam relished the challenge Marnie invariably gave him every time she walked through his doors and tonight was certainly that. It was usual for her to simply arrive unannounced and keep Sam on his toes with a random request for a dish. However, this evening was something special that had been many weeks in the making. On Marnie's prior visit to Lee's New Golden Imperial Lotus Garden, she had placed a specific order for an old favourite of hers to be enjoyed as her next meal: Chou doufu – Stinky Tofu. Moreover, for the first time ever, the request came with one other stipulation. In deference to the potent aroma of the meal, betrayed by the dish's name, Marnie had insisted that she come to dine near closing time to prevent any other potential customers being put off by the stench. Sam had been more than happy to oblige and given the pungent fumes currently filling the building - a smell reminiscent of putrid socks after having being worn for days on end hiking in the tropics - was grateful for Marnie's suggestion.

Sam plated up the Stinky Tofu and added some finishing touches to the dish - a sprinkle of coriander and chopped spring onion, a side of pickled cabbage and a serve each of both soy and garlic sauces - before carrying it out to the keenly awaiting Marnie. He proudly placed it down on the table in front of her.

"Chou dofu as requested," Sam said.

"Xiexie da chu (thank you chef)," Marnie said, beaming.

"Smells delicious, doesn't it?"

"Well, I'm hopeful it will taste much better than it smells," Sam said.

"Of that I have no doubts, Sam," Marnie said, as she picked up her chopsticks and expertly used them to navigate a piece of the tofu into her mouth. She closed her eyes and let out a soft moan of pleasure.

"Absolutely delightful."

"I'm so glad," Sam said, "I'll leave you to enjoy your meal".

Marnie was already into her next piece of tofu as Sam turned and made his way to the table closest to the door to the kitchen. He sat down and started looking through the papers he had organised into a number of piles in front of him.

The stacks of printouts were all in connection with the mayor's death. In one pile he had copies of every article from the Argus about the mayor from the past three years (a massive and tedious task he was eternally grateful to Constable Riley for undertaking) that had given the detective a new found respect for the skills of the sub editors responsible for the paper's headlines. He had also been struck by the sheer number of times the mayor had been favourably quoted about The Oasis development. Another pile had print outs of the official forensic photographs as well as the ones Sam had taken himself on his phone. The two remaining piles had copies of the eyewitness statements in one and the mayor's lengthy medical records, including Dr Cociarelli's cause of death report, in the other.

Sam had poured over each pile several times. He couldn't quite place his finger on what it was exactly but there was just something about the mayor's death that left him feeling unsettled. There was no doubt in Sam's mind that Terry McInerny was a prime candidate for a heart attack. Just looking at the man was enough evidence of that. And given that the mayor had been a regular diner at his own restaurant, with a capacity for prawn toast unmatched in the district, Sam knew that the mayor had been treating his body more like an amusement park than a temple.

Still, he felt uneasy about it.

Over his many years in the police force and particularly during his time as a detective, Sam had developed a gut feel for things. It was something that he had initially suppressed, preferring to try to remain objectively focussed on the evidence before him. One of his old sergeants had drummed into him that police work was only ever about what you could see, touch or hear. But as Sam's instincts started proving correct time and time again, he began listening more and more to what they were saying.

In recent years, he'd almost come to rely on them almost as his primary investigative tool. And in this case, his instincts were telling him that something wasn't right.

Sam picked up the printouts of the images of the scene and started flicking through them for yet another time. They told the story just as he remembered it. The mayor was lying face down in the bathroom. There was no sign of a disturbance. Nothing seemed out of place - with the exception of the mayor's gigantic, lifeless body of course. He then began studying the printouts of the shots taken with his mobile phone, in particular the flat-lay of the mayor's belongings spread out on the bed in the hotel room the mayor had used with Candy. He tapped his finger on each item, as if ticking off a mental checklist he had created in his mind.

His finger paused over one of the items.

With a sudden sense of urgency he shuffled through the stack of medical records until he found Dr Cociarelli's cause of death paperwork. He scanned the document quickly, tracing his finger along the words until he found what he was looking for. He then turned back to the flat-lay image from the hotel. He couldn't believe he'd missed it before.

"Delicious, Sam. Just delicious!" Marnie said, calling out from her table.

Sam distractedly looked over in her direction. He had almost forgotten that Marnie was still in the restaurant.

"Sorry?" Sam said.

"I'm the one who should be sorry. I can see that you are busy. It was a sad business, the death of the mayor. Very sad," Marnie said.

Sam looked at the documents spread out before him and then back at Marnie. He wore a puzzled look on his face as he tried to work out how she knew they were to do with the mayor. He could only figure that curiosity must have gotten the best of her while he had been in the kitchen preparing her food, not that he was overly concerned if she had snuck a peek while he wasn't looking.

"Now I don't mean to drag you away from your important work, detective, but I was hoping you could bring me the bill? That way I can get out of your hair and let you get on with cracking the case," Marnie said.

Sam took a moment to switch his hat from policeman back to chef. After a short beat, he smiled and placed his papers back on the table in front of him.

"Of course, Marnie," Sam said as he stood and walked behind the small reception counter by the entrance. He quickly filled out the bill on a paper receipt book before walking over and handing it to his happy diner.

"I'm glad you enjoyed it as much as I enjoyed making it for you," Sam said.

"One of the best Chou Dofu I've ever eaten. And that's saying something. You'd be hard pressed to find a tastier iteration outside of Hunan!" Marnie said.

"Flattery will get you everywhere, Marnie," Sam said, breaking into a broad grin.

He cleared the plate from her table and made his way back to his papers. Sam set the plate down temporarily on the table opposite and picked up the sheet with the photo from his phone of the mayor's belongings laid out on the bed. The report from the doctor clearly noted the presence of sildenafil citrate. In Sam's photo there was a receipt for the purchase of Viagra. Sam was kicking himself. He should have realised this before now. For while there was a receipt for Viagra, there wasn't any evidence of Viagra itself in any of the photos or paperwork documenting the scene. Not in the hotel room. Not in the bathroom. There was no half-finished pill sheet lying on the floor. Not even an empty box discarded in the rubbish.

Nothing.

Sam looked up from the images and cursed himself.

"Fuck!"

He quickly remembered Marnie and tried to swallow his expletive.

"Oh, sorry…" Sam said, looking sheepishly towards Marnie's table. Only Marnie's table was now empty. Sam scanned the restaurant but there was no sign of her. She had somehow slipped out while his attention had been otherwise occupied. He did see, however, that she had left behind some cash on the table to settle the bill.

"Marnie?" Sam called, once more just in case.

There was no response. He checked his watch. The time was approaching 11pm. Given that he had already kept the restaurant open late to accommodate Marnie's foetid meal, Sam was now keen to close up and get home. Not that sleep was going to come easily. Not now that his brain was all amped up from his discovery. He knew that the absence of evidence didn't prove the existence of other evidence but he was sure that it meant something. Sam dropped the flat lay image on the table and quickly walked over and picked up the money left by Marnie. But as he lifted up the notes something caught his eye. The bill he'd written out had been clearly amended.

Down the bottom, under 'Tip' had been added, in scrawled old lady's handwriting, the words: *Palfreeman / Oasis.*

NINE

The glow from The Oasis lit up the night's sky in the distance as Sam turned off the highway and took the access road towards the hotel's entrance. He was soon caught in a slow moving procession of vehicles, the red brake lights of the cars in front of him surging on and off like a string of Christmas lights as they crawled ever forward. Sam had expected there to be traffic - even planning his trip to arrive fashionably late - but he certainly hadn't foreseen this. Then again, the grand opening of The Oasis was always bound to draw a crowd.

Sam had flashed his badge in lieu of an official invitation to the two sharply dressed security guards standing sentry and now continued through the front gates of The Oasis. The gates were constructed to resemble a castle entrance complete with portcullis which was a portend of what was to come.

Inside the grounds, he was immediately struck by

the imposing façade of the building in front of him. Sam wasn't entirely sure what he had expected to see but had perhaps imagined something akin to the amateur theatre sets he used to help construct during his brief stint with the local performance group the Prosperity Players. By contrast, The Oasis could easily have to taken pride of place alongside Cinderella's castle in any Disney complex anywhere in the world.

Detective Chang had heard rumblings during the building's construction that it had been designed by a suite of Hollywood production designers in consultation with a world-renowned London Architecture firm. He had dismissed the talk at the time as idle town gossip but the building that now stood before him made him reconsider the merits of that chatter. For all intents and purposes, Chang felt as though he had just travelled back in time and driven onto the grounds of a medieval castle. Although, the illusion was somewhat undermined by the ostentatious Vegas-like neon green signage adorning the arch above the drawbridge entrance. If anyone was unclear about where they were, the glowing sign spelling out The Oasis removed any doubt.

Sam parked his car at the far corner of the carpark in one of the few remaining spots and joined the flow of people still making their way along the crushed gravel path, beneath the endless strings of festoon lighting criss-crossing overhead. He crossed the drawbridge and made his way inside the building beneath the illuminated sign, still marvelling at the audacious theatricality of the construction.

Aleks Keshishian lifted the cheap plastic cup to his mouth and sipped the weak margarita through a thin plastic straw. He was intently studying the large glass tank in front of him, which held about 600 litres of aquamarine coloured formaldehyde solution and the artificially conjoined bodies of what appeared to be a labrador puppy and a rooster. A small plaque identified the artwork as *Labradoodledoo,* one of the many pieces Christian Palfreeman had purchased from Dr George Hibbert's much maligned debut exhibition some years before, the vast majority of which now sat - rather incongruously given the otherwise ubiquitous medieval theme - in prominent positions around the reception area of The Oasis. Keshishian tilted his head slightly to one side, as if to see if a change of perspective would alter his opinion of the artwork, or at the very least give him some level of understanding. Before it could, however, his eyes pulled focus through the glass and zeroed in, past the milling crowd, on the arrival of a new guest. He pressed a small button that activated the microphone clamped to his collar.

"Let Christian know that Detective Chang just walked in," Keshishian said.

Detective Chang paused just inside the lobby of

The Oasis and looked around, taking in the room. The walls were all faux grey stone. Adorning them were an assortment of faux tapestries and faux lanterns, that gave the appearance of flickering flame but which the detective figured must have been programmed LED globes. There were several faux suits of armour, faux battle-axes, long swords, maces and sundry other medieval weaponry. The timber floor was covered in large woven rugs that helped soften the natural reverberation of the space. The whole place reminded Chang of the time he travelled to Las Vegas for the buck's weekend of one of his mates from the Police Academy (a wild three-days that culminated in an ill-timed phone call from the buck to the bride-to-be, an alcohol-induced confession about a lap-dance gone too far and, ultimately, the cancellation of the upcoming nuptials). Overall, the effect of the medieval detailing was impressive and quite convincing, although it didn't take much close inspection to see the artifice of it all.

What really did stand out to Chang was the placement of Dr Hibbert's animal hybrid artworks around the room. Although Sam hadn't seen any of the pieces in person before, he had definitely heard everything about them. And nothing he had heard had been particularly positive. However, regardless of whatever critique had been passed on the pieces, seeing them now for the first time they seemed wildly out of place amongst the rest of the carefully curated scene.

"Pig in a blanket, detective?"

Sam was suddenly aware of a large tray of chipolatas wrapped in bacon that was hovering under his nose. It took him a couple of moments to recognise the woman holding the delicacies. He had never seen her hair teased out like that before and the dark green outfit she was wearing – a slightly confused mix of Octoberfest maiden and Mary Elizabeth Mastriantonio's Maid Marion from *Robin Hood Price of Thieves* - was distracting at best.

"No thanks, Tracy," Sam said, politely declining the hors d'oeuvre.

"Not a fan? I think there's some devils on horseback going around somewhere if you'd prefer?" Tracy said.

"All good thanks, Tracy. I had some left over Kung Pao chicken at the restaurant before leaving. Is Mick here?"

Tracy shook her head.

"Nah. He wasn't too thrilled about me taking the job. I think he has it in his head that everyone who works here *works* here, you know? I mean it's only my first night but so far so good, you know? Jobs are hardly growing on trees round here these days – right detective?"

"I'm sure Mick'll come around," Sam said.

"Wouldn't bet on it. Male pride is a stubborn bitch."

Tracy sampled one of the tasty morsels on her tray

and made an expression that left Sam in no doubt that she quite fancied it.

Sam's attention was suddenly drawn to a commotion on the other side of the room. Dr Ricky Cociarelli had his arms around two coquettish young women dressed in suggestive, medieval garb, replete with bodices that promoted their ample bosoms to their fullest. The effect, Sam thought, was like two small bald men trying to escape each fair maiden's dress.

The girls giggled and squealed in the good doctor's arms and were putting on quite the performance. Cociarelli broke free long enough to skull a complementary glass of cheap sparkling wine - Sam guessed by his general demeanour that it wasn't his first - before corralling the women once again in his arms and leading them from the room in obnoxiously conspicuous fashion. As he went, he leaned in and whispered suggestive nothings into their ears that drew further squeals of delight. It was quite the show.

Sam's attention was then drawn closer to home. He could see Christian Palfreeman making his way through the crowd towards him, Aleks Keshishian in lock step half a pace behind.

"Detective Sam Chang - so glad you could make it to our humble opening," Christian said, offering his hand. Sam took it and shook firmly.

"It's quite the place, Mr Palfreeman."

"Please, call me Christian," Palfreeman said.

"Can I get you a drink? Or something to eat? The

arancini balls are quite something."

"I'm fine, thank you. I'm just here to take a look, really. After all the build-up it would have felt odd not coming out for the big opening," Sam said.

"Well, if that's the case, would you allow us to show you around? A grand tour if you will?" Palfreeman said.

'Sure, why not," Sam replied.

"Excellent. Follow me, detective."

"Lead the way," Sam said.

Palfreeman turned and began threading back through the crowd but Aleks hung back, waiting for Sam to pass so that he could close in behind their small party and bring up the rear. As they made their way through the milling groups of people, Sam noticed Jim Smith chatting with Debbie Clatworthy, president of the local branch of the Country Women's Association.

Sam slowed as he passed to say hello.

"Jim. Debbie."

"Detective," they replied, almost in unison.

A few steps further on and Christian began speaking to Sam over his shoulder as they walked.

"I thought it only polite to invite the delightful Mrs Clatworthy and some of her committee along this evening. It was the right thing to do after the unfortunate misunderstanding at the mayor's funeral."

Behind him, Sam heard a low grunt of displeasure emanate from Aleks Keshishian.

Jim Smith's cheeks were aching from the forced smile he had plastered on for the ten minutes he'd been cornered by Debbie Clatworthy. He cursed himself that he hadn't been quick enough to slip out of her social range the minute she had laid eyes on him. Jim had buried Debbie's late husband Des, after he tragically fell from a ladder while installing his famous annual Christmas lights display some years before. Debbie had been forever grateful to Jim, not only for organising his service with his usual low-key compassion but for his charitable act in popping around to Debbie's house afterwards to finish attaching the several hundred meters of fairy lights to the front awning and fastening Santa and his reindeer to the roof.

She had no idea that, rather than it being an extraordinary act of kindness, it had in fact been Jim's way of assuaging the guilt he felt for having swapped Des out of the mid-tier Winchester she had selected for him casket prior to burial.

Jim had been desperately looking over Debbie's shoulders in search of an escape route but so far to no avail. Detective Chang had provided a glimmer of hope - albeit tinged with apprehension given Jim's lingering concerns about the mayor's funeral - but now he was back to listening to Debbie's rather laboured account of her cat's recent health troubles.

"And the poor girl couldn't keep anything down.

Both ends mind you, Jim. Made a terrible mess in my good room. Thankfully, I keep the plastic furniture protectors on the settee. Best thing Des ever did was convince me to put those on all those years ago. I for one was always partial to feeling the texture of the fabric but Des was quite insistent. He could get his way when he wanted, my Des. Although, most of the time if I could see it was important to him I'd let him have a few wins. You know, that's the secret to a good marriage, Jim."

"Sounds like it," Jim said, politely.

"You'll make a lucky woman very happy one day, Jim Smith. Very happy indeed!" Debbie said it with a conviction that made it sound like the truest thing in the world.

Sensing a natural pause in Debbie's flow, Jim seized his chance to flee.

"That's very kind, Mrs Clatworthy. It's been lovely chatting but I'm going to have to excuse myself and find the bathroom, if you don't mind," he said.

"Of course, Jim. Look at me holding you up and keeping you all to myself when I'm sure you would much prefer to be mingling with more eligible women your own age."

Jim stretched his smile even wider, stepped past her gently and disappeared into the safety of the crowd. Once clear, his let his smile fall. Jim circled his jaw a few times to try to ease the ache in his cheeks. He kept walking through the crowd, partly to ensure he wouldn't accidentally drift back into

Debbie's conversational orbit but mainly as he was, in fact, in desperate need of the bathroom.

Jim followed the signs to the bathrooms - which were naturally in keeping with the theme of The Oasis, a knight's helmet for the men and a corset for the women - only to find a lengthy queue for both. He quickly looked around for his options and settled on the fire door at the far end of the corridor. He was relieved to find that it opened directly into a garden at the rear of the building, near where the dry riverbed wound past. It was largely shielded from view but Jim further obscured himself behind the trunk of one of the struggling gum trees that lined the riverbank, unzipped his fly and let go. The pain from the pressure in his bladder eased instantly.

The fresh air filled Jim's lungs and for the first time that night, away from the crowd inside, he felt something close to peace. The truth was, the last thing Jim wanted to be doing was 'talking to eligible women more his own age'. Not that talking to eligible men his own age filled him with any more excitement.

He reached into his jacket pocket and found the marijuana joint he had rolled in preparation for the evening. He hadn't necessary intended to smoke it but he always liked having one with him just in case. It made him feel calmer. It was his 'in case of emergency - break glass'. And tonight, Jim felt like breaking the glass.

Jim lit the joint and inhaled deeply. He held it in

his lungs for as long as he could manage before blowing the plume of sweet-smelling smoke into the night's sky. He let out a couple of small coughs before taking another deep drag.

He had known he was gay from an early age. Not that he knew what gay was. He just knew that he was different. He had tried not to be. First by kissing Felicity Houghton in grade 6, then by briefly dating Heidi Blanchard in year eight. He had subsequently lost his virginity with Erin Warburton when he was fifteen in a horribly brief, entirely unsexy encounter in the tray of a ute - the only foreplay being the best part of a bottle of Midori.

Jim had his first sexual experience with a man when he was in his early twenties at an international funeral conference in Sydney called *Downundertakers*. It was with a middle-aged American funeral director from Ohio called Hank. While it didn't involve the back of a ute it was no less awkward or alcohol fuelled. And while Jim had eventually enjoyed more fruitful sexual encounters over the years, he found by his late twenties that he just didn't seek them out anymore. And as the more time passed, the less Jim felt any real attraction to anyone. But where he sometimes thought there should be a hole, as though something was missing, there just wasn't. He was surprised how content he was without sex.

His only lingering regret was that he had never experienced having a partner - male or female - and, much to the great disappointment of Debbie

Clatworthy should she ever find out, felt fairly confident that he probably never would. The real annoyance was the constant speculation of those around Prosperity, not so much about his sexuality - although the odd rumour would bubble to the surface every now and again – but about why such an eligible bachelor as himself remained so thoroughly unattached.

While he firmly believed that his private life was nobody else's business, he had often considered putting it all out there to just bring it all to a head once and for all. Setting the record straight, so to speak. Perhaps via an article in the Argus (he even had a headline in mind: Single, Sexless and Satisfied). But he knew his life would be simpler if he didn't. So, he resigned himself to batting away enquiries about his lack of attachment with his trademark smile and variations on being 'married to his job and serving the people of Prosperity'.

Staring at the dry riverbed, Jim was starting to feel the effects of the marijuana. He decided against finishing the rest of the joint and flicked the glowing tip off into the sandy earth in front of him and scrubbed the lit end against the trunk of the tree to fully extinguish it. As much as he would have loved to have gotten completely baked and spent the rest of the evening staring at the stars, he knew for appearance's sake that he needed to head back inside. He put a couple of eye drops in each eye to ease the redness from the drugs - he would normally pass it off as hay fever but the lack of rain meant a distinct lack of flowering plants to blame - and made his way back to the fire exit. Unfortunately for Jim, it couldn't be opened from the outside.

Jim banged on the door a few times, hoping to gain the attention of someone on the other side but to no avail. Resigned, he started following the edge of the building back around to the front entrance. However, as he rounded a corner, he came across a large loading dock. The roller door was down but he spotted some stairs leading to a pedestrian access. He skipped up the stairs to the door and tried the handle. Locked. The door had a rectangular glass panel down one side of it and he pressed his face to it and looked inside. His spirits lifted as he saw a chef walk past at that very moment. He banged on the door and waited. After a moment it swung open.

"Thanks," Jim muttered, before stepping inside.

Unlike the customer focussed areas of the hotel, this part of The Oasis was entirely functional and bore none of the medieval affectations of the front of house. Nondescript corridors branched off in all directions. It reminded Jim of the famous *Spinal Tap* scene where the band take a wrong turn on the way to the stage and get lost in the bowels of the stadium. For Jim, the thought of getting lost paralysed him, his drug affected brain unable to decide which way to go.

He was about to yell out 'Hello Cleveland!' when suddenly a door opened behind him, giving him a start. A young waitress carrying a tray of hot Thai fish cakes brushed past him. The delicious aroma was like a hit of smelling salts, instantly jolting Jim from his drug-induced stupor. He figured she would be taking the food to the crowd. And that was exactly where Jim needed to be. He quickly followed her and a few twists and turns later, Jim could hear the festive hubbub of the crowd growing ever louder.

Jim rounded a final corner a few steps behind the waitress and watched her disappear through a swinging double door and into the throng gathered in the reception area on the other side. He was about to follow her when his eye was drawn down an intersecting corridor. Jim's stomach dropped and his heart started beating a little faster. He could see Tracy leaning against the wall smiling coquettishly. Returning the smile was Dr George Hibbert. He couldn't hear what the vet was saying to his brother's wife but whatever it was it made her laugh. She gently took the doctor's hand in hers and tilted her head coyly to one side. George's eyes suddenly flicked to Jim and he abruptly dropped Tracy's hand. Tracy followed the vet's gaze, straightened, and hurriedly walked up the corridor and brushed past Jim and through the double doors.

"It's not what you think, Jim," Tracy said over her shoulder, without looking back at him.

Jim looked back down the corridor at George who was standing like a shag on a rock. George didn't quite know what to do so he waved. Jim didn't quite know what to do either. So he waved back.

Sam found himself in a service corridor somewhere in the working depths of The Oasis. Palfreeman was still taking the lead but had assured Sam that the tour was almost over. He could hear the din of the crowd building as they turned a corner where he almost ran into Dr Hibbert, who was standing by himself in the middle of the passageway. Stepping around the doctor he looked up and saw Jim Smith oddly waving. Unsure why, he returned the wave so as not to appear rude before following Palfreeman through the two double doors and into the still substantial gathering of people.

"And that brings us back to where we started, detective," Palfreeman said, raising his voice to be heard.

"Thank you for the tour. It's certainly something, this place you've built here, Mr Palfreeman," Sam replied.

And that it certainly was.

The tour had begun routinely enough - a quick look at the reception desk and concierge services, followed by a brief stop off in the security room where Sam was given a cursory run through of the extensive CCTV network that covered almost every conceivable nook and cranny of the public spaces both inside and outside the building. After that, however, it had been anything but routine.

The next room they inspected was the guest services area. It resembled a mix between a medieval King's council chamber and a gentleman's club smoking room. There was a large central table surrounded by high-backed wooden chairs contrasted against plush leather armchairs positioned around the room, set up in pairs facing each other. It was here that the guests sat with their assigned 'satisfaction hostesses', as Palfreeman had called them, and set out their personal preferences, desires and expectations.

While guests were welcome to bring their own costumes and paraphernalia with them if they wished, The Oasis actively encouraged guests to take full advantage of their in-house costume hire facilities. These were located in a series of rooms down the hall from guest services. Here, aided by their hostess and being guided by their recently declared predilections, guests could choose from a vast array of outfits - everything from noble robes and furs to full suits of armour to colourful court jester attire.

From there Sam was shown some more of the themed areas. There was the torture room, filled with whips, a set of wooden stocks, steel shackles and chains and a large wooden rack that had only minor concessions to comfort in the form of a few strategically positioned, quilted leather strips. Then there was the communal suite that was dominated by the largest circular bed the detective had ever seen, meant for those patrons who preferred the company of more than just one other.

"It can easily fit fourteen. More if they are flexible," Aleks Keshishian had informed him.

Located on the subterranean level was the dungeon wing which, apart from the expected old world prison tropes - heavy wooden doors, bars, manacles chained to the wall etc. - housed the collection of spa rooms, with each cell home to its own large jacuzzi. Here, they had been unfortunate enough to walk in on Dr Cociarelli enjoying one of the spas with the two women Sam had seen earlier in reception. While Sam had witnessed plenty in his time with the police force, seeing the naked, almost emaciated doctor being fellated was an image now, regretfully, indelibly seared into the detective's mind.

Upstairs, he had been shown the banquet hall, a long communal table where guests were nightly served obscene helpings of food and drank beer and wine from oversized goblets. Palfreeman had assured the detective that all the plates and cups had been designed to be unbreakable while the cutlery was both sparing and blunt to limit the possibility of any guests taking their role-play too far and tending towards violence.

Elsewhere, the accommodation comprised a hundred or so guest rooms that were surprisingly modern. Despite the faux stone continuing throughout, the bedding itself was actually not too dissimilar to any four or five star hotel you'd find in the big cities.

"Our customer research team advised us that wooden beds with straw mattresses scored poorly with our target demographic," Palfreeman had told Sam. With a wry grin.

From there, the tour concluded with the back of house. The kitchen, which had interested Sam the most, was truly impressive. The large food prep areas and oversized burners almost brought him to the point of jealousy. The storeroom was less interesting, as were the staff change rooms and industrial laundry.

"Thanks again for the tour," Sam said, shaking Palfreeman's hand.

"Anytime. I love showing off what we've done."

Suddenly, loud music filled the room. It was Maira Muldaur's jazz-pop hit *Midnight at the Oasis*

Palfreeman stood there, beaming at the detective.

"How could we not?" he said. "We play it every evening at midnight for a bit of fun. The guests love it. I had Aleks organise for it to come on a little earlier this evening for everyone's enjoyment."

Sam returned Palfreeman's smile, courteously.

"You're welcome here any time," Palfreeman said, pulling Sam closer to him.

"Perhaps you can spend longer here next time. Get to know the place a little better," Palfreeman said softly, as he flashed a knowing look at Detective Chang. It was a look Sam recognised instantly. A look that left nothing in doubt and a look Sam wanted nothing to do with.

"I appreciate the offer, Mr Palfreeman but it's not an offer I will be taking up," Sam said, firmly.

"Understood, detective. Of course. A man of your fine reputation. However, before you leave, there is one more person I'd like you to meet," Palfreeman said.

"I really should be getting on," Sam politely protested.

"It's OK detective, it won't hold you up. In fact, she's right behind you," Palfreeman said, smiling.

"I'd like to introduce you to our, how do I put this delicately… head of staff?"

"Hello, Detective Sam Chang," a familiar voice said close behind him.

Sam spun on his heel.

There, curtsying rather theatrically before him, dressed in the same medieval maid's outfit he'd seen Tracy wearing earlier, was none other than Misty Gerrard.

"If you can't beat them, detective…"

TEN

The city he was walking through was very familiar to Detective Chang. All the buildings, the restaurants, the bars, the strange hybrid homewares and clothing warehouse; the escalators that seemed to join each area of the metropolis, as if it was all one large department store. Most of the time, Sam was never quite sure how he got there but he enjoyed visiting the city and knew all its twists and turns, lanes and side streets. The only other constant, apart from the layout, was every time he travelled to the city in his dreams, he seemed to be searching for something. And he usually only found himself there when details in a real world case were gnawing at him.

Earlier that evening, Sam had driven home from the opening of The Oasis in silence. It wasn't a conscious decision; he'd just been so preoccupied in his mind that he'd simply forgotten to turn on the car radio. He couldn't put his finger on exactly what it was that was bothering him. Christian Palfreeman had been more than pleasant. He was obviously proud of what he had built and, while it wasn't to the detective's taste, he had clearly put together an exceptionally professional operation. And there was nothing illegal about what he was doing, at least outwardly. He had also been trying to put to one side his preconceptions about Aleks Keshishian. Sam wasn't naive, he was well aware that there were some very murky corners of the sex industry, corners he was sure Aleks must have lurked in at some point. Whether he was still lurking there was something Sam was yet to determine but he didn't want that to infect his thinking. What had bothered the detective most during his almost forty-five minutes with Palfreeman was that, beyond the singular reference about the mayor's funeral when briefly mentioning inviting the CWA to the opening, he hadn't brought up Terry McInerny again. It's not so much that he expected it to be the dominant topic of conversation but more that Palfreeman seemed to be actively avoiding it as a topic at all.

Throw in the fact that Misty, one of the last people to see the mayor alive, was now working for Palfreeman and things just weren't sitting comfortably with Detective Sam Chang. And that discomfort had followed him into his dreams.

He had just walked into his dream city's tavern and was moving through the bar into a narrow pokies area when the fire alarm sprang to life. Sam looked around but couldn't see any smoke or flame and tried to tell his subconscious to turn the alarm off. Only his subconscious turned the sound up and he started to feel the ground shaking.

The detective suddenly woke with a start. His phone was ringing and vibrating loudly on the wooden side table next to his bed. He reached for it and answered, groggily. The call was brief. But Sam was now wide awake.

Sam checked the time as he slowly approached the scene ahead of him. It was just before 4.15 am. Through his windshield he could see the smouldering wreck of a car on its roof. It was illuminated by some portable work lights and the flashing red and blue emergency signals of the Rural Fire Service trucks and ambulance parked nearby. A crew of fire-fighters in breathing apparatus were spraying water mixed with retardant foam onto the vehicle to make sure any lingering flames were completely extinguished. Sam spotted the police car he was looking for and pulled off to the side of the road, parking behind it.

Constable Riley saw Sam pull up and excused herself from the captain of one of the fire brigades. She walked briskly over and met the detective at his car door.

"Sorry to get you out of bed, Sam," Riley said. She was trying her best to sound apologetic but her professional excitement was seeping through.

"I just thought you'd want to be here."

"No, you did the right thing, Riley," Sam said.

Sam climbed out and the two started walking towards the overturned car.

"The call came in about forty minutes ago. I got here about the same time as the RFS guys. The car was well and truly alight by then," Riley said, as they got closer.

"Any other vehicles involved?" Sam asked.

"None that stuck around if there were. We'll obviously have a clearer picture in a little while when the sun comes up."

"And just the one person trapped?"

"As far as we can tell. There's a body in the driver's seat still buckled in. But the firies have told me they've conducted a full search of the vehicle - no sign of anyone else," Riley said.

Sam and Riley were now standing only a few pacers behind the fire crew who were still going about their business. Detective Chang could just make out the charred human remains still strapped in the front seat of the car, surrounded by the twisted and scorched metal frame of the chassis. An acrid smell filled the air from all the burnt plastics and electrical wiring.

"Are the crash investigation team on their way?" Sam asked.

"They'll be here by sunup," Riley said.

Sam looked at the wreck again. He shook his head

- what a hell of a way to go.

"Any idea who it is?" Sam asked after a beat.

"Not so far," Riley said. "We'll need dental records for the body."

"What about the car? Plates?"

"Front plate's missing. Rear one is so charred and melted it's basically useless."

Sam stood for a moment, thinking.

"You wouldn't have a torch in your car by any chance would you?" Sam asked.

"Several," Riley replied.

The torches Riley produced weren't standard police issue. She had purchased them online after seeing a particularly convincing advertisement that touted their military grade construction, two hundred meter range and brightness of twelve hundred lumens. And they were certainly doing the trick. Sam had instructed Riley to wait at the scene while he made his way back down the road. He was scanning the bitumen for any signs of what might have caused the accident. It wasn't unusual for cars to hit kangaroos or wombats along this stretch of highway but Sam couldn't find any evidence of an impact - blood, remnants of a smashed headlight - and there was no roadkill he could see either. He kept walking about three hundred meters away from the crash scene, more than enough distance he figured to have found anything associated with the crash, but there wasn't so much as a skid mark.

Sam could see the night sky starting to lighten as the sun was now starting to come up, so Sam turned his torch off and walked back to rejoin Riley.

"That's odd," Sam said, as he reached the constable. "There's nothing that I can see that might have caused it to crash. And there's no tyre marks so it doesn't look like they've slammed the brakes on at all."

"Maybe the driver fell asleep?" Riley said.

"It could make sense, I suppose," Sam said. "I'm going to take a closer look at the car."

The firies had finished dousing the car with foam but there was still quite a bit of heat radiating from the inverted, burnt out wreck as Sam cautiously approached. Up close, he could see that the chassis was even more battered than he had first thought - the frames and what was left of the side panels were all twisted, crushed and bent. Sam had seen his share of car crashes in his time and this seemed consistent with the car having rolled more than a few times at high speed. He looked through where the rear window should have been but there was nothing in the back seats that was recognisable. As he made his way to the front, he could see the charred remains of a human body suspended upside down, still held in place by the seatbelt. The body itself had melted and merged with the seat and restraint, creating an almost amorphous blob. Sam looked past the driver and into the passenger side. Just like the back seat, it appeared empty.

"Anything?" Riley yelled from the road.

"Nothing that's going to be any use to us without forensics," Sam replied.

The car had come to rest in a scrubby area about twenty meters off the road. The scrub continued for about another twenty meters before reaching a eucalypt forest. Sam began slowly walking towards the taller trees. He cleared aside some of the shin high bushes with his legs as he went, to get a better look at anything that may be hidden on the ground beneath. He was surprised by the amount of general rubbish he found. There were soft drink bottles with labels faded by the elements, chip packets, fast food wrappers, random pieces of packing foam. But one piece was different from the rest. The detective stopped and carefully cleared the vegetation from around the license plate that was sitting in the dirt. Unlike the rest of the detritus, it was yet to show any signs of weathering. It looked like it hadn't been there for very long at all.

Sam took out his phone and quickly captured a few photos of the license plate in situ before picking it up. He was about fifteen metres from the wreck, which was well within a zone for it to have been conceivably thrown clear from a tumbling vehicle, especially if it had spun through the air like a frisbee. He held it in the air to show Riley as he started back towards her.

"Nice find, Sam!" Riley said, excitedly.

"We can't jump to conclusions," Sam said, handing it over to Riley, "but it's worth running the plate to see who it belongs to. It might give us something to start with at least."

Sam stood outside Constable Riley's police car, leaning on the open door, as Riley perched on the passenger seat and punched the details of the license plate into the data terminal mounted on the dash.

"I've got a hit," Riley said after a few seconds, "and you're not going to believe it."

Riley looked up at Sam, a look of confusion on her face.

"The car's registered to Dr Enrico Cociarelli."

Sam wasn't quite sure he'd heard Riley correctly.

"Did you say Dr Cociarelli?"

Riley nodded.

"I think I need a drink," Sam said.

Ever since he had been a probationary constable, Sam had stuck to one necessary habit without fail. Every night before bed, he prepared a thermos of coffee, just in case he was woken in the middle of the night to respond to a call - which happened remarkably often. Given he was living out in Prosperity, it was often quicker to rouse Sam to send to any local incidents rather than dispatch the duty crew from Bathurst. While it had put Sam under additional pressure from early on in his career, it had also meant he had advanced much quicker through the ranks. He was particularly thankful for his habit now as he poured himself and Riley a strong cup of Mocha Kenya.

"You look troubled, Sam," Riley said.

"Not troubled. Just thinking," he replied, as he sipped on his coffee.

"There's just a lot not adding up," he paused, then added, "actually, maybe everything is adding up a little too well."

He began to outline everything that he knew so far. He had seen Dr Cociarelli only a few hours earlier at The Oasis. According to Sam's recollection, he'd been in no fit state to put his own pants on, let alone get behind the wheel of a car. And while it would make sense that an intoxicated person might lose control of the vehicle they were driving, or fall asleep, Sam couldn't figure out why Dr Cociarelli would have been heading out this way. The road to his house ran in the opposite direction.

"You said he was pretty pissed. Maybe he took a wrong turn?" Riley said.

"Again, possible. But there's literally one t-intersection on that road. He should have gone left. Instead he's gone right," Sam said.

The detective continued talking himself through the facts as he understood them. When Dr Cociarelli had released his findings into the mayor's death, no one seemed overly surprised that it was ruled a heart attack. But Sam had been troubled by the fact that, despite the presence of Viagra being recorded in the mayor's blood stream, he had still yet to find any physical evidence of the pills themselves even though the mayor was carrying a receipt.

"And now the doctor who created that report has apparently died in a fiery car crash," Sam said, finishing his summation.

"So, what are you thinking?" Riley asked.

"I'm thinking that maybe it wasn't Viagra that the mayor took," he said quietly. "And I'm thinking that maybe Dr Cociarelli's report was less than truthful."

Sam threw the rest of his coffee onto the road and strode back to his car. He fired it up, pulled alongside Riley and wound down his window.

"I'm thinking," he said, "we need to exhume the mayor."

ELEVEN

Jim sat in his car looking out through the driver's side window at the well-worn dirt road. He turned the engine off. After a moment, he turned it back on. He put the car into drive, reached for the park brake, before sliding the gear leaver back into park and turning the engine off again. He had been repeating this sequence for the past ten minutes.

"Come on, Jim. Put your big boy pants on," Jim muttered to himself, quietly.

He held the key in the ignition and paused again.

"Fuck it!" he said, with a new found determination.

He twisted the key, put the car into gear and turned into the driveway.

"Mick's not here, Jim," Tracy said, answering the front door.

"I know, Trace. I left him at the office just now,"

Jim replied.

"Can we talk?"

"If it's about the other night…" Tracy started before being gently interrupted.

"Please, Trace?" Jim said.

Tracy looked at the ground as she stepped to one side to let Jim into the house.

Tracy put a hot cup of coffee in front of Jim as he sat at the kitchen table. She cupped her own mug of coffee in both hands and leant against the kitchen bench. They had been silent with each other since he had sat down, neither of them quite sure how to begin. Jim blew on the top of his drink to cool it slightly before taking a sip.

"Nice coffee, Trace," Jim said, breaking the silence.

"It's instant, Jim."

Jim took a deep breath.

"Look, I don't know what's going on with you and Mick. And I certainly don't want to get in the middle of things…"

"Then don't!" Tracy said, interjecting.

"…but I can't ignore what I saw the other night," Jim said, continuing.

"It's not what you think. George and I are just friends," Tracy said.

"That's not what it looked like."

"Okay then Jim, what did it look like?" Tracy said,

challenging him with a hint of defensiveness in her voice.

"I don't know. Like you're fu -- " Jim caught himself. "...sleeping with each other?"

"Fuck off, Jim!" Tracy said.

He wondered if he had gone too far as they both drank their coffee in tense silence. He could feel his anxiety rising. He touched his pocket and felt for his joint to calm himself.

"I know my brother can be difficult --."

"-- You don't know the half of it --"

" -- but I'm sure you guys can work through it."

"I'm not going to say anything to Mick," Jim said. "But I need you to fix things with him."

"It's not that easy, Jim," Tracy said, as tears started to well in her eyes.

"Mick's better with you, Tracy. You know it, I know it and I know Mick knows it. Just try."

"So it's all on me is it Jim? I have to be the one to make things better? I'm the one who has to put my happiness aside so that Mick 'The Big Local Hero' feels better about himself?" Tracy's tears began to flow freely. "What do you think I've done our whole relationship, Jim? And what have I got in return - wasting my best years as a broke farmer's wife."

She tried to wipe away her tears but they wouldn't stop coming. She simply spread them across her cheeks.

"So sue me for enjoying someone's attention for once. Someone who makes me feel good about myself."

"I didn't mean to make you upset, Trace," Jim said, unsure of whether he should try to give her a hug or make a run for his car. He opted to remained seated.

"What the fuck did you think was going to happen?" Tracy yelled through her tears.

"I'm actually not sure," Jim replied, almost to himself.

"Get out, Jim."

Jim didn't move.

"Get. Out. Jim." Tracy said, more forcefully.

Jim still refused to stand. Although he and Tracy weren't the closest of in-laws - she had never really gotten over the time Jim had, in an attempted joke about her WAG aspirations, mockingly called her Victoria Beck*Spam* in that she was kind of like the real think but a bit of a cheap knockoff - they had always considered each other family. The last thing he wanted to do was drive a wedge between the two of them now.

"I just want the best for both of you," Jim said after a silence that seemed to last an eternity. He finally stood and walked his coffee cup over to the sink.

"Just leave it on the bench, Jim. I'll wash it up," Tracy said.

"Okay," Jim said, awkwardly.

Suddenly Jim's phone rang, the chiming tones puncturing the emotionally charged atmosphere. He pulled his phone out to check who was calling.

"It's Detective Chang," Jim said. He looked at

Tracy, apologetically.

"It's okay, Jim. You can answer it," Tracy said.

Jim answered the phone. In the brief conversation with the detective, Tracy watched Jim turn from his usual ultra-white complexion to something, as impossible as it seemed, even paler. When he hung up the phone he just stared into space, a thousand miles away.

"What is it?" Tracy asked. Jim didn't answer.

"Jim? What's going on?" Tracy asked again, with growing concern.

"We're fucked."

Jim quickly scrolled for Mick's number on his phone and called him. He waited as it rang.

"Hi, you've reached the voicemail of Mick Smith. I can't come to the phone right now, which means I'm either chasing cows around a paddock or I've dropped my phone in a grave. Please leave a message."

"Fuck!" Jim said, panicked.

"What's happening, Jim? You're freaking me out," Tracy said. Jim put his hand up to ask her to wait as he tried to call Mick again.

It rang. And rang.

"Hi, you've reached the voicemail of—"

Jim hung up and immediately tried again.

"Answer your bloody phone, Mick."

Jim waited. He was about to hang up and try again so as to avoid having to hear his brother's message another time when Mick finally answered.

"Who bloody died?" Mick snapped.

"No one, yet. But we might be as good as dead," Jim said. "I just got a call from Detective Chang. He's just got a court order to exhume the mayor's body."

"Jesus!" Mick said. "Where are you, we need to figure this shit out".

Jim looked at Tracy.

"I'm just out helping Mrs Clatworthy. She needed to get a bag down from the attic."

"You're too nice, Jim. But get your arse back here now."

Mick was half-way through his second beer by the time Jim walked through the front doors of the Smith Bros. building.

"Tell me everything from your conversation with Chang." Mick said, barely giving his brother time to get inside.

"He just said he had been granted a court order to exhume the mayor's body. He wouldn't tell me why. But there's good news and bad news"

"Start with the good news, Jim." Mick said.

"He wants us to do the exhuming." Jim said.

"And the bad?"

"He wants *us* to do the exhuming."

It didn't take any explaining from either of the brothers to know the shitstorm they were in. As soon as they dug up the mayor's grave, it would be obvious that he had buried in a cheap box and not the expensive Carrington. If that wasn't bad enough, Jim was already feeling the shame of burying Terry McInerny face down. Even if they didn't end up in gaol as a result of the scam - which was a big 'if' - their business was destined for ruin once word got about how they treated their clients.

"We're cooked, Mick," Jim said. "What are we going to do?"

"First, you're going to walk over there to the fridge and get yourself a beer and calm the fuck down while I think."

Jim did as he was told. His first sip didn't seem to do anything. So he quickly took a second. Then a third. Then he just skulled the entire thing and grabbed another.

"If we dig the mayor up and he's in the Carrington, there's no issue, right?" Mick asked.

"Well, yeah. But the problem is, he's not in the Carrington," Jim said. "The Carrington is sitting in our bloody showroom!"

"No shit, Sherlock. But say he was in it. We'd be sweet, yeah? So… we just have to dig him up first, swap him back into the Carrington - put him the right way up this time - then simply bury him again. That way, when we dig him up a second time for the coppers, no one will be any the wiser," Mick said, pleased with himself.

"In theory, you're correct. In practice, how do you propose we get the digger out to the cemetery, move all that earth, do the switch and not get noticed - and all by tomorrow morning?" Jim said.

"Chang wants to dig him up tomorrow? Fuck. That's the kind of info that you might have wanted to share with me before now, don't you reckon?"

"I might have failed to mention that," Jim said.

Mick thought for a minute.

"Righto, we'll just have to head out there tonight."

"But what if we get caught?" Jim said.

"If we get caught, we're no worse off than if we do nothing, right? So, it's a no brainer."

In the security room at The Oasis, Aleks Keshishian was scanning the array of camera monitors in front of him when his phone rang. It had always been central to Keshishian's operations, wherever he was in the world, to ensure he had someone among the local police ranks, watching out for his interests. It wasn't a cheap exercise but was a necessary cost of doing business that had more than paid for itself over the years. However, Aleks had wondered if he'd picked the right Bathurst policemen this time around. Apart from making a couple of parking tickets disappear, they had proved largely useless. Until this call.

Aleks hung up the phone and returned his attention to the screens, focussing on one in particular. The camera was mounted in the corner of Christian Palfreeman's office and gave a complete picture of the space. He could see his boss sitting at his desk, working on his laptop. Aleks swung around on his chair, bounded to his feet in one fluid motion and walked purposefully from the room. A couple of minutes later, he came into view on the same screen he had just been monitoring, as he strolled into Palfreeman's office.

"Christian, we may have a problem," Aleks said.

"What kind of problem, Aleks?" Palfreeman asked. He seemed slightly annoyed by the interruption and continued reading a document on his computer.

"A dead obese mayor kind of problem. Chang is exhuming the body."

Aleks had Palfreeman's attention now.

"Shit. When?"

"First thing tomorrow morning."

Christian shut his laptop with an almost wanton disregard for its extended warranty.

"We can't let that happen, Aleks," Palfreeman said.

"How competent are you at operating an excavator?

TWELVE

Getting everything organised for the pre-exhumation exhumation had been an effort in and of itself for the brothers. First, they moved the Carrington from the showroom at Smith Bros. out the back into the waiting van. Next, they drove the van out to their storage yards near the crematorium. Jim helped Mick load the digger they kept there onto the back of a flatbed truck for transport, after which they threw shovels and a couple of large tarpaulins into the truck's cab.

Then they waited.

It was just after 1am when they departed for the cemetery. Both Jim and Mick agreed to leave it as late as possible to avoid any prying eyes. They figured that anyone up and about in Prosperity after midnight was probably up to no good - petty theft, an illicit rendezvous, perhaps - and as such, unlikely to pay them too much attention lest they draw too much themselves.

Jim drove the van, leading the way, while Mick followed in the truck. They ventured back towards the town, drove around the war memorial roundabout and into the main street. Jim was relieved to find it as deserted as he had hoped. They continued in convoy down the main street and out beyond the Royal Hotel and on to the cemetery, which was located on the far side of the football oval. Jim hoped it was far enough away from the nearest houses. Far enough, at least, so the noise they were about to make wouldn't rouse any occupants.

The brothers carefully navigated the road that weaved between the gravestones and parked as close as they could get to the mayor's final resting place. Jim positioned the van so the headlights illuminated the gravesite, while Mick began the process of unloading the mini excavator from the back of the truck. He started by unshackling the heavy-duty straps and chains that were holding the digger in place. They made loud crashing noises as they released. Jim's nerves were frayed enough already and the noise made him jump.

"Shhhhhhhh!" Jim said, in what could only be described as a shouting whisper.

"What do you want me to do, mate? If you think that's loud, wait until I actually start this puppy up!" Mick said, as he continued to prepare the back of the truck.

Once he had the chains off, Mick slid two metal

tracks out from the rear of the flatbed to create a ramp, before climbing into the small cab of the excavator and starting it up. As the diesel engine roared to life, Jim swallowed hard. It was going to be a miracle for them to get through this without being discovered. There was only one thing for it. As Jim watched Mick expertly manoeuvre the digger towards the grave, he lit the security joint he had brought for company.

Jim took a few puffs before he realised that Mick was yelling something at him. He moved closer to try to make it out over the rumbling noise of the engine.

"Bring the fucking tarps over you lazy prick!"

Jim lifted his hand to apologise and grabbed the two large tarpaulins from the cab of the truck. He held the joint in the corner of his mouth as he carried them towards the grave. The ground where Terry McInerny had been buried was still noticeably disturbed from when they had initially dug the hole. Jim spread out the tarps on either side of the grave, framing the mound of earth along each edge. Mick had made the point to Jim, quite rightly, that digging holes tends to create a mess and Chang would be sure to notice if they turned the fresh soil out straight on to the grass. This way they could catch most of the dirt on the tarps and simply tip it all back in once they were done.

Mick gave Jim a thumbs up and Jim stepped back, well clear of the arc of the digger's arm and finished off his joint. In the skilful hands of Mick Smith, the excavator made surprisingly quick work of removing the earth. Jim, thanks to the growing effect of the weed, became hypnotised watching the movement of the machine. Each repetition seemed to bring it to life. Almost as if it was moving all on its own – a mechanised alien creature. He had never before noticed just how beautiful a machine could be.

Jim was snapped from his psychoactive dreamscape by a sudden and unanticipated change in the soundtrack. Mick had stopped the engine.

"That should be deep enough, Jim. Take a look and see if I've exposed the top of the casket," Mick said.

Jim nodded to his brother and silently asked his brain to speak to his feet to get them to start walking. What happened next took them both by surprise. As a result of either his feet moving too slow for his body or his body moving too fast for his feet, Jim found himself uncontrollably leaning forward and as he built up momentum there was only one possible outcome. Mick slapped his hand on his forehead in disbelief as he watched his younger brother disappear headfirst into the hole he had just finished digging.

"For fuck's sake!" Mick said. He climbed down from the excavator and rushed to the side of the grave.

"Are you OK, Jim, you clumsy dickhead?"

Six feet below, Jim had landed face-first, the impact knocking the wind out of him. He took a moment to gather his senses. Apart from being slightly winded, Jim felt nothing else screaming out in pain. He slowly rolled himself over onto his back and looked up to the opening above him. The stars in the sky blinked and twinkled.

"Yeah. I think so," Jim said, gingerly.

Mick peered over the edge of the grave and put eyes on his brother lying on his back.

"Well, that's fucking odd," Mick said.

Jim was trying to process the last thirty seconds. He had been surprised by how soft his landing had been. He gently felt the ground around him with his hands. It was cold, soft dirt.

"Huh?" Jim said, confused.

"Huh is an understatement, Jim. The grave's fucking empty," Mick said, in a mix of anger and bemusement. "Someone's nicked the bloody mayor".

"I don't know what happened. I think the little one fell in?" The burley Kardashian said in Armenian, as he lowered his night vision binoculars.

Aleks Keshishian was crouched behind a wall in the cemetery that was covered in memorial plaques. With him were four of the Kardashians and a collection of spades and other assorted digging equipment they had brought with them in a van parked nearby. Aleks had earlier reached the conclusion that bringing a digger was too much risk, particularly when he had so much spare muscle on the payroll.

To say he was surprised to come across the Smith brothers busily digging up the mayor would have been an understatement. He had briefly considering aborting his mission before thinking better of it. He could only assume that Detective Chang had asked the Smith's to exhume the mayor and, for whatever reason, the brothers had decided to get an early start. Why they had chosen the middle of the night was anyone's guess but if they were going to do all the work, Aleks just might be able to take advantage of the situation.

"He was probably just getting in there to secure some straps to the coffin," Aleks said.

"Headfirst?" The Kardashian responded.

Aleks took the night vision binoculars from his henchman so he could get a better look for himself.

Jim had managed to pull himself to his feet and was now standing where the mayor's casket should have been.

"Maybe we're not deep enough?" Jim said.

"We didn't bury him in China," Mick replied.

Jim just couldn't understand it, who would want to steal the dead body of Terry McInerny?

"Sit tight, Jim. I'll put the head of the excavator down so you can climb out. Then we can figure out what the fuck we're going to do."

Jim knelt down and started digging with his hands to see if he could feel anything other than cool dirt beneath him, on the off chance that they really hadn't removed enough earth. But all he found was more dirt. He heard the engine of the excavator start up again and walked to the far end of the grave, pressing himself against the side wall to avoid the arm of the machine as it swung into the pit. Once the digging head was safely resting on the bottom, Jim clambered up it and pulled himself above ground.

"Well, that's put a spanner amongst the fucking pigeons!" Mick said, as Jim settled back onto terra firma.

Benefiting from being able to operate with a certain unorthodox clarity courtesy of the joint, Jim was weighing things up. He kept turning his attention from the digger, back to the grave, then back to the digger again.

"Are you with me, Jim?" Mick asked, watching his brother. Jim didn't answer.

"Jim?"

"Shhhhhhhhhh!" Jim said with a finger to his mouth.

"Shhh!"

Mick returned a *what the fuck* look at his brother.

"Maybe it's not all bad. I think I've got it."

Mick stood waiting for Jim to continue.

"Yes, Jim?"

"Sorry, I thought I was talking," Jim said, trying to compose himself before continuing. "It's simple. Just fill the hole in. When we come back here in a few hours, we dig it up again and discover the mayor is missing for a second time. Only for everyone else it'll be their first time. Then it's Chang's problem. The thing about someone taking the mayor is that someone's also taken the cheap box we put him in. They've taken the evidence."

Mick thought about it for a second.

"Well, fuck me," Mick said. He was grinning as he slapped Jim on the shoulder, hard. The force of the congratulatory contact tipped the smaller brother's balance. Jim tried to get his feet back underneath him but either his brain was too fast for his feet or his feet were too slow for his brain.

Aleks witnessed Jim fall backwards into the grave.

"I think the big one just pushed the little one back into the hole," Aleks said, giving a play-by-play report to his crew.

"What the fuck are they doing?"

He kept looking through his binoculars and saw Jim climb up the arm of the excavator a second time before watching the two brothers embrace. He then heard the rumble of the diesel engine of the excavator as it came to life. Aleks then watched on as the Smith brothers began filling in the hole again.

Aleks replayed the past half an hour in his head. He was trying to mentally confirm that he hadn't somehow missed them bringing the casket to the surface. He was one hundred percent positive he hadn't. That wasn't the kind of mistake Aleks made. As he watched the excavator swing back and forth, the piles of dirt get smaller and smaller, and presumably, the USB hidden under the mayor's body get reburied deeper and deeper, Aleks was rapidly trying to revise his plan. He quickly settled on three options.

The first option was to simply bum-rush the smith brothers, neutralise them both, then use their digger to re-excavate the mayor. The pros to this idea were speed and ease. The only con was the necessity to neutralise the brothers. Simply robbing them of their consciousness would leave two potential witnesses and inevitable police enquiries. Taking their lives, on the other hand, was a logistical nightmare - the disposing of the bodies, the hiding of their vehicles for starters - and two such prominent people suddenly disappearing without a trace was sure to rouse suspicion in Prosperity and lead to inconvenient police enquiries.

The second option was to sit tight and wait for the brothers to fill in the hole and leave, then he could proceed with his original plan to dig the casket up by hand. The pros to this were that they would have minimal chance of being discovered. Also, the soil would be much easier to shift now that it had been recently disturbed. The cons were that their original timings were now all out the window. The sun would be coming up soon and with dawn came the increased risk of their discovery. Aleks knew that a few keen locals ran laps at the oval most mornings, not to mention the early rising dog walkers.

The third and final option was to call it a night and try to gain access to the casket after the official exhumation. There were only cons to this plan. It was bound to cost a small fortune in bribes and require an equal measure of luck. Plus, there were only so many fiery car crashes that he could orchestrate - should he need to cover any more tracks - without bringing unnecessary and unwelcome heat from the local constabulary.

"So, what are we doing Aleks?"

Alex settled on option two.

"We wait".

It took Mick longer than he had thought to fill all the dirt back into hole. They had to be careful to make it look like it hadn't just been freshly dug. That required them to stop frequently and compact down the earth with the digging head. Then they had to use their shovels to shift the soil the digger couldn't scrape up. And finally, they had to cautiously tip in the remaining dirt from the tarpaulins, ensuring they didn't leave a whole lot of fresh disturbance on the ground around the grave. All in all, it took them the best part of an hour and a half. By the time they were done, the very first hints of morning were evident in the almost imperceptibly lighter sky.

"What do you think, Jim?" Mick asked, surveying his handiwork.

"If Sam isn't expecting anything untoward, I don't

think he'll notice anything untoward," Jim said. "Besides, as soon as we start digging again in a few hours, we're in the clear."

"Now we've just got to get all this gear back on the truck and all the way back to the compound. Only to turn around and do it all again," Mick said, slightly deflated.

"I think we can probably leave it here. Just say we got out early. As long as we're around when Sam turns up. It'll save us a lot of hassle," Jim said.

"Makes a shit load of sense to me," Mick replied, relieved.

"We should just run the Carrington back into the office. We can freshen up with a quick shower, grab a coffee and something to eat and be back here in plenty of time."

"Sounds like a plan," Mick said. "I'll drive."

Aleks was growing weary observing through the binoculars. But he wasn't about to look away in case he missed something important. He saw the brothers get into their van and a moment later, he watched them turn in a tight circle and drive back towards Prosperity, leaving behind the large flatbed truck and the excavator.

His brain went into overdrive.

By now, the sky was definitely growing lighter, and the air was beginning to be filled with the daily morning birdsong. The window for Aleks to do anything was growing smaller by the minute. Yet, there was now an excavator sitting by itself, exactly where he needed it. If he could hotwire it, it would cut down his worktime dramatically. The only problem was, Aleks had no idea if the brothers were gone for five minutes or two hours. If they returned halfway through any work they were doing, that presented the same set of problems as option one. But he had to get the mayor's body somehow.

"What are we doing, boss?"

Aleks had to make a decision. And he had to make it now.

"Option three."

"What's option three?" the talkative Kardashian asked.

"It's our last resort and about as appealing as kissing your ugliest sister."

"But I only have one sister?" the Kardashian replied, puzzled.

Aleks clipped him over the ear and began walking back to their van.

"Bring all the gear. We're leaving."

THIRTEEN

Detective Chang had woken early. He was loath to admit it to himself but he felt excited. It wasn't everyday he exhumed a body. Plus, he finally felt like he was getting somewhere with the mayor's case. He knew that once he had the body in his possession, he would be able to conduct a second, independent autopsy. He hoped the results would bring him at least one step closer to answering some of the doubts he held about exactly how Terry McInerny had died.

Chang had arranged to meet Constable Riley and the two Smith brothers at the cemetery at 8.30am. He was already showered and dressed and it was still only 6.45am, so he treated himself to some homemade Jianbing - Chinese fried pancakes - and a pod coffee rather than his usual instant. He cleaned up the kitchen and watched YouTube on his phone - he was half way through Ricky Gervais' 2007 stand up special *Fame* - but he was getting restless. He checked his watch. It was almost 8am. Which Sam figured was close enough to 8.30am. He grabbed his keys, wallet and gun and headed for the door.

Sam was surprised to see the Smith's truck and van already parked by the mayor's gravesite, and even more surprised to see that they had already unloaded the digger. He clearly wasn't' the only one keen to get going. Sam parked his car and started walking through the graves towards the two brothers who were standing by the truck drinking takeaway coffees.

"Morning, boys. You guys must have been up early?" Sam said as he approached.

"We figured we'd get out here and get set up so you didn't have to wait around," Jim replied.

"I appreciate it. Well, if you guys are ready, we might as well start digging," Chang said.

Jim shot Mick a furtive look.

"No time like the present. I think Terry would've been quite chuffed at being resurrected," Mick said as he climbed into the excavator. "Always did have a bit of a Jesus complex!"

The engine roared to life just as Constable Riley strode in to join the party.

"Apologies, Sam. I thought we weren't getting here 'til 8.30," Riley said, trying to catch her breath.

"I thought I was early for once!"

"It's all good, Riley. You are early," Sam said, putting her at ease.

Mick crawled the excavator over to the edge of

the gravesite and began removing the soil from it. With each load, Jim's anxiety was strangely both dissipating and increasing. On the one hand, the more Mick dug, the less obvious it was that the ground had been freshly disturbed by them only a few hours earlier. On the other, Jim knew that they were getting closer to Detective Chang discovering what he and his brother already knew.

"We should be getting close, now," Mick said, yelling over the sound of the digger. "Jim, take a look," he instructed.

Jim nodded to his brother and made his way to the edge of the hole and looked in. In his primary school days, Jim had fallen in love with drama. He always put his hand up for all the school plays and performances and even travelled to take part in regional eisteddfods – his rendition of Banjo Paterson's *The Man From Snowy River* won him many ribbons over the years. His mother had referred to him as a 'right little Peter Allen'. His crowning achievement had been winning the titular role in the end-of-year production of *Peter Pan* in grade six. Jim had reluctantly given up treading the boards in high school, where his late onset puberty had relegated him from being considered for the meatier characters to bit part player, if he made the cast at all. But Jim was about to dig deep into his acting well.

He looked into the pit then turned back to his brother and shook his head before giving a theatrical shrug.

"We should be deep enough!?!?" Mick yelled.

"Maybe the ground has sunk. Give it another foot or two," Jim said, holding his hands up to indicate how much deeper he wanted his brother to dig.

Mick responded with a thumbs up and removed another scoop of soil.

"Now?" Mick asked.

Jim took another look into the pit. He turned around and shook his head again.

"Nothing."

Mick turned the excavator off and jumped down.

"Is everything ok?" Sam asked

"We should have hit the top of the casket by now," Mick said as he walked to the edge.

"Occasionally, the ground can subside under fresh caskets," Jim said, interjecting. "But even then, I would have expected to have at least scraped the top at the depth we're at."

"What does that mean?" Sam said.

"Come take a look," Mick said, beckoning the detective over.

Sam rushed over to the edge.

"All I see is an empty hole," Sam said.

"That's the problem," Jim said.

"So what are you saying? The mayor's grave is empty?"

"I wish I could explain it differently, detective," Jim replied, "but it certainly looks that way".

"What the hell?" Sam said, in confusion, deflated.

Riley was now standing with them trying to make sense of what was happening.

"Should I call someone or something?" she asked.

Sam ignored the senior constable.

"You sure you're deep enough? Is it worth digging a little deeper?" Sam asked.

"We can do that if you want, Sam," Mick said.

"I would appreciate it."

Mick did as instructed and removed even more of the earth from the bottom of the grave while Sam supervised from the edge. Despite the additional excavation, all he could see was more earth.

"Take some more out!" Sam said, his voice rising in desperation.

"That's as deep as I can get with this digger, detective," Mick replied.

"Did you bring shovels? I'll get in there and do it by hand," Sam said, as he started rolling up his sleeves. Jim put a calming hand on his shoulder.

"I don't know how or why, Sam, but he's not in there. You could dig all the way through the Earth's mantle and hit molten lava and you still wouldn't find him."

Sam stood in silence, consumed by his thoughts.

"I gotta say, it's not a bad effort for whoever did it," Mick said "We had enough trouble getting him in there in the first place. And we had all the professional gear."

Detective Chang suddenly snapped back from his almost trance like state.

"Riley, I need you to tape this whole area off and take statements from Jim and Mick," Sam said as set off back towards the car, purposefully.

"Where are you going?" Riley asked after him.

"I need to make some calls."

An hour later, Aleks Keshishian was sitting in the security room at The Oasis finishing his breakfast, a croque monsieur with a side of grilled tomatoes, having showered to remove the smell of failure from the night's ultimately fruitless undertaking. He had turned one of the screens in front of him into a web browser and was deeply engrossed in another Gary Vaynerchuk key note on motivating employees: *Of course they fucking hate you, you're their boss.* He paused the talk as his phone rang. He glanced at the caller id. It was the phone call he had been expecting. He let it ring a couple of times as he finished his mouthful of food.

"Yes?" Aleks said, answering the phone. His face almost betrayed some emotion.

"What do you mean, empty?"

FOURTEEN

"I thought I said no loose ends?"

Christian Palfreeman and Aleks were sitting opposite each other in Palfreeman's office at The Oasis. Palfreeman had been reviewing a printout of the first week's financials - a healthy set of accounts by anyone's standards - when Aleks had interrupted him. His briefly buoyant mood was no more, replaced by a heavy presence that had brought with it a palpable tension. Palfreeman had already expressed his displeasure at Aleks's failure to secure the body prior to the exhumation. To now learn that the mayor was missing altogether had annoyed him no end.

"It is a simple inconvenience," Aleks said.

"Inconvenience?" Palfreeman replied, derisively. "A bother, a trouble, a hassle, a nuisance, an inconvenience? Just a simple inconvenience?"

Aleks simply shrugged and pursed his lips.

"That's all you have for me?"

"I already have people out looking," Aleks said, calmly. "We will find who took him."

"This is not a good situation, Aleks. We need that body. If Chang finds the mayor first… well, I don't need to tell you what that means for us."

Aleks didn't need his boss to tell him. He knew that if Chang found the casket and conducted a thorough autopsy that he would find the presence of the drugs that he had replaced the mayor's Viagra with. The drugs containing the little known compound he had personally developed with his friends in the Armenian mafia. The drugs that had caused his blood pressure to drop dramatically. The drugs that ultimately stopped his heart. However, what Aleks knew Christian didn't know was that, worse for them both, the USB that he had hidden under Terry McInerney's massive body was now also missing. The same USB that contained every incriminating document and damaging piece of correspondence between Christian Palfreeman and the mayor. It was so damning that only a small sample of that information would be sufficient to send them all to gaol for a long time should it fall into the hands of the police. Aleks quietly admonished himself. He now wished he'd just destroyed the USB when he had the chance. Why did he have to be such a romantic?

"Someone will know something. We will just keep shaking the tree," Aleks said.

"Just don't shake it too conspicuously, Aleks. We

don't need any more attention. I've worked too hard to lose it all now." Palfreeman said as he picked up the spreadsheet again and started looking through it, signalling that the meeting with Aleks was over.

Aleks stood and left Palfreeman's office. He was already making his first phone call by the time he reached the door.

Following the discovery, it had been another couple of hours before Jim had made it back to the Smith Bros. office. The first thing Constable Riley had done was to take his and his brother's statements. Jim was pretty proud of both of them for handling the situation as well as they did. Once he had control of his nerves, Jim's acting had been nothing short of a masterclass. He had played his role perfectly, expertly deploying a baffled expression with the well-practised nous of a wayward teenager. It had taken Jim a few questions to warm up but once he did, he leaned into his part with the enthusiasm of a community theatre veteran. He was revelling in it so much, in fact, that he had to reign in his routine when he caught himself postulating about who might have taken the body and then found himself on the cusp of a rant about the sanctity of the grave and how scandalous it was that someone would desecrate it in such a callous manner. However, as proud of his own act as he was, Jim had been particularly captivated by his brother's efforts. Mick had been scarily believable. So much so that Jim made a mental note of his brother's capacity for deception to ensure that he didn't fall prey to it at some time in the future.

By the end of the initial inquires by the constable and due to the flawless performances of the Smiths - modesty prevented Jim from declaring them Oscar worthy but thought them definitely in Golden Globes territory - Jim was positive that the police had no idea that they had attempted to exhume the mayor in the hours before officially exhuming the mayor. And now the body was officially missing, Jim was more than comfortable that investigators had more important and pressing enquiries in front of them than pursuing anything that could link back to the brothers.

Once Constable Riley had completed her questions, the exhausted Smith siblings had next turned their attentions to the job of packing everything up. It was only after having assisted Mick in the laborious task of getting the digger back to the compound and washed down, that Jim had then made his way back into town. After the events of the evening, he wanted to make sure everything at the office was as it should be. He also had some administration to attend to - he had long planned to re-arrange his casket display room and figured there was no time like the present. Given the goals he had already kicked today, Jim determined to finally end his procrastination and get it all done while he was on a roll. But first, a quick shut-eye was in order. After all, it had been a night.

Nobody knew that Jim often took a nap at the office. He had never been caught - Jim was hyper-conscious to only take them when he was certain the building was empty – and he had certainly never told anyone. It wasn't so much that he was concerned that some might think him lazy; he worked hard and if anyone deserved to catch a few quick zeds at work it was Jim Smith. It was more the embarrassment he was sure would burn if anyone found out where he preferred to take his siestas.

It had been during the early days of his time in the funeral business when Jim had felt almost a natural compulsion to try out the caskets. While some might have seen it as a morbid pastime, he rationalised that it served as important market research. Considering he spent much of his day talking up how comfortable the various models of casket were, it was only right that he tried them out for himself. While it had initially started out with as a quick lie-down in each new model to get a feel for their respective comfort levels, Jim soon he found himself spending more and more time in them. Before long he was using them for genuine rest and relaxation. At first it had just been the odd power nap – a quick ten to twelve minutes - but the duration had quickly increased. It was rare now for Jim to not spend at least forty minutes a day laying down in a box made for burial, catching up on sleep.

With all the focus that had been on the Carrington recently, it had been some weeks since Jim had chosen it for his worktime nap. He just hadn't felt comfortable taking it for a spin. However, given the day's recent events, he decided that it felt strangely appropriate. He also wondered, if by sleeping in the last place to house Terry McInerney, some insight into what happened to the mayor's body might come to him in a dream. A message from the other side.

However, in the haste of the morning's adventures, the brothers hadn't had time to put the Carrington away properly after their first, fruitless effort to swap the mayor back into it. As such, it was still sitting on a trolley in the loading dock. Jim wheeled the mahogany masterpiece through the corridor that linked the dock to the various rooms where the dead bodies were prepared for their final journey. He chose the first room he came to and set the Carrington up in the middle of it. Jim ducked out briefly before returning with a small travel pillow - he had found over the years that he developed a crick in his neck without one. He removed his jacket and laid it on the floor, kicked off his shoes and climbed in.

The space inside the Carrington was more than generous for Jim, not surprising given its capacity was large enough to accommodate a man the size of Terry McInerny. He stretched his legs out and placed his hands together on his stomach in a pose not to dissimilar to that in which Jim placed his clients. After a few deep breaths, he could feel himself drifting into the plush satin lining and off into the endless wonder of his dreaming sub-conscious.

Exactly forty minutes later, Jim was woken by the sounds of his alarm, the familiar rolling piano intro to Adele's *Someone Like You* coaxing him from his snooze. He kick-started his body with a large inhalation and braced his hands on either side of the casket floor to help sit up. As he pushed down, his right hand slipped on the slick, satin lining and shot into the crack between the base of the casket and the side wall. His fingers jammed into the small space and held firm.

"Fuck!" Jim yelled out in pain.

He tried to pull his fingers out but they were well and truly stuck. He shifted his weight on to his hip and grabbed the trapped wrist with his free hand and slowly started trying to ease them loose. But they wouldn't budge. The weight of Jim on the padded bottom was fighting against the leverage he needed, compounded by the awkward angle his arm was in. It was making the whole task near impossible.

"Come on you little prick," Jim said, straining harder.

With a sudden explosion of movement, Jim's hand sprung free. It flew up and slapped him square in the face.

"Ow! Shit!"

Jim took a moment to compose himself before inspecting the edge of the casket. He needed to know two things: first, how on earth such a seemingly innocuous gap had been so efficient at trapping him; and second, whether his struggle for freedom had caused any damage to the casket itself.

What he saw was not what he expected. Sitting next to where his hand had just been, was a shiny USB stick. Jim picked it up, turning it over in his fingers as he inspected it closer. He had never seen it before. Perhaps it belonged to Mick but there was nothing on it that suggested an owner. No name scrawled in permanent marker. No company logo printed on it.

Jim lifted himself out of the Carrington and studied the USB further. He racked his brain as to how he hadn't discovered the device in the casket before. He was quite proud of the effort he put into cleaning everything each time they ran their little scam. Although, if he was honest with himself, he had perhaps let things slip just a little in recent times. And, admittedly, he'd never really gotten right down into the gaps along the edges. A detail he now quietly admonished himself for.

Jim tried to recall how many times they had used this particular Carrington in recent months, apart from for the mayor. Off the top of his head, he could think of at least six or seven other funerals. If the device had been trapped like his fingers had been, he figured it could belong to any one of them. However, none of the families had come forward over that time looking for it so Jim concluded that it probably wasn't that important. He placed it in the inside pocket of his jacket for safe-keeping and resolved to plug it in to his computer later, in order to hopefully identify its rightful owner. For now though, Jim suddenly realised his already long put off chore of rearranging the casket display room had just become far more arduous. He now knew he was going to have to thoroughly double-check every recycled model on the off chance he had missed any other personal items in similar circumstances. The extra effort was surly going to require another nap. At least, that's what Jim told himself by way of motivation to begin.

Aleks Keshishian took a sip of his extra strong coffee. He was sitting in a small room in the bowels of The Oasis where he had been holed up for the best part of the day. He had most of his team of Kardashians out on the streets with their ears to the ground, trying to shake trees in order to find some information on who might have taken the mayor's body. The remaining members of his crew, his more trusted deputies, had been working directly with him. They had been meticulously going through the facts as they knew them, in the hope of identifying the individuals or organisations most likely to benefit from the mayor's disappearance. They had documented their thinking on large sheets of butchers' paper, working through the most probable scenarios in a methodical, forensic manner. With each new idea they documented the prospective motives each might have for stealing the dead mayor before systematically ruling out each scenario. In over six hours of work, and with all the evidence they had at hand, everything pointed in one direction.

Keshishian's most trusted offsider, a gruff, burly, giant of a man who insisted on being called Andre in honour of his favourite Armenia popstar of the same name - despite neither possessing the looks nor the ability to carry a tune that would warrant such a tribute - was tapping a permanent marker on his temple as he surveyed the latest sheet of paper hanging on the wall.

"I can't see how it can be anyone else," Andre said, breaking the silence in the room.

Aleks slammed his coffee down on the table.

"You idiot!" Aleks yelled.

"What?" Andre said, genuinely perplexed.

"After all the work we've done today, the best you can come up with is that the most likely person or people to have taken the mayor's body is…us?"

"Well, no one had more motivation to want to take the body than us," Andre replied.

"There's just one problem," Aleks said.

"What?" Andre asked

"We don't have the mayor's body, do we Andre? If we had the mayor's body, we wouldn't be spending all this fucking time trying to figure out who has the mayor's body would we?" Aleks said, with a calmness that bordered on menace

"Well, when you put it like that…" Andre said,

meekly.

"So what do we do now boss?"

Aleks thought for a moment.

"Tell the rest of the boys to keep chasing things. The first one of them to bring me a decent lead gets a free night at The Oasis - on me."

"And what about us?"

"We're going to check out the last place we know for a fact that the mayor's body was and go from there," Aleks said.

"And where was that?"

"Smith Bros."

FIFTEEN

Detective Chang carried a plate of freshly cooked honey chicken over to Constable Riley who was sitting at a table in the otherwise empty dining area of Lee's New Golden Imperial Lotus Garden. He wouldn't normally go for this particular dish himself but he knew that it was Riley's favourite and so had made accommodation for that in this instance. Riley was intently studying all the documents on the mayor's case, looking for any clue as to who might have taken the body. She heard Chang approaching and looked up hungrily, and clapped her hands together in excitement.

"Ohhhh, my favourite, Sam!" Riley said, inhaling the delicious aroma.

Sam placed the dish on the table and sat down as Riley cleared some of the documents to one side to make room. She enthusiastically heaped a few spoonfuls of rice and almost half the entire serve of chicken onto her plate and busily started consuming it. Sam looked at his colleague and smiled. He never tired of watching people enjoy the food he cooked.

"I can't get away from the fact that everything points to Palfreeman," Riley said, between mouthfuls.

"I know we don't have any evidence but I just can't see who else would want to steal the mayor?"

"You could be right. But until we have something concrete, we're up the proverbial without a paddle," Chang said.

Riley noticed that Sam had yet to put any food on his plate.

"You not eating Sam? It's delicious".

Sam shook his head.

"You mind if I help myself to seconds then?"

Chang looked at Riley's plate. It was still about a third covered in chicken.

"Of course. Go for it," Sam said.

Riley refilled her plate and continued eating as though she'd never been fed before in her life.

"If Palfreeman and the Kardashians had something to do with McInerny's death and had subsequently tried to cover their tracks by offing Dr Cochiarelli, it would make sense that they would want to get to the body before we did," Sam said, "but there's a lot of speculation in that whole scenario."

"Maybe we just head down to The Oasis. Have a poke around. If they were involved then surely there'd be some clues around that place," Riley said, continuing to stuff her face.

"A bit too obvious, I think. If they have got the body but haven't already disposed of it, they certainly will shortly after we show up. As unlikely as it is, I still want to get my hands on the mayor if at all possible."

"What are you thinking then, Sam?" Riley asked.

"There's one question that we still haven't answered," Sam said.

"Just one?" Riley said putting her fork down, having finished her plate of food.

"Okay, one main one, then. We're assuming that Palfreeman and The Oasis are somehow involved in the mayor's death. And Dr Cociarelli's death as well for that matter. What we still don't know is why? What did the mayor know that was enough to get him killed? In fact, what was it that warranted the deaths of two people?"

"Jesus, you're right Sam," Riley said. "Motive. That is a big one. What's our next move then?"

"We try to answer that question, obviously. If we can answer that, everything else should fall into place. But we've got to move quickly if we want any chance of getting hold of the body and conducting a new autopsy."

"Where to, boss?" Riley asked.

"We'll start at the council building first thing in the morning. The mayor's office. If there's any paper trail it will start in there."

"Sounds like a plan," Riley said, looking at the remaining chicken on the serving platter.

Sam waited a moment then nodded.

"Go on!" Sam said.

Riley grinned like a child and happily tipped the remaining chicken onto her plate and began devouring it with the grace of a pig at a trough.

The security system at the Smith Bros. offices provided little resistance to Aleks Keshishian. He had expected more from it the first time he had broken in when he had hidden the USB under the dead mayor. This second visit it had again provided no significant hindrance. Once inside, Aleks and Andre began carefully searching for any evidence. They weren't exactly sure what they were looking for but Aleks had grown more convinced the longer he thought about it, that the Smith Bros. must know something about what had happened to the body. After all, they were the last people to see the mayor prior to his burial and then there had been the odd nocturnal goings-on at the cemetery. The more he replayed that evening in his mind, the more he couldn't make sense of why they had been exhuming the mayor in the middle of the night. And he certainly couldn't reconcile why they had filled the hole in again only to excavate it once more in the company of Detective Chang a few hours later. Even if they weren't involved directly, he was certain that he would find something in their offices that would at least point him in the right direction.

"Remember, make like we were never here," Aleks

said to Andre.

Andre nodded as he quietly pulled ring binders of client information from some shelving on the wall behind a row of desks and started leafing through them. Aleks, meanwhile, was busy picking the lock to Jim Smith's office. Again, it posed little more challenge to Keshishian than unlocking his own phone. Once inside, he busied himself gaining access to Jim's computer. Aleks guessed the password in his first attempt, typing the word 'Password' into the box on the screen. He laughed at how simple and backward the people of Prosperity were.

He opened up the database that contained all the client files and searched for the mayor. He scanned the screen. Nothing jumped out at him. All the fees had been paid for by the mayor himself as part of what seemed to be a pre-paid funeral package. Aleks was quietly impressed that the mayor had the foresight to arrange his own affairs. For all his disagreeable traits, he couldn't help but acknowledge that he possessed at least some level of self-awareness about his personal health. Keshishian briefly pondered how it might have been better to leave the mayor to his own devices - his lifestyle had been bound to get the better of him sooner rather than later - thereby avoiding the current predicament they found themselves in. He quickly reviewed the cost breakdown and shook his head at the amount that was paid for the casket.

"Criminal!" Aleks said to himself.

He closed down the database and clicked on the

icon of the accounting programme on the computer's desktop. He wanted to see if there had been any unusual movements of large amounts of money in or out, anything that might provide a clue as to what was going on. He poured over the accounts for the prior six-months. They all seemed in order, with similar amounts coming and going from the accounts each week. No large amounts that were unaccounted for. No special one-off windfalls tagged 'miscellaneous income'. Nothing. Aleks kept digging. He didn't have time for a forensic audit but he wanted to get a better understanding of each line item to see if any payments could be hidden within them.

That's when it struck him. The accounting dealing with the caskets simply didn't add up. There seemed to be a significant disparity between the revenue being generated by them and the expenses attributed to their purchase. But for the world, Aleks couldn't make sense of what it meant. And it certainly didn't bring him closer to finding the mayor.

Suddenly he heard a loud crash.

"Oh fuck!" Andre said from the other side of the offices.

Aleks hopped up from the computer to see what had happened only to find Andre standing over what was, until very recently, a fish tank that was now lying smashed into a thousand pieces on the floor. Half-a-dozen colourful tropical fish were flapping about on the carpet among the blue aqua gravel and artificial plants that moments before had been their home.

"You fucking moron! What did I say? Make like we were never here!" Aleks said, annoyed.

"I just… I think I…I'm sorry…" Andre replied.

Andre knelt down and started trying to scoop up the flailing fish.

'What are you doing?" Aleks asked

"I don't like to see animals suffer," Andre said, as he chased the flopping animals around the floor.

Aleks casually walked over towards him.

"Maybe we can find a vase or a couple of glasses of water. To keep them alive," Andre continued.

Aleks suddenly stomped on the fish closest to him, squashing it dead under his heel. He then dispatched the remaining fish in a scene reminiscent of a game of whack-a-mole as Andre looked on in genuine shock.

"Now they aren't suffering anymore," Aleks said. "Clean all of this up. Find a bag or something to putt all the glass and bits in, we'll take it with us. Maybe they won't notice it's missing."

"Did you find anything?" Andre asked.

"I'm not sure. How about you?"

"Nothing."

Five minutes later, Aleks had logged out of Jim Smith's computer, closed and locked the door to his office and was resetting the alarm to the building, as Andre waited in the back lane holding what remained of the fish tank in a metal waste-paper bin he had stolen from next to one of the desks.

"I want you to set up a tail on both of the Smith brothers," Aleks said, as he and Andre climbed into his car.

"There's just something not right about them. I know they're involved. Somehow."

Detective Chang and Constable Riley were perched behind the mayoral desk inside the council building as the morning sunlight poured in through the window. Although as the standing orders and statutes demanded, council had already elected a new mayor - one Jimmy Macalister, a long-term councillor and owner / operator of Macalister's, the eponymous old-school department store in town - the mayor's office itself was yet to be occupied. This had been partly due in deference to the popular McInerny's death but had primarily been a result of no one wanting to clean out and organise all of his files and personal belongings.

Riley had switched on the mayor's computer as Chang watched over her shoulder.

"You sure you'll be able to get in?" Chang asked.

"Misspent youth, Sam. I spent way too much time holed up in my room staring at a screen. Besides, how hard can it be? I wouldn't have pegged Terry McInerny to have been the type to regularly change his passwords. And not to speak ill of the dead but I'm guessing he would have gone for the most obvious one," Riley said.

"This all above board?"

Sam held a piece of paper up to Riley.

"Judge Grant signed off on it first thing this morning," Sam said.

As the login box came up on the screen, Riley typed in eight letters that Sam couldn't read due to the computer disguising each letter as an asterisk. Riley hit enter and the computer sprang to life.

"First go!" Sam said, excitedly.

"Like I said. Not to speak ill of the dead but he used the most common password there is," Riley said

"Which is?"

"Password"

Riley started working. She opened the web browser and clicked on the search history.

"What are we looking at, Riley?" Sam asked

"Well, it looks like our old friend had a serious porn addiction. Every second website he's visited in the last month seems to have at least one 'x' in the title. But look here, Sam."

Riley pointed to the screen.

"Look how many times he's visited The Oasis website in the months before he died."

"What's odd about that?" Sam asked. "It's the biggest thing going on in town so, you can imagine he's going to show an interest. The council was all over it as well."

"That's true," Riley said, "But take another look. He's visited it at least four or five times more often than his own business, McInerny Motors and Machinery. And at least seven or eight times more often than the council's own website."

"Can we get his emails up?" Sam asked.

"If they haven't archived his account yet, we should be able to."

Riley clicked a few things on the screen and an email programme opened.

"Looks like they haven't gotten around to it yet," Riley said.

Sam leaned in closer to the screen.

"Search for any emails from Palfreeman, or Aleks or The Oasis in general," Sam said.

Riley typed in the words one after another. Nothing.

"There's nothing, Sam."

"That's strange. Not one email?"

"What's stranger is if I go to write a new email and start typing Christian Palfreeman, it auto populates the email address," Riley said.

"What does that mean?"

"It means the mayor has sent or received emails to this account from Palfreeman that are no longer here."

"Well that is interesting," Sam said. "See if you can find any documents associated with The Oasis".

Riley typed 'Oasis' into the search bar of the computer.

"There are no documents, Sam."

"Bloody hell. But there have to be?!?" Sam said, puzzled.

"What is interesting is there are about a dozen calendar meetings that are showing up. But that's it. If someone has tried to delete everything then I guess missing the calendar entries might be easy enough to do. Especially if they didn't know what they were doing."

"Is there any way to find out if someone has deleted everything off the system?"

"Let me check the logs," Riley said.

Sam watched as Riley typed away on the computer's keyboard. Her fingers were moving at such speed it was as though she had become one with the machine.

"That's interesting," Riley said after a moment or two.

"Stop saying 'that's interesting'," Sam said.

"Sorry. It looks like a large cache of data was transferred to an external device before the same amount of data was wiped from the server."

"What does that mean?"

"It means someone made a copy of whatever it was rather than just deleting it. And the date was only a few weeks before the mayor died."

"But if it was anything incriminating, why wouldn't that person just delete it?" Sam asked.

"A normal person would. Unless they wanted to keep it. For insurance perhaps."

"Is there any way we can recover the documents that were deleted?" Sam asked.

"We can try. It might take some time though.

And there's no guarantee we'll get everything. Or anything, for that matter."

"Okay. Make a note of everything you've done and shut it down. I've got an idea that might be quicker. I think it's time we had a chat with our old friend, Palfreeman."

SIXTEEN

Jim Smith took his phone from his pocket and called Mick. He was panicking.

After a few rings, Mick's voice came on the line.

"What is it, Jim?"

"I need you in the office. Now!"

Jim hung up the phone without waiting for a reply and returned his attention to the short, sobbing woman standing before him. He placed a reassuring hand on her shoulder.

Nikki Blue, known to most in town simply as Bluey, had worked reception for the Smith family since Jim's father Sid had held the reigns. She was as reliable as she was stout and possessed an unmistakable silhouette that was almost as wide as it was tall. Despite her sometimes bizarre personal stories - she claimed to be descended from German royalty among other wild fantasies - Bluey was nothing if not loveable. Never married, she had instead invested her own affection in a veritable menagerie of pets over the years. There had been the long line of dogs of course - she had a particular like for Alaskan Malamutes, an unsuitable breed for the local climate who thrived during the cold winters but were distressingly out of place during the summer months. Then there were the alpacas, followed shortly thereafter by the miniature welsh ponies. But when she moved off her acreage and into town, Bluey had taken her animal passions indoors, latterly becoming quite the aquarist. So it was only natural that she was devastated to arrive at the office to find her fish tank missing.

"I just don't know who would want to take them? My babies?" Bluey said, through thick tears.

"I have no clue," Jim said, tenderly, "But someone's obviously broken in. Have you noticed anything else missing?"

"To be honest, Jim, I came in and when I saw that the aquarium was gone, well, I just fell apart. And then you arrived."

Jim stepped forward to give Bluey a consoling embrace when something crunched under his foot, stopping him mid step. He lifted his shoe and could see a small piece of shattered glass beneath it. Jim bent down and felt the carpet. He could have sworn it felt damp.

"It's going to be ok, Bluey. Why don't you take the day off. Then tomorrow, I'll take you into Bathurst to Pappie's Pets and we'll get you some new fish,"

Jim said.

"It seems too soon to just replace them. Maybe they'll turn up?" Bluey said.

"You're right, Bluey. Maybe they will turn up."

"I'll take the day though if I can, Jim. I'll need the time to make some missing posters to put up around town," Bluey said.

"Whatever time you need, Bluey," Jim said, walking her to the door.

"You're a kind man, Jim Smith. Just like your father."

Jim smiled as he ushered her gently out the door, locking it closed behind her.

"Shit!" Jim said.

He rushed back to the spot on the carpet and felt it again. It was definitely damp. He also spotted, wedged under a filing cabinet nearby, a small, plastic tropical plant. There was no doubt about it, someone had smashed the fish tank.

Jim quickly rushed around the office to check to see if anything else was missing. The easiest picking was the petty cash tin, sitting right there in the open, right next to where the fish tank had once been. It only held about a hundred and fifty dollars but it was untouched. No meth head worth their salt would have left it behind.

He continued to make a quick inventory of the rest of the office. No computers were missing, no caskets were gone. Not even any of the fake flowers. His own office was locked, as he had left it. He opened it up and took a look inside. Everything was as it should be. His prized award for being named Best Funeral Director in Australia a few years back was still pride of place on the shelf. The organisers had tried to convince him it was Swarovski Crystal but Jim had his doubts. Regardless, if theft had been the intruder's motive, then it would have been a tempting artefact to steal.

"What the fuck's the urgency, Jim? I was half way through hand feeding the fucking cattle."

Jim exited his office and saw his brother walking in from the door to the loading dock.

"We got broken into last night," Jim said.

Mick stopped in his tracks.

"Oh for fuck's sake. That's the last thing we need. How much did they take?"

"Doesn't look like they took anything," Jim said. "Smashed poor Bluey's fish tank though. She was pretty cut up."

"What the fuck? So, what were they doing?"

That's when Jim noticed it. Along the wall behind Mick were the hard copies of their client files. They were arranged in ring binders in alphabetical order. A-D, E-K etc. However, about half-way along there was a problem. Where it should have gone L-M, N-O, P, just like the fast part of the alphabet song, instead it went L-M, P, N-O. They were in the wrong order. And if Jim was anything, it was a pedant and everyone in the office was fastidious about maintaining things, to keep their boss happy.

"They were looking for something else, Mick. Those files behind you are out of order."

"Shit, the client files?" Mick asked.

Jim nodded. He held his finger up to his mouth to ask his brother to be quiet and walked over to the nearest desk. He grabbed a pad of post-it notes from it and started writing. A few seconds later he held it up for his brother to read.

Don't say anything. Could be the police. Bugged? Meet you at the farm.

Mick read it and his eyes widened. He mouthed the word 'Fuck'.

Jim was pacing back and forth in the kitchen of Mick's house as Mick sat at the table drinking a pre-mixed rum and cola – his second.

"I just can't figure out how the police got on to us?" Jim said. "What are we going to do?"

"Look, we don't even know it was the cops."

Jim stopped pacing and looked squarely at his brother.

"Who else would it be?" Jim said, sharply.

Mick sat silent for a moment thinking, then simply sipped his drink.

"I'm pretty sure they wouldn't have found anything, not in those files at least. But the fact they're looking means they're on to us. We're fucked!" Jim said

"Don't they need a warrant or some shit to break in to places?" Mick said.

"I think so. But maybe they have due cause or something? Maybe there are loopholes? Who knows, maybe they used a private investigator?"

"Why would the cops use a private investigator?"

"I've heard they do that sometimes. It gets them around some of the intricacies of the law or something. The thing is, it doesn't really matter, does it? What does matter is what the bloody hell are we going to do now?"

Mick thought for a moment.

"We don't really have many options. We could turn ourselves in, come clean and hope for leniency…" Mick said

"Not appealing," Jim said, interjecting.

"…or we can sit tight and hope they never find enough on us. If the cops had any real evidence, they'd be driving up that drive right now and knocking on the front door."

Jim's ears pricked up at a familiar noise growing louder outside. It was the unmistakable noise of a car, driving up the drive. Mick heard it as well. The boys rushed to the window and craned their necks to see who it was.

"Oh, it's just Trace," Mick said, the relief palpable. "She's been at the vet's all morning."

Jim's throat tightened.

"The vet's?" Jim asked.

"Yeah, the bloody dog has arthritis. He's been hobbling around for the past few months. She's been taking him in to Hibbert's joint every couple of days for some new–aged stem cell treatment or something. Personally, I think a bullet would have been more humane. I swear that dog gets treated better than me!" Mick said.

Jim swallowed hard.

"Mick, there's something you should know."

"What's that?" Mick asked, casually.

Just at that moment, Tracy walked into the kitchen trailed by their dog, a thirteen-year-old blue cattle dog called Chief. Mick had named him after his childhood footy hero, Paul 'Chief' Harrigan.

"Hey Trace. How'd you go at the vet's?" Mick asked as he knelt to welcome Chief home with a vigorous scratch behind his ear.

"Yeah good. I've got to take him back in next week though, for another treatment." Tracy said. She hadn't noticed Jim standing in the kitchen until now. She could feel his eyes staring at her and her cheeks suddenly flushed red.

"I didn't know you were coming over, Jim," Tracy said, sheepishly.

"Neither did I," Jim said.

Mick finished patting the dog and turned to his brother.

"What we're you saying before, Jim? Something about me needing to know something or something?"

Jim looked at Tracy. Tracy looked back at Jim. She shook her head ever so slightly, imploring him not to say anything. Mick could feel the atmosphere change.

"What's going on?" Mick asked, switching his gaze between his brother and his wife.

Jim and Tracy stood in a silent Mexican standoff.

"Jim? Trace?"

The was a long pause. It hung thick in the air.

"It's better coming from you, Tracy." Jim said, finally.

"No," Tracy said. "I told you, there's nothing to say."

"Will someone please just tell me what's going on?" Mick said, imploring.

"I think there's something going on between Dr Hibbert and Tracy," Jim said, looking at the floor.

"Fuck you, Jim!" Tracy said, with a mix of venom and defeat.

Mick looked lost.

"What do you mean, Jim?" Mick asked

"I saw them together. At the opening of The Oasis."

"I told you there's nothing going on, Jim!" Tracy said. She took a few steps towards Mick.

"There's nothing going on, Mick. He's just been a good friend. That's all."

"I'm going to fucking kill him!" Mick said.

"I'm going to fucking kill him!"

"But he's just a friend, Mick. I swear!" Tracy said, pleadingly.

"So, is Chief even getting treatments?" Mick asked.

Tracy looked away but remained silent.

"I'm going to fucking kill him!" Mick said as he

rushed to the bowl on the bench that held his car keys, grabbed them and headed outside to his car.

Tracy looked at Jim.

"Well bloody done, Jim," Tracy said, as tears welled in her eyes.

Jim just walked past her and followed his brother outside. He broke into a run to catch up to Mick as he heard his brother's car start. He opened the passenger door and hopped in.

"What are you doing, Jim?" Mick asked.

"I'm coming with you," Jim said.

"I don't need your help to fuck this guy up, Jim. You know that, right?"

"No, but I do need to stop you from killing him," Jim said, as Mick put the car in gear and launched it down the drive, kicking a spray of dirt and gravel into the air and leaving behind a plume of dust.

SEVENTEEN

Misty Gerard greeted Detective Chang and Constable Riley in the reception area of The Oasis with a grin that would make the Cheshire Cat feel inadequate.

"Well, if it isn't my favourite Chinese-Australian chef-detective," Misty said. "To what do we owe this pleasure, Sam?"

"I need to have a word with Mr Palfreeman," Sam said, with a friendly tone.

"Let me see if I can rustle him up for you detective. Why don't you have a seat and I'll have some drinks brought over." Misty steered them to a booth positioned beneath a large wooden shield mounted imposingly on the wall.

"Non-alcoholic, of course. Unless I can tempt you with a Knightgroni? It's our take on a Negroni. I know, the name's a tad twee but it's delicious."

"Thank you, Misty. Water is fine."

Sam and Riley slid in to the booth and waited. After a few minutes, Misty returned with a jug of water and a couple of glasses. She set them down on the table and started filling them.

"Christian is just finishing up a call. He'll be right out," Misty said. "I'll be more than happy to keep you company until then."

"How are things going out here, Misty? Anything I need to know about?" Sam asked, keeping it casual.

"Only if you're interested in some of the kinks I've come across. As you know, I'm no prude, Sam. But who knew these medieval aficionados were so fucking twisted!?!" Misty laughed.

"What's Christian like to work for?" Sam continued.

"Pretty invisible to be honest. Which suits me to a tee. It's a pretty smooth operation, actually. One of the best set ups I've ever seen."

"And Keshishian?"

"I'm big enough and ugly enough to handle a man like him detective. This ain't my first rodeo. Some of his offsiders are pretty creepy but that comes with the territory a bit. Look, my first priority is my girls. Then come the guests. Everything else, is just noise."

"I'm going to level with you, Misty. I think we've always had a pretty solid relationship," Sam said, lowering his voice.

"I'd agree," Misty said, leaning in conspiratorially.

"I'm sure you've heard by now that the mayor's body is missing. I don't know in exactly what capacity, but I'm sure that your bosses are involved somehow. I need you to let me know if you see anything untoward, or out of place - even if it seems minor - I want to know."

"Ooooh, intriguing. I feel like I'm a character in a crime thriller. Or a spy in a James Bond movie!" Misty said, eyes excitedly wide.

"This is serious, Misty. What do you say?"

"Look, if I see something and you need to know, you'll know," Misty said, matter-of-fact.

"Detective Chang!"

Christian Palfreeman was striding across the room, wearing a friendly smile. He was dressed in a pastel blue polo shirt tucked into a pair of pink chinos, rolled to expose a hint of ankle and allow his neutral Loro Piana loafers to really shine. Two steps behind Palfreeman, Aleks Keshishian trailed in all black, with a stoic facial expression that betrayed nothing.

"To what do I owe the pleasure?" Palfreeman said as he reached the booth.

"I appreciate your time, Mr Palfreeman. Do you have a moment to join us?" Sam said.

Palfreeman turned to Aleks as if looking for confirmation that he did have the time to sit. Aleks returned a slight nod of his head.

"Of course, detective," Palfreeman said.

Misty rose to her feet and Christian Palfreeman took her place.

"I'll leave you to it," Misty said, before heading back across the reception area and through the double doors that led into the back offices of The Oasis.

"I'm not sure if you've met my colleague, Constable Riley. She's joining us just to make notes, if you're okay with that?" Sam said.

Christian shifted in his seat.

"Why do I get the feeling I should have my lawyer here, detective?" Palfreeman said with his usual disarming charm.

"No, it's just a friendly chat," Sam said, "A couple of questions we're hoping you can help us with." "Fire away," Palfreeman said. He opened his arms wide in an exaggerated, defenceless gesture.

Riley already had her notebook out on the table and was poised to scribe the conversation. She could feel the weight of Aleks Keshishian's glare as he stared at her.

"I'll get straight to the point, Mr Palfreeman. You are no doubt aware that the body of Mayor Terry McInerny is missing," Sam said.

"I had heard. Terrible, really."

"Can you tell me if you know anything about that?" Sam said, continuing.

Christian sat back as an incredulous expression crossed his face.

"Are you asking me if I know anything about Terry McInerney's missing body? Beyond the fact that it is no longer where it was left?" Palfreeman asked.

"Well, do you?"

"Apart from the fact that it is absent, lost, misplaced,

mislaid, gone astray, missing?" Palfreeman's gaze became steely. "Of course I don't, detective."

"How about you, Mr Keshishian?" Detective Chang asked, shifting his attention to the man in black over Palfreeman's shoulder.

Aleks sniffed, dismissively.

"He doesn't know anything, either. And to be honest, I am finding your whole line of questioning a touch rude, detective," Palfreeman said.

"Do you mind if we have a look around?" Sam asked.

Palfreeman stiffened and sat forward slightly in his seat.

"Actually, I do. Now, unless you have a warrant to be on these private premises, I would like to ask you to leave."

Christian Palfreeman stood and gestured for Detective Chang and Constable Riley to vacate the booth. Sam nodded his acceptance that the meeting was concluded and slid himself from the seat, as Riley gathered her things and joined him.

"Aleks will make sure you find your way, detective," Palfreeman said.

"We managed to find our way in. I'm sure we can find our way out," Sam said.

"No, I insist."

Aleks moved in slightly behind the two police officers, making his presence felt.

"Well, thank you for your time Mr Palfreeman. I know you're a busy man," Sam said as he started for the door.

"I hope you find the body, detective," Palfreeman said after him. And he watched as the two were hurriedly escorted from the building by his henchman.

A few moments later, Aleks Keshishian returned and found Christian Palfreeman standing in exactly the same spot.

"Are they gone?" Palfreeman asked.

Aleks nodded in the affirmative.

"What a bloody nerve. To come in here and speak to me like that!" Palfreeman said, the anger clear in his voice.

"He's desperate," Aleks said

"It's obvious that they don't have anything concrete on us. Isn't it? If they did, they'd be here with a warrant, wouldn't they?" Palfreeman said.

"Agreed," Aleks said.

"So, without the body, they have nothing?"

"Agreed."

"Well then, Aleks. You better fucking find that body."

Sam was deep in thought as he drove back into Prosperity. Constable Riley had been talking non-stop from the moment they sat back in the car. He suddenly realised he hadn't been listening to a word she had been saying.

"Sorry, I'm miles away," Sam said.

"It's ok Sam, I was just carrying on about nothing really, anyway. I'll shut up and let you think," Riley said.

Sam knew from the outset that his plan to walk into The Oasis, bluntly ask Palfreeman straight out if he was involved in the mayor's disappearance and expect an answer that wrapped everything up with a bow had been a longshot. But that wasn't really the point. The point was, he needed to let Palfreeman and Keshishian know that he was investigating them. His hope was that now they would be in even more of a hurry to cover their tracks. And Sam knew from experience - mistakes happened when people rushed.

"We're going to have to keep an eye on them, Riley," he said finally. "If our little visit has done the trick, they'll be running around trying to clean everything up as fast as they can."

"Do you reckon they have the mayor's body?" Riley asked.

"To be honest, I just don't know," Sam said. "But if they do, they'll be trying to get rid of it now. And if it wasn't them, they'll be ramping up their efforts to find it."

"Do you want me to have a chat to the Bathurst Command? I'm sure they could put some more people on it. Maybe set up a revolving tail?"

He'd already thought of that.

"It's a bit of a chicken and egg conundrum, Riley," Sam said. "There's obviously too many of them for the two of us to follow at all times. But there's so many of them we'd have to bring in multiple teams to surveil them all properly. And Prosperity isn't a big place - that sort of thing tends to get noticed."

"I think we keep it simple for now. But if they slip up, we've got to be ready."

"Understood, boss."

Sam looked through the windscreen and saw a familiar car hurtling towards him on the opposite side of the road. It must have been doing a hundred and fifty. But Sam didn't need the hassle of pulling them over right now. Instead, he flashed his lights to get the driver's attention and saw them noticeably slow down, obviously recognising the detective's car in return.

Sam could see Jim Smith waving at him from the passenger seat - a sheepish mix of apology and gratitude - as Mick Smith's car roared past.

"Where the bloody hell are they going in such a hurry?" Sam asked out loud.

"Fucking hell, that was lucky, Mick!" Jim said as he watched Detective Chang's car get smaller in his side mirror. "I wonder why he didn't pull us over?"

Mick didn't respond. Instead he slowly pressed his foot on the accelerator to increase the car's speed again.

"What if Chang didn't want to give us a ticket because he didn't want it to interfere in the cops investigation of us? Oh shit - that's probably it, Mick!"

"Shut up, Jim!" Mick snapped.

Mick knew they still had about fifteen minutes at the speed they were travelling until they reached George Hibbert's farm. And he needed about half of those to figure out what he was going to say.

And he needed the other half to figure out exactly how he was going to make him pay.

EIGHTEEN

Exactly fourteen minutes and fifty-eight seconds later, Mick pulled the car in behind a group of gum trees that provided a degree of concealment from Dr George Hibbert's house that loomed about two hundred metres further down the driveway. He turned off the engine and surveyed the scene in front of him, trying to mentally reconcile the plan he had in his head with reality. During his footy days, Mick was known as 'Sherman'', after the tank. He was famous for hurling himself at full speed into the defensive line with very little regard for his own welfare. He was brutal, quick and direct. He lived by the mantra that he tried to drum into the rest of his teammates: 'run straight and hard and hit at pace'. However, it was rare for anyone else to possess the true fearlessness required to carry it off like Mick 'Sherman' Smith. So on the drive out, Mick had formulated a plan that played to his strengths. His inclination had been to simply burst through the front door, ask the vet 'who the fuck he thought he was' then beat the shit out of him.

On arrival, however, he had unusually decided that a more cautious approach might be more appropriate. He'd never been out to Hibbert's before and had no idea of the layout. Not to mention that fact that he had no clue whether the guy had any guns on the property, although he figured, like most in the district, he would. And also like most in the district, he figured they wouldn't exactly be locked up in a gun safe as per the governing legislation.

"You don't have to do this," Jim said, breaking the silence. "It's not worth it. He's not worth it."

"You can stay here if you want," Mick said as he opened his door and stepped out into the late afternoon.

"Fuck!" Jim followed him out.

Mick took a few steps towards the trees, careful to keep them between him and the house. Safely hidden behind a trunk, he peered around, to check if the coast was clear.

"What's the plan?" Jim asked in a whisper.

"I just want to do a bit of a recon first," Mick whispered back, "have a quick look around. See if he's home. If he is, then I think we call him outside. At least that way we know he doesn't have any surprises for us and we'll be in open ground."

"And then what?"

"I guess I give him a chance to explain himself."

"That doesn't sound like you, Mick."

"And then I'll punch his face in," Mick said, matter-of-fact.

Mick started for the house. He crouched low and broke into a hunched over run, borrowing heavily from the many action movies he'd watched over the years. Although, with his size, it did little for concealment. Jim felt ridiculous copying him - he felt a bit silly pretending he was Jason Bourne - but he also didn't want to raise the ire of his brother, particularly in his current heightened state. So, he mimicked him, the two of them resembling 80's buddy cop stars, as they covered the distance to the house surprisingly quickly.

Pressing himself against the exterior weatherboards, Mick made sure to keep his head below the line of the windows as he edged along towards the front door. He lifted his head just enough to see over the sill. Through the window he saw a large loungeroom. A single lamp, sitting on a wooden sideboard, provided the only illumination inside. He waited a few minutes to see if he could see any movement but the house seemed eerily quiet.

"Can you see anything?" Jim said. He had remained squatting the entire time next to his brother and was grimacing as the muscles in his legs started feeling the strain.

"Nothing," Mick said. "It's as quiet as your sex life, brother. Let's head around the back and see if we can see anything through the other windows."

Mick led Jim around the side of the house towards the back of the dwelling, the whole time trying to keep as quite as possible - a difficult task given the ungainly squat-slash-waddle they were adopting. By the time they reached the rear landing, Jim's legs were filled with so much lactic acid that with each step he felt like he simply couldn't hold himself up anymore. His right leg buckled throwing him forward, his head ramming into the wooden cladding on the side of the house with a loud thud.

"Arrrgh!" Jim said, groggily.

"What the fuck? Why don't you just set off some fireworks to announce our arrival, you dickhead!" Mick snapped, turning to his brother. He was puzzled to see him slumped in a heap on the ground.

"You ok?" Mick asked, softer.

Jim took a moment to get his bearings. He gingerly felt his head where it had impacted the house. There was already a sizeable lump forming. He looked up at Mick with a pained expression.

"I think I'll be right. Bit of an egg but nothing too bad," Jim said, holding a hand to the top of his forehead.

"Well, at least now we'll find out if he's home. There's no way he wouldn't have heard that," Mick said. He stood out of his squat and stretched himself straight before extending a hand to Jim and helping him to his feet.

"No point continuing with any form of stealth I don't reckon."

Mick took a few steps away from the house and lined himself up directly with the back door. He adopted a fighter's stance, puffed up his chest, balled his fists by his sides and waited for the door to swing open.

But it stayed shut.

"If you're in there, Hibbert, come out here. I know about you and Tracy. I just want to talk," Mick said, raising his voice to be heard while conscious not to sound too threatening.

"Jim, you go around the front in case he makes a run for it."

"I don't think he's in, Mick."

"Just do it."

Mick turned to his brother with a look that made it clear this wasn't open for discussion.

Jim reluctantly walked back around the way they had just come and stood by the front door. He had no idea what he was going to do if a panicked Dr Hibbert burst through the doors in a desperate bid for freedom. Probably yell for Mick, he thought. Or just stand there and watch him leave, helpless to stop him. But no liberty seeking vet came bounding out of the house. Jim could hear Mick continuing to yell at the back door for Hibbert to reveal himself but Jim figured he mustn't home or there would have been some sign of him by now. A door closing; at least a light turning on if nothing else. It didn't take long before curiosity got the better of him and he tried the front door. After all, no one locked their houses around Prosperity. Not unless they were heading away for more than a night, at least. As expected, it was unlocked. Jim pushed it open and paused in the threshold. He spent a moment negotiating with his better judgement before stepping inside.

"Come out here you prick, I just want to talk you ugly-mother-fucking-wife-stealing-fuckwit!"

Mick was now yelling at the door, having dropped any effort to hide his anger. All of a sudden he tensed up. The door was opening.

"About time you gutless prick! I was going to try to hear your side of the story but that just seems like a waste of time now! So come and get your hiding, you cunt!"

Mick raised his fists in readiness, in case the doctor had a rush of ambition and tried to attack him out of the gate. To say Mick was surprised to see Jim step into the light would have been a drastic understatement.

"He's not in here, Mick. I checked the whole place. I even had a look in the cupboard under the sink," Jim said, raising his hand to shield his eyes from the lowering sun.

"You went inside? Fuck me, maybe you're carrying a bigger set than I give you credit for, Jim."

"So where is he?"

The brothers had rung the vet surgery before heading all the way out to Hibbert's home. His receptionist had said he'd left for the day, she presumed to head home, which is why they had ventured out to the property in the first place.

"House call, maybe?" Mick said.

"Maybe," Jim said. "But I saw his car out the front just now. And I can see his van over by that shedding over there."

Mick turned around and recognised the white van with Dr Hibbert's dog and cat logo on the side. It was parked by the closed door of a large machinery shed.

"Gotcha, dickhead."

Mick shelved any notions of stealth as he strode purposefully towards the machinery shed. Jim double-timed to keep up. Mick paused at the vet's van and placed his hand on the bonnet. It was still warm.

"He's here," Mick said.

Jim looked at the shed in front of them. There were two large roller doors big enough to fit some serious farm machinery - Jim figured even a harvester would be right to get in. Both were closed. In front of where the van was parked was a door that had a sign on it marked 'Authorised Personnel Only' which in such a domestic rural setting felt to Jim more like something appropriate to a teenager's bedroom door than anything anyone would take too seriously. The brothers could hear loud music coming from inside the shed. Jim focussed his attention on it and recognised the song almost immediately. It was *Sailing* by Christopher Cross.

"The music would explain why he hasn't heard all

our commotion yet," Jim said.

"I guess we go in then. No point standing out here yelling at the moon if he can't hear us," Mick replied with a shrug.

The brothers took deep breaths and looked at each other, each making sure the other was ready. Mick took hold of the doorknob.

"Count of three. One…two…three!" Mick said, as he flung the door open and the Smith brothers launched themselves inside.

The music was almost deafening as the brothers entered the shed, Christopher Cross was in the middle of singing about the canvas doing miracles. The sound seemed to fill the entire space inside and then some. It was so loud it almost felt like the air was thicker as Jim and Mick waded into the building. They weren't quite sure what they were expecting to find on the other side of the door but nothing could have prepared them for what they now faced.

Lined up along the back wall of the shed were about a dozen large tanks. Jim recognised the blue liquid that filled them as being the same formaldehyde solution he had seen used by Dr Hibbert in his previous animal hybrid artworks that adorned the public spaces of The Oasis. Only these were different.

Very different.

"What the… fuck?" Mick said, in astonished

horror.

Christopher Cross continued in his song about the fantasy getting the best of him. The timing was apt.

"Are they…?" Mick couldn't finish his sentence.

"Yep. They are," Jim said.

The brothers couldn't believe what they were looking at but it was unmistakable. Inside each of the tanks were naked, human bodies. But more horrifying, they appeared to be different bodies, dissected and reassembled into new people. Old and young, male and female, all jumbled up and reconfigured. Jim was horrified. Despite various stages of decomposition, he was sure he recognised many of the faces in the tanks. They had all been clients of Smith Bros. funerals.

Jim and Mick cautiously approached the tanks and started to make their way along them, staring at each in disbelief, until they came to the last tank and stopped. Jim felt his stomach turn and suddenly tasted bile as he caught a small involuntary vomit in his mouth. Suspended in this last tank was an extraordinarily massive head and torso, made even bigger thanks to the distortion of the glass. Except where the original arms, legs and genitals should have been were now sewn on replacements - parts that appeared to belong to an old woman.

"Well, I guess that's the mystery solved. We know who took the mayor, now," Mick said, wide eyed.

The music kept blaring. Then a raised voice cut through it.

"I call that one *Mayor-y-Magdalene*!"

The boys spun around to face the voice. Standing behind them was Dr George Hibbert, dressed in his veterinary scrubs covered by a thick pair of blood splattered leather overalls. He was brandishing a large bone saw but his face was full of pride.

"The name is a working title," Hibbert said, admiring his work. "I was hoping no one would see it before it was completely finished. But I guess best laid plans and all that. So… what do you think?"

Jim was lost for words and stood facing Dr Hibbert with his mouth wide open. Mick had no such trouble finding his words.

"What the fuck do you think you're doing, you sick motherfucking psychopath?!" Mick yelled, taking a few steps towards the vet.

Only Dr Hibbert didn't hear him as the next song on the doctor's play-list - *Hold Me Now* by Thompson Twins - blasted from the speakers mounted on the wall, drowning out all other sounds in the shed. Hibbert held up his hand, the one not holding the saw, part apology, part request for Mick's patience.

"Alexa, stop music," Hibbert said, yelling over the classic 1983 hit. After a second or two, the shed fell silent.

"Sorry, Mick. I didn't catch that?" Hibbert said, with an air of scary congeniality.

"I said -- " Mick started to repeat his thoughts but

Jim placed his hand on his brother's chest, stopping him mid-sentence.

"I'm not sure what this is, Dr Hibbert?" Jim said, trying his best to stay calm.

"It's a work in progress. My next art exhibition. I'm really exploring the duality of man juxtaposed with a deep reimagining of gender constructs through the lens of intersectionality. I'm yet to settle on a title for the Exhibition. But I'm leaning towards calling it: *The Matter of Matter, Matters*" Hibbert said.

"I'd call it 'mutilated bodies in fish tanks by some wannabe Jeffrey Dahmer cunt!'" Mick spat in reply.

"Everyone's a critic," Hibbert said, dismissively.

"Yeah but not everyone steals fucking dead people and hacks them up for art!" Mick said, barely restraining himself.

"It's illegal for a start," Jim said "Not to mention morally reprehensible. These people deserved better. They deserved to be left to rest in peace."

"Come on boys. Let's not get on our high horse just yet. *Ye who is without sin should cast the first stone*," Hibbert said.

The brothers looked at each other, trying to decipher exactly what the vet meant.

"Don't be so coy. You think I didn't notice that every single body I dug up was buried in the same shitty box just with different stickers on the outside to make it look like an expensive casket? Didn't they deserve better?" Hibbert said. His tone was changing from the cordial manner he had initially been using into something far more business-like.

"You see, we seem to be in a mutually-beneficial bind. I know what you've been doing and, well, now you know what I've been doing. If you go running to the authorities about me, I will have no option but to tell them what I know about you. And I know that if I go running to the police about you then they will no doubt end up hearing all about me."

"You do realise that when you show these… things…they won't let you get away with it. You'll be locked up straight away," Jim said.

"Maybe. But then again, great art takes great risks. And what you are looking at behind you are the riskiest artworks the world has ever seen. It's my destiny to be mentioned along with all the other greats. Van Gogh, DaVinci, Picasso, Hirst… Hibbert."

"You're mad!" Mick said

"Genius is often confused for madness."

Mick's face went hard. He took a step forward. "Well, my fists aren't mistaken for anything."

"I'd think twice if I were you, Mick," Hibbert said, backing up slightly. He raised the bone saw in front of him in an act of defensive hostility. "I've had plenty of practice with this recently."

Mick pulled himself up.

"If you go near Tracy again mate, you could be holding a fucking bazooka and I'd still fuck you up!"

"Is that what this is about?" Hibbert asked. "What can I say, every artist needs a muse."

Mick lunged towards Dr Hibbert but Jim moved faster. He shoved himself between his brother and the vet and strained to hold him back.

"He's not worth it, Mick! He's off his rocker. Let's just leave!" Jim said.

Jim was struggling to hold his brother, his shoes where scrabbling on the concrete floor in a desperate search for purchase. Mick suddenly grabbed Jim by his shoulders and threw him to one side.

"Get off me!"

At the hands of his brother, Jim took involuntary flight. He landed on the hard ground with a thud and slid headfirst into a large stainless-steel bench. The impact sent a collection of medical tools and metal trays crashing to the ground. It also opened a gash on the top of Jim's head. The loud noise seemed to snap Mick from his rage and he turned to see his brother lying on the floor, the blood from his cut already starting to turn his face crimson. It stopped him in his tracks.

"Oh fuck, Jim!" Mick said. He rushed over to check on his brother. "Sorry mate, I didn't mean it! Where are you cut?"

"Top of the head, I think," Jim managed.

Mick looked around and grabbed some paper towel that he found sitting on the bench above his brother. He tore several sheets off the roll and handed them to Jim.

"Hold these on the cut. They'll do until I can get you back into town," Mick said.

"I could take a look and pop a stitch or two in if they're needed. I am a doctor, remember," Hibbert offered, smiling.

"Fuck off!" Mick and Jim said in unison.

Mick hauled Jim to his feet and the two brothers started towards the door.

"If you wouldn't mind closing the door after you. I need to get back to work," Hibbert said. "Alexa, play *True* by Spandau Ballet."

The brothers reached the door and paused to look back at Dr Hibbert as the speakers crackled to life and the shed once again filled with music. Dr Hibbert started gliding around the room, pirouetting and dancing in time with the 80's synth chords.

The Smith brothers watched in astonishment as the vet sang along to the song, using the bone saw in his hand as a microphone, like a twelve year old girl singing in her bedroom mirror.

"He's a fucking lunatic!" Mick said, shaking his head in disbelief.

NINETEEN

The paper towel was soaked through with blood by the time Jim and Mick reached the car. Jim sat with an exhausted slump in the passenger side as Mick started rummaging around in the foot well of the back seat.

"I've got a first aid kit here somewhere," Mick said. "Here we go." Mick pulled a small green travel medical kit from underneath the front seat and set about tending to his brother.

"It's actually not as bad as it looks, Jim," Mick said, as he cleaned the wound with an alcohol swab. "I'm really sorry, mate."

Mick placed a gauze dressing on the wound and held it in place with a crudely applied bandage.

"It's not pretty, but it'll do the trick for now."

Mick jumped in the driver's seat and started the car.

"What are we going to do Mick?" Jim said "We

can't leave all those people like that. It's not right."

"I know. But he's kind of got us by the balls," Mick said

"I'd rather face the music than turn a blind eye to that, Mick. It's so fucked up."

Mick turned to his brother.

"Look, I'm with you. But let's not do anything rash. We've got to be smart about this. As soon as he goes public with his "art" the guy is going to be toast anyway. Then anything he says about us can easily be discounted as the ravings of a madman."

"It's not right!" Jim said, pleading. There were tears beginning to well in his eyes. He looked out the window as Mick reversed the car and drove out of the gates of Dr Hibbert's property and pointed the car towards Prosperity.

"They have just left. The little one was bleeding. What do you want us to do?"

In their haste to get back into town, the brothers had failed to notice the black sedan with tinted windows and two hulking Kardashians sitting in it, parked in the shade under a large blackwood tree across the road from Hibbert's entrance. The Kardashian in the passenger seat was talking on the phone. On the other end of the line was Aleks Keshishian.

"How long were they on the property?" Aleks asked from the security room at The Oasis.

"About twenty minutes. Maybe twenty-five," The

Kardashian said.

"Okay. Stay there. We'll be right out. I'll get one of the other teams to pick up the tail on the Smith brothers once they get back into town."

It was less than thirty-five minutes later that Aleks Keshishian, Andre and the two other Kardashians were standing outside the door of the large shed on Dr George Hibbert's farm. They had rendezvoused at the gate and followed the almost exact same path that the Smith brothers had taken earlier that afternoon. Finding the house empty, they had continued towards the large outbuilding, beckoned on by Yazoo's *Only You*, an evergreen hit from their 1982 debut album *Upstairs at Eric's*. The pop-synth hit called them on like a siren's song.

As they approached the door with the 'Authorised Personnel Only' sign, Aleks let Andre step ahead of him and watched as he cracked the door just enough to cautiously see what was going on inside. He peered through the crack before turning back to Aleks. He had a confused look on his face.

"What is it?" Aleks asked.

"You're going to want to take a look at this," Andre replied.

Aleks moved Andre to one side and peeked through the slit of the partially opened door.

"What the…"

Aleks pushed the door all the way open and stepped

inside.

The boppy synths and Alison Moyet's dulcet voice provided the surreal soundtrack as the Armenians crossed the threshold

Dr Hibbert was hunched over the stainless-steel bench, concentrating on stitching four thumbs onto a hand in place of where the fingers should have been. He didn't notice that he had company. Aleks calmly approached from behind, placed one arm around his neck and locked in a tight rear-naked choke. Hibbert struggled and fought, clawing at the arm around his neck as fear took over his body. Despite his desperate efforts, it only took about fifteen seconds before he fell unconscious, as Keshishian's strangulation compressed his jugular and cut the supply of oxygen to his brain. Aleks released the vet and let his body crumple to the floor.

"Search the place. If the USB stick is here, I want it."

When Dr Hibbert came to, he found himself sitting on a chair, his arms and legs bound. The shed was silent. It took him a moment to process what had happened but once the clarity returned, so did the panic. He started violently shifting around in the chair in a desperate attempt to free himself. Aleks looked over at Andre and gave him a subtle nod. Andre stepped forward and placed his hands on the doctor's shoulders and pressed down, rooting him to the spot and calming him almost instantly.

"I've seen some shit in my time, Dr Hibbert," Aleks said, "but I've got to say, this is something else."

"What do you want?" Hibbert said.

"We're looking for something. I'm hoping you might be able to help us."

"What?"

"Well, the first thing we were looking for was the mayor's body," Aleks said, looking over at the tank holding Terry McInerny's bobbing torso. "And we can all obviously see what happened to that. The second thing was a small USB stick that was inside the mayor's casket. We'd very much like that back."

On the other side of the shed, the two other Kardashians were loudly rummaging through everything they could see, knocking things off shelves, turning out drawers onto the floor.

"Hey, careful. That stuff's important!" Hibbert yelled toward them.

Aleks punched Dr Hibbert in the face. Hard.

"Attention on me, please."

Hibbert was whimpering. He spat some blood from his mouth.

"I don't know anything about any USB. I'm just an artist!"

Aleks hit him again, dislodging a tooth that clattered across the concrete floor.

"Stop hitting me…" Hibbert said, whimpering.

Aleks punched him again, opening a cut above

his right eye. The blow almost sent Dr Hibbert back into unconsciousness. He shook his head to clear the flashing stars from his vision. He groggily tried to focus on Aleks standing in front of him.

"I told you I don't know anything. I'm interested in the bodies. I dig them up and turn them into art. I'm giving them a second life. I'm making them immortal. That's all."

"Where is the mayor's casket?" Aleks asked.

"I don't know."

"What do you mean you don't know?"

"I mean I don't know. I know where the box I found him in is. But I don't know where his casket is."

"You're not making any sense doctor. Please do not make me hit you again,' Aleks said.

"It's the Smith brothers. They've been swapping caskets before burial. Every one of the bodies I've dug up has been the same. They are all in these cheap cardboard boxes. So, I don't know where the mayor's actual casket is."

Aleks processed the information. He smiled wryly. It suddenly made sense why the accounts at the Smith Bros. offices didn't add up. He was quietly impressed at their ingenuity but he was even more impressed by the balls they had to pull it off. He considered that maybe he had underestimated the two of them.

"I've got all the cheap boxes stacked up out the back. The mayor's will be the one on the top. The last one in. You can check them if you like."

"We will," Aleks said.

The cut from above the doctor's eye was leaking a trail of blood into the eye itself. It was stinging badly and making it difficult for him to see. Hibbert was blinking wildly to try to clear his vision.

"Do you have a favourite song, doctor?" Aleks asked.

"Why?"

"I'm not a monster. Everyone deserves a final moment of pleasure."

"What?"

"I'll ask again - do you have a favourite song? If you don't, I am more than happy to choose one for you."

"I don't understand?" Hibbert said. There was a desperation to his voice.

"Okay then," Aleks said "Alexa, play *Shake it Off* by Taylor Swift"

The speakers burst into life.

Aleks walked over to the stainless steel table and picked up the bone saw. He checked the blade to make sure it was sharp. He pushed the tip of his finger into it until it produced a small prick of blood.

Dr Hibbert saw Aleks walking back towards him with the saw in his hand. His eyes widened. For a moment he could have sworn his shoulders were dancing in time with the beat.

"Hey, hey, hey. We don't need to do this. If you let me go, I won't tell anyone about you and what happened here and what you're looking for. I'll say I tripped getting out of the shower or something. Or got kicked by a cow. Or a horse. Or head butted by an Alpaca!" Dr Hibbert said, rambling. He took a deep breath to try to gain some composure.

"You don't understand. I'm destined to be one of the world's great artists. I'm so close to finishing. Please, let me go. No one needs to know. Please!"

"I'm sorry. I wish I could," Aleks said.

He sat himself down, straddled across Dr George Hibbert's lap, raised the bone saw, and got to work.

TWENTY

Detective Chang had swapped his gun for a spatula and was busily preparing a simple take away order of combination chicken in the kitchen of Lee's New Golden Imperial Lotus Garden. He packaged up the meal in a container and placed it with another holding boiled rice and third with a serving of mixed entrée in a plastic bag on the counter. He stapled the order slip to the bag and walked it out into the restaurant. He handed over the meal to its eagerly waiting recipient, Col Munro the local tyre fitter - a veritable eclipse of a man - and thanked him for his order.

"Best 'chine' in the world, Sam," Munro said, with absolute conviction.

Col Munro had been a staunch patron of the restaurant for over three decades and had, in fact, been a key figure during the so-called 'Wonton Wars' of twenty years earlier. Indeed, he had caused quite the stir went he went on a self-declared 'no-hunger strike' in an effort to draw attention to Lee's cooking. Local TV news crews had even brought their cameras when he set up a table outside the old Lotus Garden and proceeded to eat every item on the menu over a rolling 48 hour period. Although he vehemently denied being the source of the rumour surrounding the rival Imperial Peking's use of roadkill.

"And boy could your mother whip up a good feed!" Munro said, before leaning in with a wink. "But some days I reckon you give her a run for her money."

"I don't know about that, Col," Sam replied.

"Don't be so modest chef," came a voice from behind Col.

As Munro lumbered out with his food, Marnie Rochambeau stepped forward with a grin.

"Lovely to see you, Marnie. But I wasn't expecting you tonight, was I?" Sam said, with uncharacteristic nervousness.

"No, this is a spontaneous drop in. I just had a hankering, Sam."

"Oh, good. With everything going I'm getting worried the wheels are going to start falling off," Sam said. "Take a seat and I'll bring you over a menu, unless you had something in mind?"

"You know what, I'm feeling adventurous, Sam - surprise me. But nothing fancy. Just something off the menu is fine. Whatever you feel like cooking,"

Marnie said.

She reached out and touched Sam's arm and gave it a friendly squeeze before heading to her usual table at the rear of the restaurant.

Sam was relieved that Marnie hadn't requested some obscure regional Chinese dish as she usually did. It wasn't that he didn't relish the challenges she gave him, it was just that he didn't feel like he had the mental bandwidth to stretch himself too far just at the minute. Sam had considered closing the restaurant for a day or two to focus on working out his next steps. He still had to figure out how to find the mayor and was also yet to decide how he could further rattle the cages at The Oasis. However, he also knew that he needed to cook to give his mind some time to breathe. It was his meditation. Concentrating on preparing the meal at hand allowed his thoughts to tick along in the background, subliminally. It always surprised him the amount of clarity he could gain in his police work at the end of a cook, without having put too much conscious effort into it.

Sam paused to have a quick think about what item on his menu would prove the most suitable dish for Marnie. He briefly tossed up playing a very straight bat and simply plating up some sizzling beef but quickly changed his mind. That was a lazy option and Marnie deserved something special, even if she hadn't requested it. He decided to share the meal he had been preparing for himself - Dong Po Rou - braised pork belly. He lifted the lid on the pot the pork belly had been cooking in for the past two-and-a-half hours. The ginger and soy hit his nostrils - it was smelling amazing.

"Dinner is still probably about fifteen to twenty minutes away, Marnie," Sam said, as he brought some water over to her table.

"Not a problem at all, Sam," Marnie said.

"Would you like anything stronger while you wait? A beer perhaps? Whisky?"

"An icy cold beer would be a delight," Marnie said, "But just bring the bottle. No need for a glass."

"Of course. I'll be right back."

Sam walked over to the fridge near the front door and took a cold Tsing Tao from it and wondered if it was too early to grab a second for himself. The idea of sharing the braised pork belly and a beer with Marnie was an appealing one, so he reached back into the fridge and grabbed a second beer.

The front door suddenly opened and three young men entered. They were partly adorned in cheap medieval costumes, the type you might find in a discount store. 'Doggy', 'Bushido' and 'Snipper' were three mates from Sydney who had travelled to Prosperity having heard about the various offerings at The Oasis. Only they had soon found themselves kicked out. Apparently, the management frowned upon Snipper urinating in the middle of the banquet hall. Despite their protestations that they were merely leaning into the theme of the joint - getting heavily into character - the Kardashians had other opinions and escorted them swiftly from the premises. Forced to take up lodgings in the Golden Nugget Motel on the edge of town, the gang had polished off the best part of a case of beer and more than a few of the "dexies" Bushido had stolen from his younger, ADHD-diagnosed brother, before looking for a meal.

Sam sized them up. He had dealt with drunks plenty of times over his years in the force. There were always two ways to go - react forcefully or play along.

"Evening fellas," Sam said. "You here to grab some takeaway?"

He hoped by planting the suggestion that they would take up the opportunity to order and leave.

"Nah mate, table for three," Bushido, a short rat-faced man in his mid-thirties, replied.

"Okay. Take a seat, I'll be over in a minute."

The three slapped hands on each other's backs, bums and arms as they rowdily laughed at jokes no sober person would find funny, and took up chairs at a table opposite where Marnie was sitting.

Sam reluctantly put the second beer back in the fridge in quiet defeat, realising the opportunity to share a drink and a meal with Marnie had now evaporated. He took the other bottle over to her table. He felt one of the men - the one who went by Snipper - reach out and grab his shirt sleeve as he passed. Sam pulled his arm away.

"Oi, buddy. Can you bring us a menu and three of

those chink beers?" Snipper yelled at Sam.

"I'll be with you in a minute," Sam said. His teeth were gritted. He placed Marnie's beer in front of her on the table.

"Thank you, Sam," Marnie said. "Why don't you join me?"

Sam looked over his shoulder at the table of blokes.

"I can probably only spare a moment or two."

Sam pulled a chair out and sat down.

"You look tired Sam. Is everything OK?" Marnie asked.

"Just work stuff, Marnie. But thank you for asking," Sam said.

"I don't mean to pry Sam, but it's important that you take some time to look after yourself. Do something just for you."

Sam smiled.

"That's what I'm doing right now, Marnie."

A voice suddenly cut through the restaurant.

"Oi, you speaka da engrish?" Doggy yelled at Sam. "B.E.E.R."

Sam didn't turn around.

"I said - I'll be with you in a minute."

"There's all sorts of rumours going around town, Sam. About the mayor. That his body has gone missing," Marnie said in a hushed voice.

"I can't really talk about it."

"Oh of course, Sam. I get it. But there's some pretty wild stuff flying about. Everything from satanic grave robbers to Eastern European organ harvesters to conjecture that Terry faked his own death and was never in there in the first place. Just thought you should know."

"Small towns, hey?" Sam said, smiling. "At least it's given everyone something to talk about."

"You know what I think -- " Marnie started before being interrupted.

"-- Hey, Bruce Lee, sorry to cock block your romantic little dinner date but… beer! Now!"

Marnie looked past Sam at the table of inebriated men.

"He already told you - in a minute!" Marnie said, sternly.

"Shut ya gob, grandma. No one asked you, lady," Snipper replied causing his two mates to snigger.

Sam closed his eyes and tried to centre himself. The last thing he needed was trouble in the restaurant. He stood and turned to face the men.

"Look, I know you guys have had a bit of a night. That's clear. No judgement from me about that - everyone needs to let their hair down from time to time. But I can't have you behaving like that in here," Sam said. "I'm happy to serve you take away if you'd like but I'm going to have to ask you to leave."

The mood instantly changed. The expressions on the faces of the three troublemakers hardened. The air suddenly felt dangerous, like a fight was brewing.

"Nah, nah, nah, Jackie Chan. We told you, we want to dine in," Bushido said.

"And I just told you - you have to leave," Sam replied, coolly.

Bushido stood and puffed his weaselly chest out.

"Make us."

The room went quiet. The hum of the fridge suddenly seemed very loud.

Bushido kicked his chair to the ground. The others followed, emboldened. Sam knew at once that Bushido was the alpha of the gang. He decided to focus his attention on him.

"Okay, here's the deal," Sam said, directing his words to the drunken rat of a man in front of him, "I don't want any trouble. If you just leave now, no harm, no foul. There's no need to get silly."

"Let me guess, you're a fucking kung-fu-karate-tai-chi-judo-master!" Bushido said. He started theatrically chopping the air with his hands and making swishing noises to accentuate them slicing through the air.

"Hiya!"

"Like I said fellas. I don't want any trouble. Look, I'll give you guys a couple of beers on the way out. Free of charge," Sam said.

He put his hands up in deference and started to walk towards the fridge at the front of the restaurant. He wanted to deescalate the situation and avoid any further confrontation. His training had taught him that people will often acquiesce if they feel like they have won the altercation. The free beers, Sam hoped, would be seen by the trio as the spoils of war. But as he walked past the drunks' table, he forgot another part of his training - never turn your back on a threat.

"Sam!" There was an urgency to Marnie's voice that spun Sam around. He saw the chair arcing through the air towards him but it was too late to react. Sam's world instantly went black.

It was the smell of braised pork belly that Sam first noticed. He slowly opened his eyes, blinking them a few times to regain some focus. Sam was lying on the floor of his restaurant. He was aware of something soft under his head. It took him a moment to realise that it was a satin cushion. He slid it out from under his head as he propped himself up on his elbow. He stared at it, trying to place it, before realising it came from the bench by the door that people sat on while waiting for takeaway. How the hell had it ended up here? Had he fallen on it or had someone put it there? All Sam knew for sure was that his head was pounding. He gingerly traced his skull with his hand and was relieved to confirm that there wasn't any blood, as far as he could tell.

Sam cautiously pulled himself up to his feet and stood for a moment to get his legs back underneath him. He was swaying slightly, the ground beneath him rolling as if he was on a boat. His legs couldn't quite get balanced. The whole room felt on tilt. Sam looked around the restaurant for Marnie. His stomach dropped. She was nowhere to be seen and the three men were also gone from sight.

"Shit," Sam said.

Sam's police brain kicked in. He knew that if they had taken Marnie, there wasn't much time to stop something terrible happening to her. He searched his pockets for his phone but came up empty.

"Shit!"

He rushed for the front counter, heading for the landline but failed to see the legs sticking out from next to one of the other tables. His foot clipped it and given his already compromised balance, Sam found himself straight back on the floor with a thud.

"Shit!" Sam said, groaning.

He looked back to try to figure out what had happened.

"Huh?"

Sam got to his feet and slowly walked back, blinking his eyes to make sure he was seeing what he thought he was seeing. Lying on the floor between the tables were the three drunks. They had each been hogtied and gagged with gaffer tape. Sam was struggling to process the scene. He looked around the restaurant again to see if anyone else was present, anyone that might be able to shed some light on what had happened. Had the cops already turned up? A tactical team perhaps? But there was no one there. Even more confusing, Sam was pretty sure he didn't keep any gaffer tape in the place.

He quickly checked the three men for pulses. They were all alive which pleased Sam, if for no other reason than it meant less paperwork. That's when he saw it. Stapled to one of the guy's shirt was a slip of paper. Sam recognised it immediately - it had been torn from his restaurant bill pad. He plucked it from the man's chest and took a closer look. It was mostly blank.

Only down the bottom, under 'Tip' was written one word: *Vet*

TWENTY-ONE

Detective Chang looked out the windscreen of his car. He could see some headlights coming down the road, approaching at speed. It was Riley. After Chang had rung for a unit to come and collect the three drunks tied up on the floor of Lee's New Golden Imperial Lotus Garden, he had rung her and told her to meet him at the entrance to Dr George Hibbert's farm. As she pulled up alongside him, Sam wound down his window.

"Thanks for coming out," Sam said.

"You know me - Miss twenty-four-seven. What's the go?" Riley asked.

"I'm not quite sure yet," Sam replied. "I can't really explain it but I think it's worth us having a chat with Hibbert. If you follow me in, we'll head straight up to the house."

Sam turned his car into the driveway and Riley pulled her car in behind him. His headlights bounced down the road, illuminating the farmhouse in front of him. Sam pulled his car up near the front door and parked it next to a car he recognised. It belonged to the vet. Riley swung in next to him. Sam turned his engine off followed by his lights. Everything went dark. There were no lights on inside the house. Sam switched the headlights back on again and got out of the car.

"Hey Riley, have you still got those torches in your car?"

"One step ahead, boss," Riley said, holding up the two tactical flashlights, one in each hand.

Sam grabbed a torch and approached the front door. He tried to look inside through the window next to the entrance, however the darkness both outside and inside made it hard to make out anything beyond some shapes of furniture. Sam stepped forward and knocked three times on the door, loudly. He then stepped back and waited.

"I don't think anyone's home," Riley said, after a minute or two.

Sam turned his torch on and shone it through the window. He swept it back and forth before quickly dropping the beam to his side.

"We're going in," Sam said, with a sudden urgency.

He grabbed the door handle and turned; it was unlocked and the door swung open with unintentional violence. Sam's eagerness to enter translating into kinetic energy that flung it backwards and sent it straining against its hinges.

Once inside, Sam raised the torch again to provide some light while he reached with one hand along the wall behind him in search of the switch he was certain would be there. His fingers quickly found a familiar shape and the room lit up.

"Wow!" Riley said. "Someone's really done a number on this place."

The lounge room they were standing in had been turned upside down. Cushions from the couches were strewn across the room after being slashed open. Paintings on the wall were askew on their hooks. Drawers from the sideboard had been turned out on the floor. It was a textbook ransacking.

"Don't touch anything, Riley," Sam said. "You go that way. I'll check out the other end of the house. Yell out if you find anything. Or anyone."

Riley left the lounge room through the door at one end, while Sam took a corridor in the other direction. The first room Sam came to was a bedroom. It was in a similar state to the lounge, the mattress from the bed had been tossed against the far wall and clothing had been tipped all over the bed base. It was a pattern repeated in every room throughout Dr Hibbert's house. Sam met up with Riley again in the kitchen at the rear of the building.

"No sign of anyone, boss. Hell of a mess though. Someone was keen to find whatever they were looking for," Riley said.

"But I don't think they found it." Sam said.

"What makes you say that?"

"The whole house is trashed. Unless they found it in the very last place they looked. If they found it earlier, why keep turning over the joint?" Sam said.

Riley smiled. She hadn't considered that.

"That's why you get paid the big bucks."

"Let's take a look around outside," Sam said, opening the back door. He switched his torch back on to light up his path. Riley followed Sam as they completed a circumnavigation of the house looking for anything out of place. They returned to their starting point having found nothing. Sam swept his torch through the night's sky beyond the back of Hibbert's house and paused on the large machinery shed.

"Worth a look, Sam?" Riley asked.

But Sam was already walking. As he approached he could hear muted bass coming from music playing inside. When he reached the door of the shed, he stopped. He could feel the bass now through his feet and in his chest. Sam knocked loudly on the door with the base of the torch. The metallic noise reverberated around the inside of the shed.

"Dr Hibbert? Are you in there?" Sam asked, making sure to yell loud enough to be heard over the music if, indeed, Dr Hibbert was inside. Again, there was no response. Sam checked the door, just like the main house, it was unlocked. There was no need to find a light switch this time as the shed was fully lit up. Sam stepped inside, took a few steps then came to a halt.

The music was clear now to Detective Chang. It was 2Pac's *To Live and Die in L.A.* The melodic chorus kicked in as he took in the horror show before him.

Sam couldn't believe what he was looking at. Riley entered the shed and stood behind the detective, her mouth and eyes wide. They both stared in mutual shock at the tanks filled with the blue formaldehyde solution and the mutilated bodies.

"What's going on, Sam?" Riley asked, a noticeable quiver present in her voice.

"I have no idea. But whatever it is, it's not good."

"And one of these things is not like the others, Sam. Look."

Riley pointed to the last tank in the row. The liquid inside this one wasn't blue. It was bright red.

"And check that out," Riley said.

Riley pointed again. Sitting in the middle of the shed was a single chair that looked from a distance as though it was splattered with blood. On the floor around the chair was a large dark stain. The whole scene was like something out of a Quentin Tarantino film.

Detective Chang approached the chair for a closer look. He bent down and touched the stain. It was still tacky.

"That's a hell of a lot of blood," Riley said, looking over the detective's shoulder.

Sam didn't answer. Instead he made his way past all the tanks to the last one. The one that was red.

In the background the music slowly faded out, momentarily leaving the only sound in the shed being Sam's feet scuffing on the ground as he walked, before *To Live and Die in L.A.* blared out of the speakers once again. The song was on repeat.

"Please, make that stop, Riley!" Sam said, as he started inspecting the crimson tank. Even through the murky liquid, it didn't take him long to identify the massive head and body suspended in the middle of it.

"We might never know who killed 2Pac but we've found Biggie," Sam said to himself. "We can call off the search for Mayor McInerny."

The music stopped mid-verse. Riley had pulled the plug to the speakers.

Sam looked harder at the tank. He could see something floating around inside it. He pressed his face against the glass to see if he could get a better view. Something slowly resolved as it drifted towards him. Sam suddenly jumped back, stumbling, his stomach in knots, as the severed head of Dr George Hibbert squished against the side of the tank. Sam watched it bounce back into the opaque liquid once again and disappear behind the mayor's massive torso.

"Get on the phone, Riley. We need everyone out here. Right now!" Sam said, urgently.

"Everyone?"

"Yes, Riley. Everyone! Someone's murdered the vet."

TWENTY-TWO

Jim Smith woke groggily. It took him a moment or two to get his bearings. His head was pounding and he gingerly put his hand to the heart of the throbbing. As his fingers traced the bandage on his head, the memory of what had happened at the vet's came flooding back. Slowly, he re-traced the steps that followed.

By the time the boys got back into Prosperity from Dr Hibbert's farm the doctor's general practice had already closed, so Mick had rung Jane Kikkarachi, a nurse who lived locally but worked at the hospital in Bathurst. Jane, a matronly woman in her sixties, had in many ways acted as a proxy mother figure in the boys' lives after their mother had absconded. While there were rumours around town that Jane had also provided Sid a more adult proxy of his runaway wife, there had never been anything formal. Regardless of any potential romantic connection with their father,

Jane had always kept an eye over the boys.

Mick had been right about the gash on Jim's head, it hadn't been as bad as the blood might have suggested. A bit of domestic superglue, a clean dressing and a bandage and he'd been good to go. However, it was going to take more than a dab of Tarzan Grip to dull his raging headache.

Jim slowly sat up in his bed. He swung his feet over the side of the mattress and let them settle on the floor. He made sure they had a good understanding of the ground beneath him before he stood up and cautiously walked into the kitchen. He searched one of the drawers for some pain relief, read the back of the box for the recommended dose and doubled it. He drank directly from the kitchen tap to wash the tablets down, before he leant on the sink and ran over the events at Dr Hibbert's one more time to make sure it hadn't been a dream. Unfortunately, he was sure that the nightmare was real. His brain was incapable of making something like that up.

"Fucking hell," Jim said quietly to himself.

Mick had been up early. He didn't have any specific chores to do but still found himself in his favourite spot on the farm around sunrise. It was a rocky outcrop on top of a small hill and it provided a good vantage point over the entire property. It was the place Mick always gravitated towards when he had thinking to do. Sleep hadn't come easily. By the time he had made it back to the farm after getting Jim all patched up, Tracy had already left for her shift at The Oasis, which left him no one to share the conversation that had been running through his head. Consequently, he'd spent the best part of the night staring at the ceiling waiting for her to return. By the time Tracy sent Mick a text saying that Misty had let her spend the night in one of the rooms and that she'd taken an extra shift the next day, it was almost morning anyway. It was easier just to get up and start the day.

Mick reached for the thermos next to him and poured a strong coffee, topped up with a nip of whisky from the hipflask he had also made sure to bring. He couldn't focus on what needed his immediate attention. On the one hand, there was the matter of his marriage and what he was to do about trying to save it. That was, if he even wanted to save it. Then on the other, he was in a serious quandary about what to do about Dr Hibbert. On a moral level, he knew that what the vet had been doing was so far past being wrong that he didn't quite have the vocabulary to describe it. On a personal level, he would have liked nothing more than to dob the guy in and have him get the legal comeuppance he so thoroughly deserved. Mick was dirty at himself that he hadn't taken the opportunity to give Dr Hibbert a hiding when he had the chance, not only for what he had done with Tracy but by some way of revenge for the desecrated deceased. However, Mick couldn't for the life of him figure out how he could send Hibbert down without also exposing him and Jim to inevitable prosecution themselves. All he kept doing was circling back to the idea that their best course of action was to simply leave Hibbert to his devices and hope that when he produced his art for the world to see, he would get what was coming to him and that the boys' crimes would pale into such insignificance, that they would barely encourage investigation.

Mick took another sip of his extra strong coffee and took in the spectacular sunrise. His brain quietened finally as he watched the flocks of birds greet the new day with raucous birdsong as they swept through the pink and orange sky above the farm. Mick felt his pocket buzz. A message. He looked and his brain went haywire again.

I need to see you and Jim immediately. I'll be at your office at 8am. Det. Chang

Mick read the text several more times. His brain was now yelling. What on earth could Chang want with them? His phone buzzed again as a second message came through.

Did you just get a text from Chang? Fuck, what does he want? Shit!!!

Mick sent a reply to Jim.

Let's not panic. I'll meet you there at 7.30 so we can get ready for him.

He threw the remaining coffee from his cup into the dirt and quickly started for town.

Mick and Jim approached the Smith Bros. offices on Prosperity's main street from opposite directions at exactly the same time, which meant they also saw Detective Sam Chang already parked outside the building at exactly the same time. Even though the brothers were punctual for their early 7.30 arrival time, Sam Chang was even earlier. It was too late for either of them to turn around. Prosperity in the mornings was hardly the Sydney CBD in terms of peak hour traffic, and as such the detective had clocked both of them the minute they had each turned on to the main drag. Mick could see him swivelling his head between the two brother's vehicles as they approached.

"Well, this is less than fucking ideal," Mick said to himself.

The brothers pulled up outside their offices and parked, one on each side of Detective Chang's car, and climbed out.

"Thanks for coming so quickly," Sam said, "I know I said 8 but I thought I'd get here early just in case. There's a shit load going on in my world right now so the sooner I can get back to it, the better. But first I need you guys to get started on something for me."

Jim and Mick looked at each other. This didn't sound like they were getting in trouble.

"What's going on, Sam?" Jim asked, trying to play

it cool.

Detective Chang's gaze fell to the large bandage wrapped around Jim's head.

"What happened to you? Are you ok?"

"Oh this?" Jim could feel a warm blush in his cheeks. He tried to stop it but the more he tried, the hotter his cheeks got. "Nothing really. Clumsy accident. I was trying to get a stepladder down from on top of my cupboard and had to get on my tippy toes to reach it," Jim said. He wasn't sure why he was saying what he was saying but he couldn't stop the words coming out of his mouth.

"Stupid really to keep a stepladder somewhere you need a stepladder to reach. Anyway, I dropped it on my own head. But no permanent damage. But enough about me - you we're saying?"

"Look, we have a hell of a situation fellas," Sam said. "Something terrible has gone down out at Dr Hibbert's place."

Mick and Jim shot each other another look. It was filled with shared apprehension.

"I can't go into too much detail but it looks like Hibbert has been moonlighting as a bit of a grave-robber."

"A grave-robber?" Mick said, trying his best to feign surprise.

"Yeah. There's more to it. A lot more. But we're still putting the pieces together. Literally. We've at least solved the mystery of what happened to Mayor McInerny."

"The vet took him? Why?" Jim asked, taking his brother's lead acting surprised.

"Well, we're still figuring all that out. What I can say is that it's not just the mayor's body. By the looks of things there could be about a dozen others. Possibly more. Which is where you two come in. I need you to dig out - pardon the pun - all the files of your customers from the past eighteen months. We're going to need to cross-reference them."

"The last eighteen months? That's quite a few people detective," Jim said.

"That's only the start of it, Jim. We're also going to need you guys to start exhuming everyone as well."

"Exhume them all?" Mick said, genuinely surprised.

"It's the only way we can be sure who he's messed with. I've got Riley over at the courthouse now to get the judge up to speed. Which is why I need those names. He's not going to sign off on anything without having the names."

"When do you need them?" Jim asked.

"Yesterday," Sam replied. "I'll leave you boys to get on with it. Call me when you have the list. I need to head back out to Hibbert's farm. It's like something out of a horror movie out there."

Sam opened his car door and slid into the driver's seat. Mick took a step towards him.

"What about the vet, detective?" Mick asked. "Has he been locked up yet?"

Sam stood thinking for a beat.

"I guess you guys will hear it soon enough, anyway," Sam said.

"Hear what?" Mick asked.

"You can't tell anyone. Not yet at least."

Mick looked at Jim and they both shrugged in agreement.

"George Hibbert was killed last night."

Mick didn't know what to say, for one of the first times in his entire life, Mick Smith was genuinely rattled.

"So, get me those names. Pronto."

Sam shut the car door, performed a u-turn and disappeared down the main street of Prosperity back in the direction of Dr Hibbert's farm, leaving the Smith brothers standing like one o'clock half-struck on the footpath behind him.

TWENTY-THREE

The Smith brothers rushed through the doors of their office building in a panic. Jim fumbled with the lock behind him, finally managing to secure it before turning off the alarm by entering the six-digit code. Mick was manically pacing back and forth between the front doors and the reception desk.

"I think we're fucked, Jim," Mick said. "I think we're really fucked this time."

Jim reflexively reached for his breast pocket for his calming joint but quickly realised there wasn't one. In his rush to leave the house he hadn't put a jacket on. He quickly walked past Mick and burst into his office. He often left behind a jacket in the office, just in case. Thankfully for Jim, hanging up on a stand just inside the door was exactly what he was looking for. He grabbed the jacket and slid it on before checking the inside pocket. His whole body almost instantly relaxed. Jim removed the joint and ran it under his nose, smelling the sweet marijuana within it.

"You don't have a lighter on you, do you Mick?" Jim said, exiting his office.

"What are you talking about? We're fucked mate. Do you not understand that?"

Jim continued as if unable to hear his brother, hyper-focussed on his task, in his own world.

"I think Bluey used to keep a box of matches for the candles in her desk," Jim said, as he started rifling through the draws at reception.

"I don't think I have to explain to you just how fucked we are, Jim," Mick said, "but just in case you haven't worked it out yet let me do the paint-by-numbers. If we start having to dig up bodies, eventually we're going to dig one up that Hibbert didn't steal. And when Detective Chang finds someone buried in one of the cheapo, shitty boxes we put them in, he isn't going to stop until he's dug every fucking corpse in that entire, god-forsaken cemetery up!"

"Bingo!" Jim said. He proudly held up a box of matches for his brother to see.

"Jim!" Mick said, as he slammed his hands on the top of the reception desk in utter frustration. Jim jumped.

"Sorry, Mick. Just give me a second to…calm my nerves. Then we'll figure out what to do."

Jim put the joint in his mouth and lit it up.

"Would you like some?" Jim said, offering it to his

brother.

"No, I don't want any fucking weed."

Mick began pacing again as Jim puffed away.

"How many people have we buried in the last eighteen months that we haven't swapped the caskets on do you reckon?" Mick asked.

"Can't be many. Three. Maybe four."

"Okay, if we put them at the top of the list, that'll buy us some time."

"Time for what?" Jim asked.

"I don't know. Just time!" Mick said, his frustration was boiling over.

"Okay. Got it. I'll put them on the top of the list," Jim said.

"Is there any way we can fill the rest of the list with people from way back. You know, from before we started swapping things. We must have a list of those people and where they're buried, don't we?"

Jim looked around for somewhere to put out the almost finished joint. He hesitated, before taking a few halting steps in each direction until giving up and simply extinguishing it on the top of the reception desk.

"That won't work. Sam's no idiot. He'll take one look at the graves and notice the dates," Jim said.

"Well what do you suggest?" Mick asked.

"I think we just give Sam the list of everyone we've buried in the last eighteen months. Then we start digging them up. We might get lucky."

"Lucky?"

"The way I see it, they're looking for confirmation of specific people that the deranged vet dug up. What's to say we can't fluke it and dig up the exact people he's taken? I recognised some of the faces in the tanks so we can start with them. Once their graves are all confirmed empty, maybe Chang'll have no reason to keep digging," Jim said.

"But what if he doesn't stop at those?" Mick said. "We don't even know how many bodies Hibbert took. What if they check all those fucked up stitched together bodies in those tanks and discover it's like a dozen more than the one's we already know about? The odds of digging the next dozen or so in a row would be like winning fucking Powerball. Twice."

"Yeah, but that doesn't mean it's impossible."

Mick shot his brother a withering glare.

"Well. It's not," Jim said, suitable chastened.

"Oh, Jesus!" Mick said, slapping his forehead at a sudden realisation.

"What?" Jim asked

"Oh we're really fucked. Like, really stupidly bent over and fucked!" Mick said. "Hibbert!"

Jim took a moment to catch up with his brother before it hit him as well.

"Someone killed Hibbert!" Jim said, realising.

"Not only that, Jim. We were there yesterday and your blood is all over the floor. Remember? From when you cracked your blood head open!"

"I didn't exactly do it on purpose," Jim said.

We're totally screwed," Mick said, barely hearing

his brother.

Jim checked his pockets looking for his phone.

"I'll have a quick look online and see if there's anything about it on the news. You never know, they might have someone arrested for it already."

Jim's hand felt something inside one of pockets but it wasn't his phone. He pulled the object out and held it between his fingers and stared at it. Jim experienced another moment of THC-induced clarity. He had intended to plug the USB stick he had found inside the casket into his computer to try to identify who it belonged to. But it had simply slipped his mind (or more accurately, on the day he found it he had got super high after cleaning and rearranging the caskets and promptly forgot all about it.) And now, looking at it once again, things started falling into place in his mind like pieces in a jigsaw puzzle.

"Follow me, Mick," Jim said as he rushed into his office. Mick reluctantly followed.

"We don't have time for this Jim. We need to figure out a plan."

Jim walked around his desk and started up his desktop computer, as Mick dragged his feet into the room.

"Jim?" Mick said.

Jim ushered him over to join him. Mick watched as Jim plugged the USB stick into one of the ports on the machine.

"What's that?" Mick asked.

"I'm not exactly sure. But I'm hoping whatever is

on this can explain some things."

Jim clicked on the icon of the USB stick and waited for it to open. Suddenly, the screen was filled with a seemingly endless number of files.

"Jesus, it's like a WikiLeaks dump," Jim said. He started randomly clicking on files and skim reading them.

"What are they?" Mick asked.

"I'm not a hundred percent sure. There seems to be a shit load of emails between Palfreeman and Terry McInerny. Stuff to do with The Oasis. Plus, a whole heap of documents. It'd take forever to go through all this properly but first impressions tell me there was something dodgy going on to get The Oasis through council and the mayor was up to his neck in it."

"No wonder that fat fuck was able to afford the funeral he had. I mean, fucking Morris dancers and a pipe band!?" Mick said.

"It's all starting to make sense. The break in here wasn't the cops. It was the Kardashians looking for this. Except, I'd already found it in the mayor's casket," Jim said. "They must have somehow found out about Hibbert's habit for human corpses and gone out in search for the USB stick at his place and knocked him off in the process. If we thought we were fucked before… Mick, I don't even think there's a word in the English language to describe how fucked we are now. If they find out we have this…"

Mick yanked the USB stick from the computer.

"Oh shit! Mick, you've got to eject it first. You can damage the drive if you do that!"

Mick smiled.

"Brother, that has never happened in the history of… ever."

Mick held up the USB stick in front of his eyes and inspected it like it was a rare Jewel in an Indiana Jones film.

"This could very well be the solution to all our problems."

TWENTY-FOUR

Mick was playing with the USB stick, tossing it up the in the air and catching it repeatedly. Jim watched on, mesmerised.

"Look, Jim. You know me, I'm always one to call a spade a shovel," Mick said. "And there's no way around it, we're going to have to do something drastic if we want to get out of this."

"When you say drastic, what exactly do you mean?"

"We make a run for it. I figure the cops are going to be so tied up dealing with all the shenanigans out at Hibbert's that they won't even know we're gone for at least a couple of days. We can get pretty far in a couple of days," Mick said. There was an undeniable air of excitement in his voice.

Jim rubbed his hand across his face, trying to massage into it a proper understanding of what his brother was proposing.

"Where would we go?" Jim asked.

"I dunno. Western Australia. Bali. Thailand. Fucking Timbuktu. Just somewhere not called Prosperity."

"We can't leave, Mick. At least, I can't leave. This place is my home."

"If you don't leave, Jim, you'll soon have a new home. Behind bars."

Jim turned his attention back to the computer in front of him. He started clicking his mouse and typing purposefully on his keyboard.

"What are you doing?" Mick said. Jim didn't answer him. He kept clicking. He kept typing.

"Jim?"

Mick tried to look over his shoulder but Jim shifted his seat to shield his brother from the screen. Jim's fingers were getting audibly louder and louder, click-clacking with increasing impetus. He moved the mouse and clicked it again several times and then stopped. Mick heard a small whooshing noise. It was the sound of an email being sent.

"What have you just done, Jim?" Mick asked, physically pushing his brother out of the way to get a look.

"I just emailed Chang a list of everyone we've buried in the past eighteen months. I put the ones we're certain will be missing at the top."

"I don't believe you," Mick said. His hand grabbed the mouse on the desk and he opened up the e-mail programme on the computer. Mick searched in the sent mail folder. The last email was addressed to Detective Sam Chang with a subject line that simply read: *The Names you were after.* Mick threw the mouse off the table violently, but it only went as far as the chord attaching it to the computer would allow. It pulled tight and crashed loudly into the desk itself.

"You do realise you have just completely screwed us, Jim! Why would you do that?" Mick said, turning angrily to his brother.

"We can't run from this, Mick."

"Yes we bloody well can!"

"Here's the thing. We give Chang that USB stick in exchange for coming clean. We plead for some sort of immunity. Or leniency at the very least. With The Oasis, the mayor, Hibbert we'll be way down the list in terms of bad guys. Particularly if we help the authorities," Jim said. He was trying to sound as calm as he possibly could.

"So, your idea is we just walk into the cop shop and put our hands up in the air, hand over the USB stick - which is the one piece of leverage we have - and just hope for some sort of deal?" Mick said.

Jim looked straight at his brother.

"Yeah."

"Brilliant!"

Mick could feel the anger boiling in his veins. The valve burst with a sudden eruption of violence as Mick pushed the computer from the top of Jim's desk. It crashed to the ground in a discordant explosion of broken plastic and glass. Mick angrily stormed from the office.

"Fuck, Mick, that comes out of both of our pockets!"

Jim hastily stood up and rushed after his brother.

"Mick, what are you doing?"

Mick didn't break stride. He was making a beeline for the front door of the office.

"I know someone who wants this USB stick back. And I'm sure they'll pay good money for it!" Mick spat.

"Who? Palfreeman?"

"If we want to get out of this, we're going to need money to leave. If giving those pricks what's on this device will get me that, then so be it."

Mick reached the door and started trying to unlock it. He spun the lock clockwise as far as it would go and tried to pull the door but it was still locked. He tried turning it all the other way but it still wouldn't open. In the delay, Jim had managed to catch up to his brother.

"It's a bad idea. Let's just give it to Chang and face what comes," Jim said, pleading. He grabbed his brother's arm gently to try to calm him, a gentle way to grab his attention. But Mick reactively spun his arm back to break the grip. He lifted his elbow and it caught his brother square on the temple. Jim Smith was unconscious before he even hit the ground.

Mick had felt his elbow hit something hard and heard the body crash to the ground but at the same moment, the lock clicked open and he impatiently thrust the door open. Only then did he turn and look back at his brother. He saw him lying motionless on the floor. Mick watched him for a second, momentarily worried, until Jim started slowly moving his feet and let out a soft groan.

"Sorry, brother," Mick said quietly, before closing the door behind him and jumping in his car outside.

Jim could feel the now familiar throbbing of his head as he pulled himself slowly from the darkness of yet another concussion. If he had been a professional sportsman he'd no doubt be declared medically unfit to play for a period of months after all his recent head knocks. A potential candidate for CTE, even. He propped himself up on one elbow as he strained to pull focus through the frosted glass doors of the Smith Bros. office to the street beyond. He could just make out the blurry shape of Mick's car as it reversed backwards and whipped around onto the main street. Jim tried to call out but could only manage a feeble croak.

"Mick…"

Jim rolled himself over and pulled himself onto on to all fours. He crawled slowly over to the doors and braced himself against them with his hands, drawing himself up into a praying position. He rocked forward on his knees, sending all his weight down through his hands onto the door. It slowly started to open, before reaching its tipping point where it swung wide, robbing Jim of any support. He fell forward, face first into the street, his body now acting as a doorstop, lying half inside and half outside through the threshold.

Jim lifted his head and looked up and down the footpath. It was still early in Prosperity and there was no one coming in either direction. Although Jim could have used some assistance, he was somewhat relieved to not have to explain the situation he found himself in. He rolled onto his back and sat up and his world immediately started spinning. Everything started going sideways and Jim knew he was going to go down again. He pressed his palm into the concrete to brace himself and waited for the horizon to level like an instrument panel in an plane cockpit. Only it didn't.

Jim could hear his ears begin to buzz and his head become light. The buzzing grew ever louder as he lost all strength in his arms and fell back onto the hard ground again. Jim closed his eyes but it made no difference, the spinning only worsened. He had just enough time to turn his head as the vomit erupted from deep within him. It splattered on to the footpath and down his shirt front. The smell caused Jim to heave again before he lay back and surrendered to the wholly unedifying experience.

He knew he wasn't going anywhere in a hurry.

The phone rang on the desk inside the security

room of The Oasis. It was vibrating across the table, getting closer to the edge with each buzz. Aleks Keshishian suddenly reached across and saved the shiny black mirror from tumbling off. He slid it back into the middle of the desk where it continued to ring. Aleks was otherwise occupied. Although he had always tried his best to separate business and pleasure, there were the odd occasions when he felt the temptation to break the rules and 'get high on his own supply' so to speak. The adrenaline rush from his recent dismembering of the vet had found Aleks looking for a different kind of release. As the phone kept ringing, he roughly thrust himself into one of the girls who had recently arrived from his famous city brothel, The Red Room. It wasn't her first time with Aleks and she met his efforts with her usual indifferent professionalism, despite Aleks's obvious enthusiasm. He suddenly finished with a guttural groan before reaching back for the still ringing mobile. He answered it, putting the phone on speaker.

"Yes?" Aleks said, breathing heavily.

As he listened, he pulled up his trousers and dismissively shooed the woman from the room.

"The big one left the office about five minutes ago in a hurry. The little one is lying in the street. It looked like the big one hit him. Hard."

It was Andre. He was parked up the main street in Prosperity and had been watched the morning's proceedings through his binoculars.

"And Chang?" Aleks asked.

"He spoke with them for one, maybe two minutes then left. Looked like he was heading back out to the freakshow at the vets."

Aleks zipped up his fly and buckled his belt.

"Do you still have two cars there?"

"Yeah. The crew assigned to the big one and me," Andre said.

"Okay, send the big one's crew after him. See where he's off to."

"And what do you want me to do?"

"Sit tight and stay with the little one. See what happens. But don't let him out of your sight," Aleks said.

He leaned across and hit the button on the screen to end the call and continued to straighten himself up. He had just finished tucking his shirt in when the phone started ringing again. Annoyed, he forcefully hit the screen with his finger. "What now? Surely you don't need me to explain it again do you? Watch the little one and send the other car after the big one!"

There was a pause. It made Aleks uneasy. An unfamiliar voice finally broke the silence.

"I have something of yours that I think you and your boss will be very keen to get back."

"Who is this?" Aleks asked.

"I'm guessing I must be the 'Big One.'"

TWENTY-FIVE

"How did you get this number?" Aleks said, as he picked up the phone.

"It was surprisingly easy. The front desk wouldn't give me your boss' number but they were more than happy to give me yours," Mick said. He was behind the wheel flying down the road, his foot pressed almost to the floor. Mick hadn't felt this amped up for years. It reminded him of the way he used to feel before running out for a big game. The excitement had him repeatedly gripping the steering wheel, turning his knuckles white, as he brought the vehicle to almost a hundred and sixty kilometres per hour.

"Interesting. But why do you want to talk to my boss?"

"Let's just say that I have found what you've been looking for. And for the right price, I'd even consider giving it to you," Mick said.

"That's very interesting, Mr Smith."

"I'd say it's a bit more than fucking interesting mate!" Mick said. He couldn't help but laugh.

"What did you want for its safe delivery to us?" Aleks asked.

"Mate, no offense but I want to do the negotiating directly with your boss, Palfreeman," Mick said.

"That won't be necessary. You can rest assured that I have the authority -- " Mick cut Aleks off mid-sentence.

"-- Listen here, it's Palfreeman of Palfuck-off! Get the hors d'oeuvres ready. I'll see you in less than ten minutes."

Mick hung up and let a broad grin light up his face. He knew he was playing a serious game with serious people but he was just enjoying it all way too much not to smile.

Aleks knocked on the door of Christian Palfreeman's office and entered without waiting for an invite. Palfreeman was watching premier league highlights on his phone – he was a lifelong Arsenal supporter - and jumped at the surprise entrance. He quickly hid his phone under a pile of documents like a schoolboy caught watching something he shouldn't.

"I'm not quite sure you fully understand the purpose of knocking, Aleks," Palfreeman said, trying not to look flustered.

"I paused," Aleks said, defending himself.

"Do you have any updates on the unfortunate events at the vets? I honestly can't believe you sometimes, Aleks. Talk about taking a simple task and complicating it."

"My sources tell me that they have found nothing yet. And they won't," Aleks said. "They might have suspicions but as we both know, suspicions don't mean anything without evidence."

"That may be the case Aleks, but suspicions do bring with them a whole shitload of unnecessary heat!" Palfreeman said in a forceful whisper, trying to communicate his displeasure without shouting.

"Please tell me though you have some news about the USB stick?"

It had been an awkward conversation earlier that morning. Aleks had finally come clean to his boss about the existence of the USB stick and the unfortunate situation of it being missing. He had tried to keep quiet about it for as long as he possibly could. However, having created such a grizzly scene out at Dr Hibbert's, Keshishian had felt compelled to fess up. After all, even by Aleks's standards, he knew his performance in the machinery shed was on the extreme side. Given that, he figured that providing some explanation of his motivation beyond mere psychopathic bloodlust was required.

Christian Palfreeman had taken the news better than expected. His threat to have Keshishian locked in a cage with a pack of starving Bullmastiffs unless he recovered the device, or secured one hundred percent proof of its destruction, came off as more Hollywood than 'hood. His subsequent dressing down of Aleks with a colourful use of some very Anglo-Saxon words came across as slightly performative and similarly unthreatening. Unfortunately for Palfreeman, they both knew how indispensable Aleks was to the operation - and to Christian Palfreeman personally - such that the outbursts failed to carry any real threat.

Aleks sat down in a long green sofa that ran along the side wall of Palfreeman's office and crossed his legs. The pause in the conversation made Palfreeman uncomfortable. It was the Armenian's way of taking back some control of the dynamic between them.

"Aleks?"

"I just received a very interesting phone call. It looks like the Smith brothers have what we have been looking for. In fact, one of them is on their way here right now to negotiate," Aleks said, coolly.

"Negotiate?" Palfreeman said.

"Yes, haggle, thrash out, broker, come to terms… negotiate," Aleks said. He was thoroughly pleased with himself, though he betrayed little emotion outwardly. He had been waiting a very long time for this moment. Aleks had longed for an opportunity to mimic Palfreeman's fondness for synonymic explanation and his boss had just put this one on a tee. While nothing could compare to the joy he derived from physical violence, the rush of pleasure he was experiencing in that few seconds was a close second. Christian Palfreeman wasn't so joy-filled.

"Been reading the thesaurus, Aleks, when you're not trying to fuck up my business? Interesting you have so much goddamn time on your hands!"

Aleks tried not to let Christian's petulance ruin his buzz.

"But these guys are amateurs. Rule number one of any negotiation is to understand exactly what cards the other side is holding."

The doors to Palfreeman's office swung open a second time and two of Aleks' Kardashians entered the room.

"Jesus Christ, does anyone in Armenia know how to knock on a fucking door properly?"

The two Kardashians stepped to one side and a third person entered behind them. Palfreeman looked at the new arrival with curiosity. As it fully dawned on him, he smiled and noticeably relaxed.

"Sorry to disturb, Mr Palfreeman. These guys said you asked to see me? I hope I'm not in any trouble. If it's about me staying here last night, I cleared it with Misty," Tracy Smith said, her voice full of nervous conciliation.

"Close the door," Aleks said. "Let's have a chat."

The Kardashians pulled the door shut and stood either side of it like two strip club bouncers, preventing anyone from coming or going.

Mick Smith slowed his car as he turned through

the portcullis entrance of The Oasis and followed the road around to the car park. He pulled up in a spot closest to the pedestrian path and turned the engine off. Mick bent the rear vision mirror to be able to see his reflection and looked deep into his own eyes.

"It's game day, Sherman!" Mick said.

He stepped out of the car and started confidently striding towards the draw bridge that crossed the moat into the reception area. Once inside he paused and took in his surroundings. His reaction was the same as most when they first laid eyes on the interiors: general astonishment. It was like nothing he'd ever seen before.

"Holy Game of Thrones, Batman," Mick said quietly to himself.

He looked around the room and noticed a few guests dressed in various medieval costumes, enjoying the company of buxom young women whom he assumed were paid by the hour for their amorous attentions. Mick spied the reception desk and made a beeline for it. He'd barely made it two steps before three Kardashians moved in, a pincer movement Rommel would have been proud of.

"Mr Palfreeman is expecting you, Mr Smith."

"Well, better not keep the man waiting then. We're not here to fuck spiders," Mick said. He gestured for his large, suited escorts to lead the way. As two of the Kardashians fell in behind him, he experienced a moment of doubt. This suddenly didn't feel like a big footy match as he had psyched himself up for.

Mick hoped he wasn't suddenly an all too willing participant in his own march to the gallows. He was still banking on the fact that whatever was on that USB stick meant he was worth more to them above ground than below it.

The Kardashians led Mick down a series of corridors until they reached a door that held a plaque that read 'Christian Palfreeman, CEO'. As it swung open the cool, stale air from the office hit Mick in the face, and the atmosphere changed. His remaining confidence all but evaporated as he spotted Tracy sitting on a green couch against the wall, her hands bound behind her back.

"Tracy!" Mick yelled. He tried to rush to her side but a large arm appeared from behind him. It looped over his shoulder like a seat belt, holding him back.

"Mate, I've felt harder tackles from a half-back!" Mick said, as he brushed off the Kardashian's attempt to stop him with ease. He made it to the couch in a few quick strides but the room rapidly closed around him, as half a dozen goons advanced from every corner.

"Are you OK? Have they hurt you?" Mick said, frantically checking over Tracy for any signs of injury.

"I'm ok. I'm ok. What's going on Mick? What do they want?" Tracy asked, her voice shaking.

"It's going to be ok. I'm here now. It'll be all over soon."

The cabal of Kardashians were now encircling

Mick. He stood, chest out, and sized up the situation. He was a handy brawler in his playing days and was pretty sure he could take out one or two of them - maybe a third if he was lucky - but there was no way he could account for all of them. And he was sure that at least some of them would be carrying weapons. Mick eased himself out of his fighting stance and let the tension drain from his muscles. He looked past the henchmen and saw Christian Palfreeman sitting behind his desk, steely, with Aleks Keshishian standing over his right shoulder. It was like a scene out of a Bond film.

"I'm not sure if this is how you conduct all your business dealings, Mr Palfreeman, but I can honestly say I wish I had you as my agent back in my playing days - that's for sure," Mick said trying to alleviate the tension.

"Mr Smith, I believe you have something of great importance to us," Palfreeman said.

"Yes. I believe I do."

Christian smiled.

"Wonderful. If you would be so kind as to hand it over to my associate here, we can conclude our business," Palfreeman said.

"And what do I get in return?" Mick asked. "You've obviously gone to a lot of trouble to get your hands on it. I'd say about half-a-mills worth of trouble, wouldn't you think?"

Christian Palfreeman started laughing. He turned to Aleks.

"How about this guy!?!"

Palfreeman stood from his chair.

"You obviously don't quite understand the situation you find yourself in if you think we'd hand over a half a million dollars."

"Oh, I understand the situation perfectly well. Before I saw you had Tracy, I was going to ask for a million," Mick said.

Aleks gave a slight nod to the Kardashian standing nearest to Mick who swung a thunderous fist into his stomach with brutal force. It knocked the wind clean out of him, bringing him to his knees.

"Mick!" Tracy screamed.

Mick grabbed at his body as he struggled to breathe. He stretched himself upright and lifted his chest, doing his best to get air back into his lungs as quickly as he could.

"Now, I'm not some street hood so I'll ask one more time, politely. If you could be so good as to hand over the USB device," Palfreeman said as his right hand opened the top drawer of his desk and removed a shiny, nickel-plated Baretta 92FS 9mm handgun which he pointed squarely at Mick.

"Pretty please."

TWENTY-SIX

Jim splashed some more water on his face and checked the mirror again to ensure that he had successfully removed all traces vomit from himself. He had remained on the footpath outside for what he estimated was about five minutes. It was only when he started to feel as though he could stand without fear of toppling over again did he try to get up. He was thankful that no one had come past during that time - although he could have sworn he'd seen some movement in the windows of the church op-shop across the road. He suspected the ladies who ran it had noticed him but chosen not to make any further enquiries about his wellbeing. Perhaps they assumed he was merely experiencing the self-induced repercussions of ungodly behaviour after a big night out. However, a part of Jim felt that their lack of interest was at best uncharitable. And certainly lacked the community spirit Prosperity normally prided itself on.

However, when Jim had eventually pulled himself up and made it back into the restroom inside, catching himself in the mirror he could hardly blame them. He looked in a right state.

He now turned his face from side to side and studied his reflection carefully. Only once satisfied that his face was one-hundred percent certified vomit free, did he turn his attention to his shirt front. Jim pulled a few sheets of hand towel from the dispenser and soaked them under the tap. He tried to scrub the bile stains from his top as best he could but his efforts only succeeded in spreading the marks further. Plus, he now had the added bonus of a soaking wet shirt. Jim removed his top and held it under the hand dryer. Putting it through several cycles, he blasted the hot air onto the shirt until it was dry enough to put back on. After all the effort, the stains looked barely changed.

Jim picked up the suit jacket from where he had laid it on the floor of the bathroom and slid it on. It served to cover up some of the worst of the blemishes. He then turned his attention back to his phone. Jim had tried unsuccessfully to call Mick several times already. He checked now to see if he had somehow missed a return call or text message. But there was nothing. He decided to try to call again. Jim waited with the phone to his ear, listening as it rang. And rang. He was just about to hang up when the line answered.

Except it wasn't Mick on the other end of the phone.

"Mr Smith, what impeccable timing."

"Who is this? Where's Mick?" Jim asked.

"Your brother is right here. I'm just about to pass the phone to him. He's going to ask you to do something. It's important that you follow his instructions precisely. I don't want this to get any more complicated than it already is."

"What do you mean complicated?" Jim said, confused.

"Involved, convoluted, tricky, thorny, complex. Complicated."

Christian Palfreeman handed the phone to Aleks Keshishian who in turn walked across Palfreeman's office and held it to Mick's ear. Mick was now seated next to Tracy on the green couch and had been restrained in a similar manner to his wife, his hands tied together behind his back with cable ties.

"Jim?" Mick said.

"Where are you Mick? What's going on? Should I call Chang?" Jim asked, rapid-fire.

"Let's just say I may have been a touch hasty in executing my plans, brother," Mick said. "I'm all good though. This Palfreeman bloke and his Southern European mates are simply entertaining Tracy and I for the moment. If we're lucky they might even dance for us."

Jim started rushing for the door of the office. He wasn't quite sure where exactly he was heading but he knew that he needed to get in his car as fast as possible and go somewhere.

"Shit, Mick. Are you guys OK? Have they hurt either of you?"

"We're fine. But I need you to do something for me. I need you to grab the USB stick we found and bring it out to The Oasis and hand it over to these guys."

Jim stopped in his tracks. He couldn't make any sense of what his brother was saying. Unless the latest concussion had scrambled his brains even more than he thought, Jim was certain that Mick had left with the USB stick in his possession. It was the entire reason he tried to stop him leaving in the first place after all.

"Are you on speaker?" Jim asked.

Mick sat in the office and forced a broad smile. He was trying to stay relaxed and play it cool.

"We're all good, Jim," Mick said, trying to let Jim know that they weren't being listened to. "But you need to get that USB stick out here as quick as you can. No funny business. No cops. Then once you've handed it over you can destroy all the copies."

This last line made Christian Palfreeman straighten in his seat. It also caught the attention of Aleks Keshishian who aggressively snatched the phone from Mick's ear and brought it to his own.

"If you show up with anyone else we will not hesitate to kill the two of them. You have an hour," Aleks said before hanging up the phone, ending the conversation.

"Copies? How very interesting. I must say, you're far more resourceful than I gave you credit for," Palfreeman said.

"Look, I'll level with you… I have watched my fair share of spy and action movies in my time and it seems to be digital blackmail 101 to make sure there are copies," Mick said.

He was growing quite pleased with himself and was impressed at how he was operating so well under the circumstances. The idea about the copies had come to him like a bolt of lightning while he was on the phone with his brother. He figured, if Palfreeman and the Kardashians could be placed under the misapprehension that there were copies of all the incriminating evidence, then it might just buy him and Tracy some valuable time. He was less sure about the predicament he had now placed his brother in, however. Considering the USB stick Jim had been asked to bring was sitting under the floor mat of Mick's car that currently sat outside in the car park of The Oasis where he had left it, he had no idea what Jim would come up with. Mick had at least had sense enough to realise that it probably wasn't the smartest idea in the world to boldly stroll into Palfreeman's office with the device still on his person. However, he did wish he had taken more time to think through his approach slightly more strategically. Although the creativity of the fictional copies had evidently caused quite a reaction and thrown a potential spanner in the works for his captors, with the benefit of hindsight, Mick couldn't help but think that actually making copies might have been a prudent idea.

Christian Palfreeman stood from his desk and started pacing back and forth, his brain working so furiously it was almost audible. Everyone else in the room watched and waited for him to speak.

"Aleks, we still have a surveillance team on the Smith still out there, yes?" Palfreeman said.

"Yes. As instructed," Aleks replied.

"Good. Have them follow him. When they are clear of the town, I want them to intercept his car, take possession of the USB stick and then supervise the destruction of any copies. No point waiting until he's all the way out here. We don't need to be inviting even more mess into this place. We've got enough to deal with already."

"Agreed. I'll contact them straight away."

Aleks started for the door of the office before turning back to his boss.

"What would you like done after we have what we need?"

"I'll leave that up to you. But just make it cleaner than the vet. Drowning. Missing person. Perhaps another car accident? Like Cociarelli?"

"And these two?"

Christian looked over at Mick and Tracy sitting on the couch.

"They can stay here for now. It always pays to

have a little insurance."

Aleks Keshishian was already dialling Andre by the time he left the room.

Jim had been sitting at the wheel of his car for the past seven minutes with the engine running. He knew it was exactly seven minutes because he had set a timer on his phone for one hour the instant the call with his brother had ended. He had fifty-three minutes left. Jim knew the drive out to The Oasis was about twenty, which meant he still had about half an hour up his sleeve to figure out exactly what he was going to do. So far, his mind was drawing a blank.

Mick had really put Jim in a bind by making Palfreeman believe that he had the USB stick in his possession. He thought about rummaging around in the office to find another device that he could try to pass off for the one with all The Oasis documents on it but quickly ruled that out. He knew that Palfreeman would be sure to check its contents almost immediately and discover it was merely a prop. Then he'd still be without the USB stick except he would now also be facing a very angry mob of bloodthirsty gangsters.

He also briefly considered handing over control of the situation to the police by calling detective Chang. But the coolness of the way Aleks had instructed him to come alone, had left him feeling certain that he was serious about following through on his threat to kill Mick and Tracy if he heard so much as a distant siren, so he ruled that option out as well.

Jim checked his timer. He had forty-seven minutes remaining.

He decided that the only course of action left to him was to simply head out to The Oasis empty-handed and come clean, in the hope that Mick would tell them all where the USB stick was. He knew that his brother would have hoped that he had been able to come up with a better solution but short of going via the farm to pick up the shotgun and try to blast his way in to free them, he was shit out of ideas. Jim took the handbrake off and pointed the car out of town in the direction of The Oasis.

At the same time a few hundred meters down the road, Andre eased his car out on to Prosperity's main street and followed Jim out of town.

Mick was lost deep in his thoughts. He was trying to process the fact that the Kardashians following Jim had just been given the green light to kill his brother. But he knew if he told them where the USB stick was then they'd more than likely kill him and Tracy once they had possession of it, and with them out of the way there was probably no need to leave Jim above ground either - why leave any loose ends? He was now not quite as proud of his lie about making copies of the device. Now that the idea was planted, there was no way that Keshishian and Palfreeman would believe that there weren't any and Mick was convinced they'd keep looking until they found them, no matter what they had to do, or who they had to hurt. And even if he managed to sway them towards believing that he'd made the whole thing up, they'd be mad not to at least put the blowtorch to Jim - and he couldn't rule out a literal interpretation of this phrase - before being completely convinced either way. He tried desperately to navigate his thinking but wherever he went ended up with them all - him, Jim and Tracy - lying dead in a shallow grave, or worse.

"Mick?" Tracy said. He turned towards her and tried to force a smile.

"Are we going to be ok?"

"Of course," Mick said "Of course we're going to be ok. I'm going to figure out a way out of this."

Mick wasn't sure who he was trying to reassure more, Tracy or himself.

It was probably the slowest that Jim Smith had ever driven along the road out of Prosperity. He was for once sticking to the one hundred kilometre per hour speed limit. The last thing he needed was to get out to The Oasis early. He still needed to figure out what exactly he was going to say on arrival. He glanced down at the phone on the seat next to him. The timer was still running. He had thirty-two minutes left. It was more than enough time to get out to the brothel before his allotted hour was up. In fact, it was, despite his cautious driving, still far too much time.

Jim pressed his foot on the brake and slowed the car sufficiently to be able to pull off the bitumen and onto the gravel verge on the side of the road, where he brought the car to a complete stop.

"This is madness," Jim said out loud to himself. "What do I do? What do I do?" He said over and over again as if trying to conjure a magical response from the universe.

"Fuck it!"

Jim made up his mind. This was too big a deal for him to face alone. He needed to call Chang. He reached for his phone just as a large black sedan pulled up alongside him. It was so close that the side mirrors of the cars collided, snapping Jim's from its mount and sending a shower of glass into the air.

"Jesus Christ!" Jim said, in a sudden panic. He looked out his side window and watched as the tinted window of the car that just pulled up slowly lowered. His eyes grew wider as he recognised the pointy end of a large revolver. It was being aimed directly at him. Jim tried to open his door but the cars were so close together that his door wouldn't move more than a few centimetres. He frantically unbuckled his seat belt and tried to scramble over the centre console to make his escape through the passenger side door. He scratched for the door handle in a desperate attempt to open it. But before he could, the door suddenly opened a large hand reached into the car and took a firm grip on the back of Jim's shirt collar. Before Jim could do anything to resist, Andre had dragged him from the car.

"I believe you have something that belongs to us," Andre said as he stood Jim up and pushed him back firmly against the side of his car.

"No, I don't know what you mean? Who are you --"

Andre slapped him with an open palm across his face. The force split the corner of Jim's mouth and he quickly tasted blood.

"Look, I was told to bring it out to your boss. So that's what I'm going to do."

"Change of plan. I have new instructions," Andre said. He slapped Jim again, this time from the other direction with his other hand. Unfortunately for Jim, this hand also sported a large ring. The impact had almost the same effect of a set of brass knuckles.

Given all his recent head trauma, Jim could sense his legs getting weak again. He could hear the buzzing rising in his ears once more. However, this time it seemed to be getting louder. And louder. And louder. But there was something different about it. Andre suddenly looked to his right. He took a couple of steps away from Jim and tried to first shuffle one way, then the other as if trying to avoid something that was coming at him fast. Finally, he planted his feet and braced. It did two-fifths of fuck all. He was far too late to avoid the large branch that thundered into his chest. It knocked the wind from him, picked his feet off the ground and knocked him flat onto the hard bitumen. On the other end of the branch was the helmeted rider of a bright red Honda CT110 postie bike, which explained the buzzing. From Jim's vantage point the whole thing reminded him, quite appropriately, of a medieval jousting battle, albeit a one-sided one. The bike shot past the parked cars as the rider tossed the branch to one side where it cartwheeled off into the bush beyond the verge.

Jim could hear a commotion coming from the other car as the remaining Kardashian - the one who had levelled the gun at Jim - began frantically trying to get himself out. Only, he faced the same dilemma as Jim had moments before - the positioning of the two vehicles made it impossible for him to exit through the nearside door. He wildly banged the door against the side of Jim's car a few times before giving up and changing tack. He scrambled over to the driver's side and tumbled out on to the road through the door Andre had left open. Jim spun around as he heard the postie bike begin to rev its engine again. The rider dropped the clutch and the bike sprung to life.

The little red machine leaped down the road in a direct path towards the Kardashian who was struggling to his feet. As he finally stood upright, he raised his gun and swung it in a wide arc through the air until it was aimed directly at the rapidly approaching motorised steed. He squeezed the trigger and gunshots exploded from the barrel, sending a barrage of deadly projectiles hurtling through the air. At the same time, the postie bike kicked back onto its rear wheel, lifting the front clear off the ground. The few bullets that were on target deflected in showers of sparks from the undercarriage while the majority sprayed well wide of their intended target. Although the Kardashian carried the weapon daily, it was mostly for show. He had actually only fired the thing on a handful of occasions and each time had displayed almost zero natural talent for marksmanship.

Having threaded the hail of poorly aimed bullets, the rider skilfully kept the bike on a one-wheel collision course with the still firing Kardashian, before gracefully dismounting the hurtling machine moments before it impacted. The gun became silent as the Honda smashed into the henchman, knocking him over like a skittle in an alley. It impacted with such devastation that months of rehabilitation and pureed food would have been considered an optimistic prognosis.

Jim was struggling to make sense of what he was witnessing as he watched the rider casually walk back over to Andre who was still lying on the ground, grasping for air. The rider stood over him, removed their helmet and with one forceful blow, brought it down onto Andre's head, removing him of his consciousness. The whole thing was over in seconds.

"Hey, I've got nothing to do with these guys!" Jim said, panic creeping in. He didn't want to be mistaken for one of the suited Armenian gangsters. "In fact, that one you just clobbered with your helmet was hitting me!" Jim pleaded as he pointed to his bloodied lip.

"Of course I know that, Jim."

It was a female voice. The woman turned around, smiled, and Jim finally saw her face.

"You?" Jim said, in genuine astonishment.

TWENTY-SEVEN

"You don't have any cable-ties in your car by any chance do you?" Marnie Rochambeau said as she walked towards Jim.

"I don't think so," Jim replied, still in a state of shock.

"It's all good. I'm sure these fellas will have some. Any good gangster worth their salt should have pliers, gaffer tape, a boxcutter, three lengths of rope and half a dozen cable ties at a bare minimum.'"

Marnie reached inside the Kardashian's car and popped open the boot. She rummaged around inside before removing a small black canvas gym bag. She propped it on the rear bumper of the car and unzipped it.

"Now this is what I'm talking about!" Marnie said, letting out a whistle as she sifted through the bag's contents. "Cable-ties, gaffer tape, box cutter, hand file, pepper-spray, taser, knuckle dusters, three sizes of wrench and what looks like a hand-held reciprocating saw… wow! Now that's a real goon bag don't you reckon?" Marnie said with a laugh. She shut the boot and carried the bag over to the still prone Kardashian nearby. The only signs of life were coming from the still purring engine of the postie bike, lying on its side close to the body. Marnie leant over and turned off the bike's ignition before checking the Kardashian for a pulse. It was weak but he was alive. She roughly pulled his arms together behind his back and bound them together with one of the cable-ties from the bag, her smoothness with the manoeuvre making it clear to Jim that she'd done this many times before. Marnie then turned her attention to Andre.

The large Armenian was still exactly where Marnie had left him, only now his face was covered in blood. The blow from the helmet had opened a nasty slice above his eye. She knelt down and took the gaffer tape from the bag and tore a large strip from the roll. With one hand she pinched the two edges of the wound together to close the cut while she used her free hand to stick the gaffer tape over the skin to hold it in place. Jim heard the cable tie zip tight around Andre's wrists moments before Marnie stood up and double-checked her work.

"Okay, let's get out of here," Marnie said, matter-of-fact.

She calmly walked towards Jim's car but Jim remained rooted to the spot.

"Who the bloody hell are you?" Jim asked.

"Oh calm down petal. I'll explain on the way. But you have about two minutes before another car is bound to drive past. It's astonishing, actually, that there hasn't been one yet," Marnie said, as she waved Jim over to the car. "Trust me, it's much better for everyone if we're not here when this whole scene gets discovered."

Marnie stood at the passenger door and held it open for Jim but he remained still.

"Well, you get in first, dummy. You have to drive. I don't have a license," Marnie said, with a cheeky smile.

Jim reluctantly shuffled his way over to the door before stopping, unsure.

"Go on. It'll be fun," she said with a wink.

He climbed in over the centre console and sat behind the wheel as Marnie slid into the passenger seat and closed the door. She perched the gym bag on her lap like an old lady on her way to church might do with her purse.

"To The Oasis, driver," Marnie said.

Jim carefully eased the car back onto the highway, making sure not to run over Andre in the process, and slowly accelerated the car. Marnie shifted uncomfortably in her seat and reached beneath her leg and pulled out Jim's phone.

"Is this yours?"

She held it up for Jim to confirm. The timer was still going. There were twenty-four minutes left. Jim pressed down on the accelerator and the car sped up.

"Hello, police?"

Jim snapped his head. Marnie was talking on the phone but it didn't sound like her. It sounded much younger, almost like someone in their twenties. And it was filled with a heightened sense of urgency and panic.

"There's been a terrible accident!"

Marnie went on to give the police on the other end of the line the exact location of the two Kardashians they had just left by the side of the road. She hung up the phone and noticed Jim looking at her, concern etched on his face.

"Don't worry, that wasn't from your phone. I always carry a burner."

"Who are you?" Jim asked again, before turning his eyes back to the road.

"I keep telling people you don't get to my age without picking up a thing or two along the way."

"I don't understand what's going on."

"Let's just say I spent a considerable amount of time working in the Attorney General's Department. I came out to Prosperity to find the quiet life. And to make it hard for some international organisations - who I may or may not have inconvenienced from time to time - to be able to find me. How was I to know that so much unseemly shit was going on out here?!" Marnie laughed.

"But how did you know I was in trouble. How did you know where I was?"

"Oh, I've been watching those boys for some time. It wasn't hard to spot the tails they had on you and your brother. Pretty basic stuff really, when it comes to surveillance. It was only a matter of time before they tried something. I assume you and your brother have some dirt on Palfreeman - probably courtesy of the mayor's shady dealings - and Mick tried to get some sort of payout from them but it's all gone to shit? Stop me when I'm wrong."

Jim didn't stop her.

"Now you're in a bind because of the little casket swap-a-roo you two have been running, which means you're too shit scared to bring Detective Chang up to speed."

"You know about that?" Jim said.

Marnie just looked at him and raised her eyebrows - as if she wouldn't know about that.

"Look, I've always said there's a hierarchy of criminality. Murder, paedophilia, rape, etc down to petty theft. And within that hierarchy there are two subsets of crimes - those that cause a physical harm to the victims and those that cause financial and emotional harm. While I in no way condone your behaviour - in fact I'd say that taking advantage of grieving families is pretty fucking despicable - on the hierarchical matrix of crime severity and harm your acts sit well down the list and significantly further down than anything Palfreeman and the Kardashians are up to. I didn't want to get involved but I couldn't sit back and let more residents of this delightful little town turn up dead."

Marnie looked out the windshield. They were rapidly approaching the turn off to The Oasis.

"Pull over up here. I'll head in the rest of the way on foot. I gather they've told you to come alone?"

"Are you sure? The sign says it's one kilometre to the entrance."

"I might be old but there's some running left in these old legs yet."

Jim turned the car onto the dirt road and stopped.

"What's the plan?" Jim asked, nervously.

"Don't know, really. Wait here a couple of minutes to let me get a head start. Then I guess you head on in as expected."

"Then what?" Jim asked.

"I guess I've got a one kilometre run to try to figure that out."

TWENTY-EIGHT

Detective Sam Chang stood in the middle of Dr George Hibbert's oversized machinery shed. The scene was vastly different to the one he had faced when he had first arrived with Riley. After careful forensic examination, all the bodies had been removed from the formaldehyde filled tanks and carefully transported to Sydney to begin the process of formal identification. The tanks themselves had been drained, loaded on to the back of a number of flatbed trucks and moved to a police-controlled warehouse on the outskirts of Bathurst for further examination and secure storage. Most of the rest of the contents of the shed had also been seized and removed as potential evidence, leaving the large blood stain in the middle of the floor and the myriad forensic markings around the building as the only testament to the horrors of the building's recent past.

While the police had uncovered a treasure trove

of evidence concerning the vet's sordid pastime - including an extensive artistic vision board that laid out in an almost too-good-to-be-true fashion a simple and clear explanation of the exactly how he obtained and and assembled his artworks - they had yet to find anything that could directly connect Palfreeman or any of the Kardashians. And whatever evidence contained within the tissues of the mayor was now redundant. There wasn't a court in the country that would allow any posthumous evidence to be admitted given how extensively the body had been interfered with. And while the blood stain on the floor had been provisionally matched with Dr Hibbert, apart from his dismembered body, there were nothing else for the police to go on that might provide any clues as to who might have been responsible for the late vet's demise.

However, despite drawing blanks finding any hard evidence, Chang remained convinced that the most likely suspects of the vet's murder could be found out at The Oasis and he had been developing a theory that seemed to support that proposition. Although he had been cautious to avoid any sort of confirmation bias in his thinking, Chang was almost certain that Mayor McInerny had met an unnatural end rather than a lifestyle induced heart attack, probably due to either knowledge of, or active involvement in, deep corruption associated with The Oasis development. He wouldn't have been the first elected council official to have taken a brown paper bag full of cash from a property developer. The mayor's lavish funeral bore testament to the fact that he wasn't short of money. As to why he needed to be killed, maybe McInerny had started applying the screws to Palfreeman, wanting additional compensation in exchange for his silence. Or maybe they just wanted the mayor out of the way to minimise any chance that he might big note himself around town and let things slip. Either seemed plausible motives.

Then there was Dr Enrico Cociarelli's untimely demise. While it was possible that Dr Cociarelli's car crash had been a coincidental accident - the crash investigation unit was still conducting their investigations and had yet to provide a conclusive report - Chang couldn't help but find it suspicious that the doctor who signed off on the mayor's cause of death would himself meet a sudden, unexpected end. Who would benefit from the doctor's death more than Palfreeman and Keshishian if they had paid him to falsify the death certificate?

Chang admitted to himself that there was a lot of speculation and conjecture in his theory. However, if Palfreeman's people were involved, then it would have made complete sense once word got out about the mayor's body going missing, for the Kardashians to want to find the corpse before the police did, in order to dispose of any remaining evidence. How they managed to track the body all the way to the vet's machinery shed was still a mystery but at best guess, Chang figured that Dr Hibbert had simply been in the wrong place, admittedly doing very wrong things, at the wrong time.

If he was correct in his proposition, Detective Sam Chang was now looking at Christian Palfreeman and Aleks Keshishian for at least three murders.

However, Sam now also faced the prospect of his workload become so significant that he would have no meaningful time to spend in pursuit of the elusive piece of evidence that he was certain would unlock the case. He had already forwarded the list of names provided to him by the Smith brothers to the court in order to finalise the exact plots set for exhumation. Then there was the duty he felt to take the time to properly visit each of the families involved in Hibbert's 'art' project and to keep them up to date on the investigations.

Sam felt that he had no other choice but to hand over investigation of The Oasis to a bigger team with far greater resources, probably some sort of major crimes squad based out of Sydney. But that idea filled Sam with apprehension. While the salacious nature of the recent deaths in Prosperity might attract some interest from his city colleagues, Chang had been around long enough to know that there were always ways for investigations to be put in the slow lane. And he had also been around long enough to know that people like Aleks Keshishian and Christian Palfreeman were exactly the kinds of individuals who more than likely had the connections to make that happen. The notion that Christian Palfreeman and Aleks Keshishian might get away with their murderous contributions to his hometown made Sam sick to his stomach.

But what could he do?

Chang took one more look around the shed before walking to the door. He stepped outside and locked the shed behind him, making sure to replace the police tape to prevent any unauthorised entry. He spent a moment taking in the quiet and trying to reconcile it with the horrors that had taken place, before heading back to his car. Sam had just sat down behind the wheel when his phone rang.

It was Riley.

"Hey Riley, if it's about that list of names for the Judge, I've already shot them through…" Riley stopped him mid-sentence.

"That's being sorted, Sam, it's not about that," Riley said. Sam noticed the urgency in her voice. His body involuntarily started flooding with cortisol, quickening his heart rate. He was in 'fight or flight' mode.

"What is it, Riley?"

"One of the cars heading back to Bathurst from Hibbert's was redirected to a call out to an accident out towards The Oasis. Except there wasn't an accident. Well, not one like they were expecting anyway."

"Go on," Sam said.

"They found two of the Kardashians in a pretty bad way. They'll live…just… but someone's given them a real working over. Not only that, they'd been tied up and left by the side of the road. Their car was there, along with, get this, an old postie bike that looks like it had taken about half a dozen rounds. There was no evidence of anyone else in the vicinity. I tell you Sam, the guys on scene said they can't remember seeing anything quite like it. None of it makes any sense. But I thought you'd want to know," Riley said.

Sam took about half a second to process the information and decide on his next course of action.

"Where are you?" Sam asked

"At the station," Riley replied.

"Be out the front in ten. We're going to pay Palfreeman another visit."

TWENTY-NINE

Christian Palfreeman sat in his office, kicked back in his chair resting his feet on his desk. He slid up the French cuff on his left wrist and checked the time. They should have heard something from Andre by now.

"Aleks, try Andre again, will you?"

Aleks hit redial on his phone and waited.

"No answer."

Aleks looked at his phone and checked the app that he had secretly installed on Andre's phone. He'd done the same to all the henchmen. It allowed for their location to be shared at all times with Alek's own device. He had kept it a secret as he knew that had Andre known, he would have objected forcefully at the very least. After all he had become physically violent and thrown his brand new iPhone from a sixteenth-floor balcony when he discovered iTunes had put U2's *Song of Innocence* on his device without his permission, and that was despite the fact that Bono was his second favourite front man behind his Armenian namesake. Regardless, it provided great utility for Aleks as it allowed him to gain a quick snapshot whenever he needed, of where everyone was, like chess pieces on a board. Right now it showed that Andre, or at least his phone, was in the same place it had been for the last twenty or so minutes.

"He still hasn't moved from the spot out on the road leading here," Aleks said to Palfreeman.

"We don't need everyone here to watch these two. Send some to go check on him. And if the other brother is there, no more mucking around. Just kill the son of a bitch," Palfreeman said.

Aleks singled out four of the Kardashians in the room by simply looking at them in turn. All four left hurriedly in a bustling mass of hulking cheap suits. It left only Palfreeman, Aleks and two henchmen behind. Mick was starting to feel better about his and Tracy's odds. He wasn't feeling that good about Jim's though. He needed to buy his brother some time.

"Do you know what one of my footy coaches used to always say to me Mr Palfreeman?" Mick said, piping up from the couch where he and Tracy remained bound.

"I couldn't possibly imagine," Palfreeman replied, with a gentle roll of his eyes.

"He used to say that tackling opponents bigger than

yourself was like clipping the toenails of a tiger: the more committed you are going in, the less chance there is of getting hurt."

Everyone in the room looked at Mick. They each shared the same perplexed look.

"Now I've got your attention, he also used to say that 'Pressure causes panic, and panic causes pain so never let pressure, throw you off your game.' I'll admit, he wasn't much of a poet but his point had merit. Changing your plans and killing Jim straight away won't solve your problems."

"Oh, and why is that?" Palfreeman said, growing tired of the conversation.

"Because he's the only one who knows where the copies are. And if I know my brother, he'll have those pretty well hid. Not only that, but he's also probably got some sort of technology set up so that if he disappears then the copies automatically get sent to the cops. Or some journalists in the big smoke. Probably both."

Mick was worried he might have overplayed his hand a little. He tried his best to put back on the same cloak of confidence he had possessed when he first walked in.

"You're bluffing," Aleks said. He turned to Palfreeman. "I'll have them rip his fingernails out one by one. And if he's still reluctant to talk we'll move on to a taser on his testicles. Trust me, he'll soon tell us where the copies are."

Aleks started typing out a text on his phone,

conveying the torture instructions to Andre. Mick's invisible cloak started slipping towards the floor. He couldn't help but think that every time he opened his mouth, he was doing nothing more than putting Jim further and further into the shit. Mick decided to change his focus.

"Look, at least let Tracy go. She's got nothing to do with any of this. She won't tell anyone, will you babe?"

Tracy looked at Mick with worried eyes.

"Will you Trace? You won't tell anyone. In fact you'll move. Go and live in Thailand. As far away from Prosperity as you can. Won't you?"

Tracy slowly started nodding.

"Yeah, far away. Won't say a word," Tracy said, barely audible.

Christian Palfreeman started clapping, a slow, taunting round of applause.

"True love. Ain't it grand?!?" Palfreeman said. "Unfortunately, the prospect of anyone leaving here until I have what I want is about as high as Calvin Klein signing up my good Armenian friend Mr Keshishian here for their next underwear campaign."

Palfreeman stopped clapping.

"Aleks, call Andre again."

Aleks did as instructed. There was still no answer.

Jim cautiously slowed the car as he approached the entrance to The Oasis. He was wary that he might be driving into an ambush. But everything seemed normal. So he accelerated the car back up to speed, pulled through the portcullis gate and continued around towards the carpark. He didn't notice the two black sedans accelerating out through the gate behind him, back down the dirt road towards Prosperity. It was lucky for Jim that the occupants, the Kardashians dispatched by Aleks to go and find Andre, also didn't notice him either. As Jim reached the carpark, he recognised Mick's car sitting by itself and decided to pull in beside it. He still had no idea what the plan was, and Jim wished he and Marnie had hashed out some more detail before committing to the rescue effort. They didn't even have any means by which they could contact each other.

"I guess I just go on in as expected," Jim said, echoing Marnie's last instructions to him.

Jim could feel his anxiety suddenly start to rise, the feeling of someone sitting on his chest was growing stronger by the second. He opened the glove box and pulled out a small, ornately decorated miniature casket, the lid of which hinged open. It was the kind of trinket designed as a receptacle for jewellery or perhaps for loose change. Jim had used a novelty gift company he'd found online to manufacture them a few years back. The idea was to use them to hand out as Smith Bros. corporate gifts. However, they had proved to be less than popular. Jim still had about five hundred of them stored in the cleaning cupboard at the office. One unexpected upside was that they were the perfect size to hold a couple of joints and a small lighter.

Jim quickly lit up a joint and feverishly smoked it halfway down before stubbing it out and placing the remaining roach back in the small box.

"Okay, I guess we're doing this," Jim said. He took a moment to steel himself, before he opened the car door and started to make the same walk towards the entrance of The Oasis that his brother had made only a few hours before.

Aleks Keshishian was perched on the edge of Christian Palfreeman's desk. He was deep into another Garry Vee keynote address on his phone. He had the sound down so as not to disturb the room and was relying on the subtitles. Aleks was proud of his grasp of the English language - he felt he had a commanding handle on effective verbal communication in particular - however, reading took more of an effort and he had to constantly pause and replay sections to fully grasp the nuances of Gary's talk titled *There is an 'I' in Winner*. He was just going back to hear the fourth of five ways to embrace your inner C'ME'O when his phone rang. It was one of the Kardashians who had been sent to find Andre.

"Fuck!" Aleks said in frustration.

He answered the phone but before he could speak he was bombarded with shouting from the other end. He lifted the phone away from his ear slightly to shield his hearing from the blast of noise emanating from the handset and listened. His face remained stony but Christian Palfreeman could sense that something was wrong. Very wrong. He could hear the muffled sounds of a roaring car engine and what sounded like distant sirens in the background behind the screeching Armenian monologue.

"Is everything ok, Aleks?" Palfreeman asked.

Aleks cut off the still excitedly shouting Kardashian mid-sentence, as he hung up the phone. His eyes focused on the floor in front of him.

"Aleks?" Palfreeman said

"Fucking idiots!" Aleks said. He threw his phone across the room. It hurtled through the air and violently smashed into the far wall, sending one of the remaining Kardashians ducking for cover.

"Aleks!" Palfreeman said, with a rare sternness.

Aleks took a deep breath.

"When they got there, they could see Andre being loaded into an ambulance," Aleks began. "There were police everywhere. Our guys had no idea what had happened so were trying to get a better look. But somehow, they made it too fucking obvious and raised the suspicions of the police who tried to stop them to ask them some questions. But instead of complying, it looks like our guys put their foot to the floor instead. They're now being chased all over the local area by at least three police vehicles."

"Well, that's just brilliant, Aleks!" Christian said with mock enthusiasm.

"By the sounds of it, there was no sign of the other brother either," Aleks continued.

Mick started to smile.

"Well I'll be a monkey's uncle. The little prick has more lives than a fucking Teflon, bullet proof cat! Looks like you're little plan didn't fucking work…"

Aleks took a few steps and collected Mick with a thundering right hook that loosened one of his bottom teeth and split his lip wide. A burst of stars flashed in his eyes.

"Why don't I just kill these two and we can get out of here?" Aleks asked of Palfreeman.

The landline phone on Christian's desk buzzed, he could see a flashing light indicating it was inbound from reception. Christian answered and put it on speaker.

"I thought I said no interruptions!" Christian barked.

"I'm so sorry to disturb, Mr Palfreeman but you have a visitor."

Palfreeman paused a beat, thinking.

"I'm not expecting any visitors. Who is it?"

The receptionist lowered her voice almost to a whisper.

"I don't know if it's his real name, but he's calling himself Mr Smith."

THIRTY

"You two, go and bring him here," Palfreeman said, instructing the two remaining Kardashians in the room to head out to reception and escort Jim Smith back to the office. They swiftly obeyed, leaving only Aleks and Palfreeman remaining in the office. Mick edged himself forward on the couch and coiled his legs beneath him, ready for action should an opportunity present itself. Christian caught his subtle movement from the corner of his eye. He casually lifted the nickel-plated Beretta and pointed it at Mick.

"Now's not the time to develop a hero complex, Mr Smith," Palfreeman said. "Unlike those action movies you're so fond of, these bullets are real." He waved his gun to usher Mick into his former position. Mick obliged and settled back next to Tracy, who leant her head over to rest on his shoulder.

"I love you, Mick," Tracy said, softly.

"I love you too, Trace. And I'm sorry - about everything."

Jim was still standing at the front desk of The Oasis nervously waiting. He couldn't work out if he was being soothed or annoyed by the music piping through the foyer sound system. It was *Centrefold* by J. Gelis Band, the number one hit from their 1981 album, *Freeze Frame*.

The familiarity of the song was a comfort but the jangly, sharp-edged tune had his nerves beginning to fray. Either way, Jim's blood went cold the minute the two round-shouldered Kardashians appeared in a doorway beyond the reception desk and beckoned him to join them. Jim took a deep breath, thanked the receptionist and crossed the foyer towards the two men and all the unknowns that they represented.

Jim switched into full funeral mode. He mustered up his best saccharine funeral smile and extended his hand to greet the nearest of the gangsters. He needn't have bothered. His offer was met with nothing but air and aggressive indifference.

"This way," one of the Kardashians grunted.

"After you," Jim said, politely.

The Kardashian shook his head.

"No. After you."

The Kardashian pointed down a hall that led away from the common areas towards the rear of the building. Jim looked at each of the men in turn and took stock of his situation before beginning his march down the corridor as the music faded behind him.

Jim continued down the corridor until it reached a Y-junction with an option to turn head either left or right. He paused.

"Um…which way?" Jim asked.

He felt a large hand roughly push on his right shoulder. It steered him around to the left.

"I guess we're going this way," Jim said.

He had taken only a couple more steps when he heard what sounded like a hard object on bone. It was an impact that was dull, wet, and final. It was followed by something that resembled a large sack of potatoes hitting the ground. Jim turned around just in time to see the nearest Kardashian crumple to the deck just footsteps behind him. Jim saw the expression of the remaining Kardashian flash from confusion to agony, as Marnie delivered a forceful boot to his groin. The impact and the instantaneous pain doubled the huge man over. Marnie swung her right hand in an aggressively efficient arc and connected the already debilitated man directly in the temple. His body switched off as if someone had pulled out his plug. He toppled like a giant old-growth tree, almost in slow motion, and slumped next to his partner on the floor. Marnie wiped some sweat from her brow, looked up and smiled at Jim.

"Well, these came in handy," Marnie said, admiring the brass knuckle-dusters she had procured from the gym bag salvaged from Andre's car. She searched the two unconscious henchmen and removed their wallets. Quickly flicking through both, she removed their photo IDs before throwing the wallets on the floor.

"In the words of Hannibal from *The A-Team*: 'I love it when a plan comes together'."

Marnie's plan had been simple by almost all measures. She had settled on her strategy about five hundred meters into her one kilometre run to The Oasis, an endeavour which she had completed with surprising ease. Marnie had figured that, unless either of the two Kardashians she had neutralised while first rescuing Jim on the main road had risen like Lazarus, she had the ultimate advantage - the element of surprise. Not even the most suspicious of criminals would be on the lookout for a diminutive, grey-haired, pearl-clad woman. Moments after Jim had been led away, Marnie had simply strolled into the reception area of The Oasis and approached the front desk with a story about being there to pick up her wayward nephew. She had sought permission to wait for him in one of the booths but first she was in desperate need for the bathroom. Keen to avoid an incontinence incident, the staff had eagerly pointed her in the direction of the toilets.

Only Marnie wasn't looking for the toilets.

When she had first entered the building, she had made a mental note of the positioning of the security cameras around the room. She had performed a rough mental triangulation and used her best guestimate to figure out the most likely direction to the security room. Once out of site of the front desk, she had quickly ducked through some double doors and followed her nose. It led her straight where she was wanting to go.

Marnie knew that every successful operation required equal measures of detailed planning and good fortune. As this particular mission had almost none of the former, it was going to rely on plenty of the latter. The first piece of luck was finding the security room unattended. Its bank of screens, which gave her a rapid overview of the entire building, told her everything she had needed to know. Luckily for Jim, that had included his exact whereabouts.

"I tell you, Jim, I expected a little more from this lot," Marnie said. "With these two down, it just leaves the big boss Palfreeman and his enforcer Keshishian."

"How do you know that?" Jim asked.

"I've seen the cameras. They have your brother and Tracy holed up in what looks like Palfreeman's office."

"So what do we do?"

"We bring the fight to us. We'll have a better chance out here than rushing in and confronting them on their turf."

"How?" Jim asked.

"Simple. We knock on the door and announce our arrival."

Marnie held up the two photo IDs and started walking down the corridor in the direction of Palfreeman's office. Jim followed, still unsure of exactly what he was meant to do. But he figured, based on what he had just witnessed first-hand, the safest place for him to be right now was as close by Marnie Rochambeau as he could get.

Marnie stopped just short of Palfreeman's office and turned to Jim.

"Okay, things might get a little exciting from this moment on. I'll draw one of them out, I assume it will be Keshishian. That'll leave Palfreeman inside guarding your brother and sister-in-law. You lay low over in the shadows in that corner and once I've drawn Keshishian away, you enter the office," Marnie said, her voice barely above a whisper.

"Then what do I do?" Jim said, barely able to concentrate.

"Palfreeman still thinks you have what he wants. Buy some time by making him think you'll give it to him. Then when you see an opportunity, try to subdue him."

"Subdue him? Fuck me. I'm not Jason Bourne. I'm a bloody stoned undertaker!"

"It'll be three on one. You'll be fine. He can only shoot one of you at a time," Marnie said with a quiet laugh. "Now go over there and put your big boy pants on. I've got work to do."

Marnie sent Jim off to hide in the shadows, before approaching the door to the office. She rapped loudly on the dark wood, just beneath Palfreeman's nameplate.

On the other side of the door, the sudden, unexpected knock spun all four heads around. Eight expectant eyes trained, unblinking, in the same direction.

Only nobody entered.

"Finally, your lot are getting the hang of this knocking business, Aleks," Palfreeman said, with a sense of accomplishment.

"Come in!"

The door remained closed.

"Enter. Entrez-vous por-favour. Come the fuck in!" Palfreeman shouted. "Jesus Christ almighty! It's gone from one extreme to the other. First, I couldn't keep the fucking idiots out, now I can't get the morons to come in. What are they waiting for? A fucking red-carpet?"

Finally, the door jerked open. But only a crack. It was just wide enough for Marnie to flick the two IDs belonging to the unconscious Kardashians into the room before quickly shutting the door again. The plastic rectangles flew through the air, spinning like playing cards before landing in the middle of the floor. Aleks rushed over and picked them up. He instantly recognised the faces and just as immediately knew what it meant. He'd lost his back up muscle.

Aleks hurled the two sets of identification on Palfreeman's desk before removing a large painting from the wall behind - a rather naïve rendition of a pair of breasts that Palfreeman had bought at auction believing it's young creator to be destined for great things, only for the artist to soon after fall out of favour with the art cognoscenti following his rather crude exhibition of 'cock and ball' paintings - to reveal a large concealed gun safe. Aleks pulled out a Heckler and Koch MP5 submachine gun. He removed the ammunition clip to quickly check it was fully loaded before clicking it back into place and cocking the gun, slapping the bolt into place with his right hand.

"What are you doing, Aleks? We have guests in the building, remember? We can't go around shooting up the place!" Palfreeman yelled. "For Christ's sake, think of the TripAdvisor reviews!"

"Fuck the TripAdvisor reviews," Aleks shot back at his boss, cooly, before marching to the door. He paused for a second before swinging it open wildly and stepping out into the corridor, submachine gun poised on his hip.

Aleks cautiously stalked down the hallway, slowly sweeping the barrel of the gun left and right as he scanned the corridor ahead of him. He soon came to the two Kardashians lying in a heap on the floor. He carefully stepped over them, his eyes remaining focussed ahead, as his feet felt their way through the obstacle beneath him. Aleks reached the y-intersection and opted to head right and back out towards the reception area. He quickened his pace as he noticed someone up ahead.

"Hey! What are you doing back here?!" Aleks

cried out as the woman slowly turned around.

"I'm sorry, I was looking for the bathroom, I must have taken a wrong turn," Marnie said, adding a convincing quiver to her voice, playing up her elderly befuddlement. "Oh my, is that a gun?!?"

"Get out of here. Or you'll find out!" Aleks said, gruffly. His eyes locked back down the corridor searching for danger, as he started to push past Marnie. But he failed to notice the danger right in front of him.

Quick as a featherweight boxer, Marnie's hand reached for the barrel of the MP5. She gripped it hard and pushed it away. Instinctively, Alek's finger squeezed on the trigger, sending a hail of bullets in an arc up the wall. At first, Aleks couldn't comprehend what was happening before the realisation dawned on him - this old lady wasn't as innocent as she might have first appeared. He struggled to regain control of his weapon, pushing the barrel back towards Marnie and unleashing a fresh volley of gunfire. The barrage tore through the ceiling, shattering the lighting above them and sending a shower of fine glass everywhere. Decades of muscle memory kicked in as Marnie used her free arm to drive in behind the stock of the sub-machinegun and use the momentum created by Aleks against him. The subsequent torque was too much for Aleks and the weapon wrenched from his grip. It spun, cartwheeling towards Marnie, who expertly plucked it from the air mid spin. It couldn't have gone better on a Hollywood soundstage.

"Well, that's a turn up for the books, isn't it Mr Keshishian?" Marnie said, training the gun on Aleks, stony-faced.

Aleks reacted swiftly. He reached for his belt and found the small throwing knife he kept concealed there for just such unexpected circumstances. Without a moment's hesitation, he deftly flicked the blade at Marnie. It sliced through the air, on target to hit her square between the eyes. At the last minute, Marnie managed to duck her head out of the way. The knife whistled past her ear, taking a few strands of her hair on the way, pinning them to the wall of the corridor behind her. The momentary distraction granted Aleks just enough time to sprint down the corridor and launch himself through the double doors, out into the reception area.

As the doors swung open, Marnie caught the screams and confusion coming from beyond the doors, no doubt a reaction to the unexpected sound of gunfire. She quickly removed the ammunition clip from the gun and expelled the round that was already lodged in the chamber to completely unload the weapon. She then stripped the gun, breaking it down into its component parts and letting them fall impotently to the ground at her feet. In less than fifteen seconds the Heckler and Koch MP5 had gone from deadly instrument to completely inoperable.

"Never much liked guns, personally. Brutish things," Marnie said to herself, before calmly pushing open the doors and heading out in pursuit of

Aleks Keshishian.

Jim was still cowered in the shadows outside Palfreeman's office when the loud bursts of gunshots rang out. They had shaken him into action, like a starter's gun in a foot race. He now found himself standing flat against the wall beside the still open door to Palfreeman's office, talking himself into what he knew had to happen next.

"Ok Jim. Count of three, One. Two, Three!"

He rushed the door and flung himself through the opening but somehow managed to catch the door frame with his trailing leg. He felt himself launching forward, airborne and headfirst, before landing on the carpeted floor and sliding just enough to give himself nasty friction burns on his knees and elbows. He looked up to see Christian Palfreeman leaning over his desk pointing a large, shiny handgun at him.

"Nice of you to finally join us," Palfreeman said. "You seem to have caused us a great deal of trouble."

Jim pushed himself up to his knees and stared straight at Palfreeman.

"Sorry I took so long. I was doing my best to get out here as quickly as I could but I could swear you did everything humanly possible to stop me," Jim said, with an almost cathartic laugh. "But when my brother asks me to do something, well, I do it."

He placed his hand on his pants pocket and felt for the outline of his lighter that was still inside. It was the approximate size of a USB stick and was almost indistinguishable from the real thing through the material. He gripped his fingers on either side of it to better define the lighter's outline.

"And I still think there's a way out of this. I have what you're so desperate for after all."

Christian gestured with the tip of the gun for Jim to stand.

"Well, well, well. I'm not sure if it's bravery or stupidity but here we are," Palfreeman said. "Hand it over."

Mick suddenly rose to his feet.

"Not so fast. Remember the copies," Mick said. "Good to see you brother."

Jim looked at Mick.

"Good to see you too. And yes. The copies. The many copies," Jim said, trying his best to play along.

"Enough mucking around. The USB stick. Now! Then we can talk about these copies, if they exist."

Mick took a couple of steps towards Palfreeman, who swung the gun around to hold him back.

"Stay where you are!"

"The thing is, Christian, you seem to be in a bit of a pickle. You can't shoot Jim, because he knows where the copies all are," Mick said, as he stepped even closer.

"But that doesn't stop me shooting you though, does it?"

"Well - and here's a turn up for the books - it's just I'm the only one who knows where the actual USB stick is. Show him, Jim."

Jim took the lighter from his pocket and held it out in his palm.

"Fuck!" Palfreeman yelled. He started taking deep breaths.

"These feelings are real but they will not hurt me."

"What?" Mick said, perplexed.

"These feelings are real but they will not hurt me!" Palfreeman said, loudly. He took a deep breath, composed himself and fired the gun twice in quick succession. The first bullet tore through Mick's upper thigh, the second hit Jim squarely in the foot. The echo from the gunshots bounced around the walls as the brothers both cried out in pain and collapsed to the floor.

Tracy screamed. Christian Palfreeman calmly aimed the gun directly at her.

"Don't make me pull the trigger a third time. Rest assured, I won't be aiming for a limb."

The common areas of The Oasis near the reception area were in chaos. Scantily clad women and ridiculously dressed patrons were scampering for cover in all directions. The scene was made even more surreal by George Michael's 1984 hit *Careless Whisper* which was loudly providing the soundtrack. Marnie strolled through the bedlam as calmly as if taking a casual Sunday stroll. As she scanned the room for Keshishian, she nonchalantly slid the brass knuckle dusters back onto her hand.

Out of nowhere, Aleks shot out from his hiding place behind the plinth of one of Dr Hibbert's artworks - the sheep paired with the sheep dog - and tackled Marnie, hitting her with full force just below the ribs. The two crashed to the ground with Aleks ending up on top. He began raining down elbows onto Marnie, like a UFC fighter. She did her best to block the blows with her forearms, but she still felt every blow. She tried desperately to shrimp her hips away enough to get some separation from the Armenian's assault, eventually creating just enough space to reach into her pocket and grab the can of pepper spray she had also taken from Andre's gym bag. She couldn't quite pull her arm free but managed to spray the contents in the general direction of Aleks' face. It was a haphazard stream but enough of it hit him in the face to back him up slightly. It was all Marnie needed. She swung her other hand as hard as she could towards her assailant's head. The brass knuckles impacted Aleks just below his eye and he immediately felt the world start to shift off kilter. He sensed himself toppling sideways and instinctively braced himself on the ground with his hand, barely managing to keep from going all the way over.

Although dazed herself from the blows she had taken, Marnie used the moment to her advantage. She pushed Aleks off and jumped to her feet. She rushed over to the far wall, reached up and pulled down a large mace that was hanging next to a shield for decoration. She felt the weight of it in her hands before slowly turning back to face Aleks. He had managed to regain some of his senses and was struggling to his feet. His vision cleared just in time to see the spiked end of the mace thunder into his chest. The impact spun him around and robbed his body of air. He felt a second blow thump into his back. It staggered him forward, momentarily forcing him to one knee before he regained his footing. He turned around to face his attacker.

"Who are you?" Aleks struggled to say.

He would never find out.

Marnie swung the mace for a third time, crashing the steel ball into Aleks's temple. The Armenian lifted from the ground and flew through the air backwards, straight into the large glass tank holding Hibbert's *Kangamoo*. The glass shattered as Aleks Keshishian's lifeless body crashed through it, flooding the floor of the reception with the blue formaldehyde solution.

"What the fuck is going on!?!?!"

Detective Sam Chang and Constable Riley had burst through the front doors just in time to see the Armenian slam into and subsequently through, the artwork.

Marnie looked up at the detective. She was breathing heavily from her exertion.

"I'm not sure. I think he must have slipped."

She smiled at Sam before starting to laugh. She was soon laughing uncontrollably as George Michael continued to sing in the background about how he was never going to dance again.

THIRTY-ONE

Detective Chang rushed towards Marnie who was leaning on the mace to hold herself upright, as Constable Riley ran towards the lifeless body of Aleks Keshishian. Sam arrived just in time to catch Marnie as the exhaustion of her fight with Aleks overwhelmed her and her legs threatened to give way.

"Easy, Marnie," Sam said gently as he slowly assisted her down to the floor. "I'll get an ambulance."

Marnie waived the suggestion off.

"Don't be silly. I've never needed an ambulance before and I've been in much worse scraps than this! I just need a second to catch my breath."

Riley appeared behind Sam having checked Aleks for vital signs.

"He's a goner, Sam," Riley said.

"And there'll be more goners if you don't get moving," Marnie said. "Palfreeman has the Smiths holed up in his office. And he has a gun. I can't vouch for how useful he is with it. But any idiot with a firearm can cause damage."

"Which way?"

Marnie pointed in the direction of the corridor.

"Head down there. Stick left. His office is all the way at the end."

Sam looked to Riley to see if she was ready but the young constable was already moving towards Palfreeman's office. Sam followed a half a pace behind.

"Sam!" Marnie called out after them. Sam turned back.

"If you need a hand, just give me a shout!"

Marnie started laughing again. Sam could hear her chuckle slowly fade behind him as he and Riley ventured down the corridor and took the left at the Y-junction. Sam tapped Riley on the arm and motioned for her to take out her weapon, as he drew his own service revolver from his holster. The two cops reached the door of Palfreeman's office and paused.

Tracy was leaning over Mick who was lying on the floor writhing in pain from the gunshot wound to his thigh. She was trying her best to apply pressure to slow the blood loss but was struggling as her hands were still bound. Jim, meanwhile, was staring at his own bleeding foot in shocked disbelief. On some level he knew he was experiencing searing pain but he was surprised that he wasn't screaming out in agony. He felt a detachment, as though he was watching it all through a screen. All his senses were overwhelmed to the point that his brain had temporarily shut down messages from his pain receptors.

"I'm not entirely sure why it took me to shoot you both for you to realise that I am being serious," Palfreeman said, proudly appreciating his handiwork. He bounced around slightly on his feet, excited and quietly impressed with himself that he had the nerve to fire at them at all, let alone actually hit them both roughly where he was aiming.

"So, unless you would like me to pull the trigger again. Hand over the USB stick and tell me where the copies are."

Mick grimaced and tried to control his rapid breathing.

"Okay. Okay. I'll tell you where it is. But you have to let Tracy go first."

"I don't know what makes you think you are in any position to negotiate? I just shot you and your brother and if I'm not mistaken, the only one with a gun in this room right now is yours truly. So just stop all this nonsense and hand over the fucking USB stick!"

"No. Only if you let Tracy go."

Tracy started shaking her head.

"It doesn't matter, Mick. I'll stay. I need to look after you."

"I've been shot," Jim said quietly, still transfixed

on his foot.

"No, Trace. I want to get you out. You had nothing to do with any of this."

"The USB stick, Mr Smith!" Palfreeman yelled.

"I've been shot!" Jim said again, louder.

"Not until Tracy is let go!" Mick yelled back.

"That's not happening!" Palfreeman shouted, starting to lose control of his emotions. "Tell me where it is. I'm going to count to three!"

"I've been shot!" Jim screamed, the realisation of what had just happened dawning on him fully.

"One…"

"Not until Tracy is safe"

"Two…"

"I've been shot in the fucking foot!"

"Three…"

Suddenly the door to the office flew open. Riley burst into the room, her gun held in a firing position in front of her.

"Stop, police!" Riley shouted. It was loud and self-assured.

Christian Palfreeman answered. His gun fired three quick shots in the direction of the door. The first two bullets bit into the door frame, sending splinters of wood flying everywhere. The third thundered into Riley's shoulder, the force of the impact spinning her around and sending her crashing to the floor. Despite the gunshots, Detective Chang was already committed to following Riley into the room. Palfreeman caught sight of the detective. He fired several more shots but snatched at the trigger, sending the bullets well wide. Chang had just enough time to hastily reverse course and dive back into the safety of the corridor as Palfreeman fired again through the open doorway after him.

Palfreeman wasn't too concerned about hitting the detective, he just needed some covering fire to buy a few essential seconds. As the sound of the gunshots still lingered in the air, he quickly turned around and ran his finger along a small groove on the wall at the back of the office behind his desk. It activated a handle that appeared as if by magic. Christian grabbed the handle and pulled. A secret door, it's outline almost imperceptible to the naked eye, opened and Christian Palfreeman rushed through it and disappeared down a narrow dark passageway.

Sam crouched low against the wall of the corridor. He waited a second or two after the volley of shots exploded through the open door to see if any further gunfire was forthcoming. But nothing else came through the opening except for the sounds of moaning. He took a deep breath and launched himself back through the door. He tucked into a surprisingly agile combat roll that saw him end up crouching on one knee, his gun aimed in the direction he had last seen Palfreeman. He quickly scanned the room for threats but couldn't see Christian Palfreeman anywhere.

"It's okay, detective. He took off down there," Tracy said, pointing Chang towards the secret passage.

Sam turned his attention to Riley who was groaning on the floor next to him. He rolled her over so he could get a better look at her wound. The bullet had passed straight through her shoulder. Sam grabbed Riley's hand and pressed it up against the entry wound.

"Keep pressure on it," Sam said, "it's going to be fine. I know it hurts like hell but this one won't kill you."

Sam reached around and grabbed his police radio from his belt.

"This is Detective Chang. Shots fired. I need immediate back up of all available resources and an ambulance. Riley's been shot," Sam said into the handset.

"I've also been shot!" Jim said, raising his hand.

"Make that a trifecta," Mick said, arm also in the air.

Chang jumped back on the radio. "Correction, send all the ambulances you can. We have multiple wounded."

Sam clipped the radio back in its housing and took out the multi-tool that he always kept on the side of his belt. He quickly set about removing the bindings on Mick and Tracy.

"How bad are you hit?" Sam asked the brothers.

"We're fine. Don't worry about us. Just go get that bastard," Mick replied, through gritted teeth.

"Okay, the cavalry is coming. Sit tight," Sam said.

Detective Chang started to make his way into the

secret corridor. He cautiously stuck his head into the void. The space beyond was completely dark. He felt around on the walls near the entrance in the hope of finding a light switch but there was nothing. He strained his eyes, willing them to adjust. Gradually, he started to be able to make out the walls of the passage and he noticed a dim shaft of light in the distance. Sam started walking forward, with each step he gained greater confidence that there was no one hiding in a dark corner ready to ambush him. His gait quickened. Soon he was running. Before long, he reached the shaft of light. It was at a point where the passage took a sharp right turn. Sam cautiously peered around the corner to check what awaited him. He could see nothing but another door. It was open. Sam could see out to the brightness of the building beyond. Without hesitation, Sam broke back into a run and propelled himself straight through the door with barely a thought for personal wellbeing.

It was a mistake.

Pop! Pop! Pop! Pop!

The bullets whistled through the air past Detective Chang, who threw himself behind an ornate chaise lounge. It provided only the smallest amount of cover. Sam cursed himself for being so reckless. Palfreeman had been waiting for whoever came through the door and Sam should have known better. He double-checked that the safety on his gun was off. Sam had never had to shoot anyone before. However, he knew that he just might have to, if he was to have any chance of getting out of this unharmed.

"It pains me to have this all end this way, detective," Palfreeman said as he advanced on Sam's position.

Pop!

Stuffing flew out from the couch next to Sam's head. That one was too close.

"You see, I know what killing a cop means to my future but you leave me no choice."

Pop!

More stuffing puffed into the air.

"So let's just get this over with shall we?"

Sam gripped the handle of his gun tightly. His knuckles went white as he prepared himself to beat Christian to the punch. He knew that he couldn't afford to stand straight up. Palfreeman would have too much time to shoot him before he would be able to get his gun into position. His only hope was to dive to his right and fire up from the ground and hope that he hit Palfreeman before he was shot himself. Sam picked out his landing spot on the carpet. He was milliseconds away from committing to tumbling through the air when he heard a loud, high-pitched, terrified scream. It stopped Chang in his tracks.

"Well, this just got more interesting," Palfreeman said. There was an unmistakeable air of satisfaction in his voice.

Chang's eyes were drawn to some movement and he noticed a picture hanging on the wall to his right. He could see Palfreeman's reflection in the glass. His heart sank. Palfreeman's arm was now wrapped around a young woman. She was dressed in an Oasis buxom wench uniform. Sam recognised her. It was Candy – not her real name – and she was now providing Palfreeman with a perfect human shield. The opportunity for Sam Chang to take out Christian Palfreeman, as slim as it might have been, had now well and truly passed.

"Okay, Christian. You win. I'm going to stand up slowly but you have to let the girl go," Chang said as calmly as he could.

"Throw your gun away first!" Palfreeman snapped.

Sam hesitated.

"Your gun, Detective Chang."

Sam checked the reflection again. Palfreeman was pressing the barrel of his shiny Beretta to Candy's head. Sam had already seen Christian's willingness to use it and, even if he might be about to die himself, he knew that he couldn't be responsible for the death of an innocent bystander. Sam clicked the safety back into place on his pistol and threw it out from behind the couch.

Sam heard a slight chuckle coming from Palfreeman.

"What a shame," Palfreeman said, the note of glee in his voice gratingly smug.

"You don't need to do this, Christian. You'll never get away with it. There's half the police force in the state on their way here right now," Sam pleaded "Don't make it worse on yourself than it already is."

"Oh, but I will get away with it, detective. Do you really think that I wouldn't have a contingency plan for just such a turn of events? And you and I both know that your reinforcements, even if it is half the entire police force - which I doubt - are twenty minutes away at best. The last chance you had of preventing the inevitable was that gun. That you just threw away."

Palfreeman forced the squirming Candy to move as he started walking closer to the Sam who remained crouched behind the couch.

"You said you'd let her go," Sam said.

"Call it extra insurance," Palfreeman replied. "One can never be too careful. Now, I take it you did maths at school, detective?" He laughed. "What am I saying, you're Asian, of course you did maths. So I'll just say Quod Erat Demonstrandum."

Christian Palfreeman peered over the edge of the couch and saw Detective Chang looking up at him. He could see the fear in the policeman's eyes. Palfreeman smiled his Cheshire smile and slowly levelled the gun at the detective.

"Q. E. D."

Sam closed his eyes and held them tightly shut as

he braced for the gunshot. He waited to hear the loud bang that would be the last thing he ever experienced. Only, all he heard was a dull thud.

Sam opened his eyes and saw Christian Palfreeman listing sideways. His eyes looked blank as he slowly fell, first onto the back of the chaise lounge before sliding - almost comically slowly - to the floor, where he remained in a motionless heap. Chang cautiously stood up and saw Misty Gerard standing in the hall, a large medieval war hammer in her hands.

"Don't be such a fucking racist!" Misty said, standing over the unconscious Palfreeman. She spied the gun near his hand, kicked it and watched it slide across the floor out of harm's way.

Candy burst into tears and rushed into Misty's arms.

"I told you, detective. I'll do anything for my girls."

THIRTY-TWO

The past four weeks had been the busiest of Detective Sam Chang's career. The arrests of Christian Palfreeman and the remaining Kardashians had occupied much of his time. On top of that, he had still been working through the process of identifying the bodies that Hibbert had been using for his artistic monstrosities. And when not busy with either of those tasks, he had been tied up in seemingly endless briefings to get the major crimes and homicide squads up to speed concerning the suspected murders of Mayor Terry McInerny, Dr Enricio Cociarelli and Dr George Hibbert. The Sydney boys had become quite excited to get involved following the media interest surrounding the shoot-out at The Oasis. It had been headline news around the country, leading television bulletins and filling the front pages of most of the daily metro papers. However, despite the big-city interest, Sam's favourite coverage had been the Argus' investigation that called for an entire dedicated issue - save for the all-important classifieds and local sports results, of course. The souvenir paper bore the banner 'Murder, Murky Machinations and Medieval Mayhem'. Sam thought it worthy of a Walkley award. It was truly the Argus' opus.

Palfreeman had been transported to Sydney and was now facing multiple serious charges. Following a forensic investigation of the files that Mick had handed over to Detective Chang on the USB stick, a litany of briefs related to corruption and money laundering were being prepared. He was also up on kidnapping and attempted murder offences with additional murder charges possible, pending the outcome of the homicide investigations. Palfreeman was also suffering from a loss of smell and taste courtesy of the blow inflicted by Misty. Whether by design or happenstance, the impact had been in the perfect spot to create the exact head trauma required to rob him of those faculties. While Palfreeman's lawyers planned to defend all of their client's charges aggressively, it was looking more than probable that Christian Palfreeman was going to spend a large part of his remaining days in gaol and never enjoy a glass of his favoured Sangiovese again.

The Oasis itself was slated for a makeover, with plans afoot to soften the medieval aspects of the establishment while keeping the overall theme in place. The women working there had been instrumental in providing input into the new direction, with a focus on ensuring it would be a supportive and safe environment for them to ply their trade. The new owners, a consortium calling themselves the Rooney Group, made up of wealthy Sydney businessmen (who may or may not have frequented the establishment on more than one occasion), were more than happy to listen. They had moved swiftly to install a new general manager to run the operation in their stead. Misty Gerard had been quick to accept their offer.

Sam sat behind the wheel of his car as he drove down the main street of Prosperity. There was still one loose end he needed to tie up. He wasn't sure if it was just that it was raining for the first time in months but the town felt different. Lighter. As if it was on the cusp of a new era. He pulled his car over and parked outside the Smith Bros. offices. He turned off his car and contemplated how he could make it to the door without getting wet. He had looked everywhere for his umbrella that morning when word of the expected weather had reached him but for the life of him couldn't find it anywhere.

"It's just water, Sam," he said to himself as he opened the door and half ran, half skipped across the footpath and into the building.

Bluey looked up from the reception desk at the slightly damp detective who was standing just inside the doorway, brushing the beading water from his clothing.

"Detective Chang. So good to see you. The boys are waiting for you in the conference room," Bluey said, with a cheery disposition.

Sam smiled at Bluey. He noticed a large aquarium sitting pride-of-place behind the desk. It was filled with an assortment of brightly coloured fish.

"Nice tank, Bluey. It's looking good," Sam said.

"Thank you, detective. I named one after you," Bluey replied, beaming.

"I couldn't be prouder if it had been your first born child," Sam said as he headed for the door to the conference room. It was a rather grandiose term for what amounted to an office with two desks pushed together and a few chairs around them. He entered to find Jim and Mick Smith already seated at the makeshift table facing the door.

"Welcome Sam, you won't mind if we don't get up?" Mick said.

Both Jim and Mick were still recovering from their respective gunshot wounds. Mick had required surgery to repair his leg. The bullet had nicked his femur on the way through and cracked it sufficiently to warrant the insertion of a couple of screws and a titanium plate to hold it in place. Jim had had to have many of the bones in his foot pieced back together like a 3D puzzle. Both were still many weeks from getting off crutches.

"Take a seat," Jim said.

Sam pulled out the chair nearest to him and sat down.

"Look, I won't pad this out. Obviously, you know why I'm here."

"We have a fair idea," Jim said. His eyes fell to the desk in front of him, unable to hold the detective's gaze.

"During our investigations into Doctor Hibbert, we uncovered the operation that you two have been running."

"Should we have a lawyer here?" Mick asked, interjecting. "Jim, you said we didn't need a lawyer."

"Just hear him out!" Jim said, imploring his brother.

"It's okay, I told Jim on the phone that you don't need a lawyer, Mick. At least not yet," Sam said. "Obviously you guys have been through a lot. Most of it not of your own making. But what you two did was not only highly illegal - fraud, obtaining monies by deception for starters - but how you could do that to members of your own community, people you have known and who have known you for your entire lives is beyond me."

Jim and Mick both shuffled uncomfortably in their chairs. They felt every word of Sam's dressing down.

"It's obviously not something we're particularly proud of, Sam," Jim said. "It just kind of took on a life of its own."

"But here's the thing," Sam said, continuing, "I have enough on my plate right now. Coming after you guys is that last thing I need."

"So you're not going to charge us?" Mick asked. His face registered his surprise.

"No. But you're not off the hook just yet. Firstly, once you're both up and running again, you're going to conduct all the exhumations I need."

"Sure," Jim said.

"What, for free?" Mick started. Jim leant over and punched his brother in the arm.

"Sorry. Go on," Mick said, rubbing his arm, suitable chastened.

"Then, obviously everybody that we have found out at Hibbert's is going to need to be reburied. You're going to bury them in the best bloody caskets you have. And you're going to do it without charging the families. They have been through enough already. Agreed?"

"Agreed," Jim said.

"But…" Mick started before thinking better.

"Agreed."

"Good. It goes without saying that if I ever catch wind of you guys getting up to your old tricks, this little deal goes away quicker than you can say Universal Serial Bus," Sam said, as he stood from his chair and made for the door.

"Sorry, universal what?" Mick asked.

Sam turned back to answer.

"USB Mick. USB."

THIRTY-THREE

Detective Sam Chang stood in the kitchen of Lee's New Golden Imperial Lotus Garden and tossed the portion of honey chicken in the wok over the stove in front of him. Given who his guests were this evening, he had been sure to make an extra-large serving. Sam picked a piece of the chicken in the tips of his fingers and blew on it to cool it down slightly before popping it into his mouth. It was scalding hot but even Sam had to admit that it was delicious. He set the chicken out onto a platter already covered with fried vermicelli noodles and finished the dish off with a liberal sprinkling of sesame seeds and chopped spring onion.

"Here you go, ladies!" Sam said as he placed the heaving dish down on the table. Constable Riley almost couldn't contain her excitement.

"Can I start?" Riley asked, eagerly.

"Of course. Go for it," Sam said. "I'll be interested

to see if your arm slows you down."

Riley's arm was strapped tightly against her chest in a heavy duty sling designed to aid the ongoing recovery from her gunshot wound. All things considered, she had been pretty lucky in terms of damage to the shoulder. Although she faced the prospect of a solid six months of rehabilitation, the long-term prognosis was looking favourable and her doctors expected her to make a full recovery in time.

"Not likely, Sam," Riley said with a grin, as her one good hand began shovelling the chicken onto her plate.

"Now, I'm not normally one to go for this particular delicacy but I have to say, it does look pretty mouth-watering, Sam," Marnie Rochambeau said, with a hungry smile.

She waited for Riley to return the serving spoon to the platter before placing a few pieces on her own plate in front of her. She placed a single morsel into her mouth and groaned with delight.

"Delightful, chef. I could almost become a convert," Marnie said.

"It's the least I can do after all of your…help," Sam replied. "Speaking of which, I have an update for you. The coroner has accepted the explanation that Aleks Keshishian died as a result of a tragic accident, most probably as the result of a trip and fall. Unfortunately, the lack of any CCTV footage to show otherwise aided in his decision. There is apparently a two hour gap in the recording," Sam said.

Marnie smiled.

"I do find that odd," Marnie said, with a wink.

"I don't want to know what happened to that footage, Marnie," Sam said, smiling back. "Oh, and it looks like the two Kardashians from the roadside have no idea what happened to them either. The one that can talk has no memory of the incident and we're not expecting much to come from the other one if he every regains his faculties. So as far as we're concerned, on the law-enforcement side of things anyway, it's pretty much all done and dusted."

"Which just leaves one question," Sam continued. "If you don't mind me asking - who are you?"

Sam had tried to do some digging around to get some answers about Marnie. He'd always known that she was not your average retiree but it was only after she escaped so easily from the drunks who had knocked him out in the restaurant that he'd first placed a call. He had some friends in Canberra who he thought might be able to help but everyone came back drawing blanks. That or they were prevented from passing on whatever they found. Either way, he was no closer to putting the puzzle together.

Marnie smiled. She placed her hand softly on Sam's.

"Oh Sam. Who is anyone, really?"

Sam smiled at Marnie. He knew he would never get an answer.

Riley was almost finished with her first plate of

chicken, she'd barely been paying attention.

"Is it okay if I have seconds?" Riley asked.

"Of course," Sam replied, "and don't you go anywhere, Marnie, I've actually got a surprise for you. Give me a second."

Sam stood from the table and rushed back into the kitchen while Marnie watched, amused, as Riley heaped even more food onto her plate.

Sam quickly returned carrying another small dish in his hand.

"I've been working on this. I wanted you to be the first one to try it," Sam said, as he proudly placed the dish in front of Marnie.

"Oohhhh, if I'm not mistaken this looks like Duo Jiao Yu Tou - Spicy Steamed Fish head!" Marnie said excitedly. She picked up her chopsticks and sampled the sweet flesh from the cheek of the fish.

"Mmmm. I'm transported straight back to Hunan, Sam," Marnie said.

"I'm glad you like it. Actually, what would go well with that is an icy cold beer," Sam said.

"I'd be down for that, boss," Riley said, through a mouthful of food.

Sam approached the beer fridge and pulled three Tsing Taos from it. He went to pop their tops with a bottle opener tied to the fridge handle, only the condensation from the bottles made them hard to hold. Before he could readjust his grip, two of the three bottles of beer had slipped from his grasp and smashed onto the floor in a fountain of glass and beer.

"Bugger me!" Sam said.

Riley heard the sudden commotion, stopped eating and looked up. Like a good lieutenant, she sprang into action, leaping from the table.

"Let me help you with that, Sam," Riley said, hurrying over to Sam.

"There's a mop and a dustpan and broom in the kitchen," Sam said, as he gingerly picked up the larger pieces of broken bottle, careful not to cut himself.

"Whereabouts are they, Sam?" Riley yelled from the kitchen.

"Gimme a sec. I'll come look."

Sam placed the broken glass on the top of the front counter and made his way into the kitchen in search of the domestic tools he needed to complete the clean-up. Less than a minute later, Sam and Riley walked back into the restaurant holding the mop and dustpan respectively.

"Sorry to leave you by yourself, Marnie. We'll be all done in a minute," Sam said.

But when he looked up, Marnie was nowhere to be seen.

"Where'd she go?" Riley asked, confused.

Sam noticed something on the table. From a distance it looked like a small piece of paper. On closer inspection he realised that it was a sheet torn from his bill pad. He walked over to the table slowly and picked it up. There was a note that read: *Thank*

you for the lovely dinner and company, as always.
Then, down the bottom under 'Tip' had been added, simply:

More chilli.

www.ingramcontent.com/pod-product-compliance
Lightning Source LLC
Chambersburg PA
CBHW021217220726
48287CB00015B/1574